#BLOCKED

A Social Media Love Story

SAVANNAH THOMAS

#BLOCKED

ISBN: 978-1-953735-19-5

Published by Satin Romance
An Imprint of Melange Books, LLC
White Bear Lake, MN 55110
www.satinromance.com

Published in the United States of America.

Cover Design by Caroline Andrus

For Greg, who supported and encouraged me in every way possible. And Jessie the Cat, who only walked over my laptop two or three times throughout the course of writing this book. He would also stare at me in that judgmental manner that cats do... pushing me to work harder.

I'm glad I never #blocked either of you.

Btw, Greg thinks it's funny that the cat got a longer dedication than he did.

CHAPTER ONE

Winter Smith was in the midst of an anxiety storm, scrambling to find her mother's heather gray Stanford University sweater with crisp maroon lettering. She borrowed it the prior week and hid it somewhere for safekeeping, knowing very well that her mother would have a complete meltdown if she discovered it wasn't in her closet. Winter wondered if it could be considered a talent to hide an item so well from oneself that it stopped existing in reality altogether.

She looked at the clock. Her makeup had taken longer than expected, and the time blindsided her like a sneaky running back–or was it, fullback? She didn't watch much football. It was already 9:30 p.m. *9:30!* According to her extensive research into social marketing, the best time to post on Mondays was in the evening between 7:00 p.m. and 10:00 p.m. She'd already posted a few inspiring quotes to Nanogram and Twitter, and uploaded some workout clips to all the platforms, but she still had #ClassicStyleMondays to post to StyleSlap, the app that was singlehandedly paying for her rent.

It was that damn sinus infection that made her lay around all day. She wanted to kick herself for shaking hands and fist bumping with that germ-infested fraternity two days before at the mall. But they were pushy and a little drunk. Couldn't risk the online trash talking that would occur if she had turned a cold shoulder to the brotherly testosterone. Wouldn't be too good for her girl next door brand. To tell the truth, they were actually really sweet guys and she enjoyed meeting them. So, whatever.

She finally found the sweater in her closet, neatly folded behind a box of Polar Bear Smile Teeth Whitening Strips. Thankfully, she'd already posted that month's teeth advertisement, consisting of a seemingly candid yet overly set up scene that conveyed how happy she was to have "teeth as white as a polar bear." It had become one of her silliest posts to produce.

The comments were usually filled with people pointing out that polar bears don't exactly have the whitest teeth, so why would they use the product? One time she stated in a video that the strips would make teeth as white as a polar bear's fur, and people replied with hilarious photos and gifs of dirty, sometimes even yellow, polar bears. It was kind of an inside joke with her and her fans.

She held out the pristine, oversized, V-neck sweater, and for a brief moment, imagined her mother as a college student, happily walking through campus, probably getting checked out by all the boys, with her whole life ahead of her. Winter's stomach did a quick somersault as she realized her mother's actual future consisted of wine hangovers and a permanent scowl that silently signaled her lifetime of regrets to the world.

10:00 p.m. was fast approaching. She threw on the sweater over a stark white camisole, carefully making sure not to mess up the top half of her hair, which was braided and pinned into a crown. She pulled down one side of the sweater so her right shoulder and camisole strap peaked out.

Despite feeling icky, and having zero energy to shower, Winter's hair somehow looked amazing. Her dark hair was shiny and boasted natural looking waves. In reality, it was all thanks to a magic recipe consisting of a three-day old salon blowout and forgetting to sleep in a silk cap the previous night. Though she looked like she had just walked off a shampoo commercial, her nose was so red it could light Santa's sleigh in a snowstorm. After sneezing five times in a row, she trudged through onset lightheadedness to exchange her comfy cotton unicorn pajama bottoms with a short denim skirt and white and blue tube socks. She took one more glance in her bedroom mirror, winced at the blotchy mess staring back at her, then turned on the ring light and set her phone on the tripod.

Usually, she would shoot at some interesting location or in some elaborate scene she set up in her one bedroom bungalow, but due to her poor health, all she could manage was a backdrop of a string of cactus lights, haphazardly taped to the wall.

Taking a deep breath and waiting for the tickling sensation of another potential sneeze to pass, she set the timer and did a variety of poses, all the while making sure her face was turned away from the camera. She repeated this process about thirty times before she was happy with only one shot that she was actually kinda iffy about but too tired to continue. Just like that, her perfect posture morphed into a slouch.

She turned off the ring light, grabbed her phone, and stumbled over to her bed, landing with her best impression of a fainting damsel in distress, half drama queen, half genuinely feeling miserable. Her eyes felt heavier and heavier the second her head hit that pink satin pillow, and just as she was about to float off to dream island, her five-minute Monday posting warning timer went off.

With a huff, she enhanced the saturation in her chosen photo making the gray sweater, crimson letters, white and blue socks, and green back lights pop and edited out any imperfections. That bruise on her left knee? Click, click, gone! That scuff mark on the wall behind her? Click, click, sayonara, sucker! *If this career doesn't pan out*, she thought, *I could definitely be a photo editor or something*.

Finally, she clicked **Post to StyleSlap** and her latest creation was up. Within a few seconds, her phone buzzed with notifications. One comment read: "**I love your outfit! Where can I buy it?**" and it made Winter realize she forgot the description. She quickly edited in the hashtag **#ClassicStyleMondays** and the caption: **Mama's favorite sweater from college. Shhh! 🤫 Don't tell her I borrowed it. XOXO, Winter.**

Winter slept from last night's wild posting party (insert sarcasm here), to 8:00 a.m. the next morning. Immediately, she looked at her phone, sadly displaying the red battery icon.

Her throwback outfit was a hit, with 90,389 love slaps. Somehow, it had already been blogged about, and included in a couple style articles. One short read, for example, referenced Winter's post in a list of the best and easiest throwback styles of the year. They even talked about the history of hand-me-down, vintage, and repurposed fashion.

How do these things get published so fast? Are the writers working all night? Or is it just some algorithm creating an article from the newest popular postings? The usual questions swirled in her mind whenever she had that kind of good feedback from a style she shared, though she was grateful for the phenomenon getting her brand out to more people.

She pulled the curtains and opened the window. The sounds of life streamed in: birds chirping, kids playing, cars honking, trees shaking their branch fists at the random gusts of wind. Despite her name, fall was one of her favorite seasons. Yes, it rained a lot in Tigard, Oregon, but on dry days it was a comfortable temperature, not too hot nor too cold. Well… *usually.* It could get a little chilly at night, but nothing a cute sweater, maybe layered with a light jacket, couldn't fix. The changing colors of the leaves reminded her of the long drives she would take with her mother as a kid, both happy and in awe of the various shades of reds, oranges, and yellows that lined the streets.

Winter made some oatmeal and poured it into her new white, pink, and gold cat-shaped bowl that a fan sent to her P.O. Box. She sliced a half banana and arranged each slice on the oatmeal to look like a smiling face. She placed it on the kitchen counter, under the natural light glow of the kitchen window. Then she took a photo...and another one… and there it was. She posted the photo to Nanogram with the caption

Starting the day off right, adding a few breakfast worthy hashtags before sitting down to eat.

Though she had only been living on her own for six months, Winter felt loneliness engulf her like an unwanted hug. She blew her nose, realizing that her cold was actually kind of going away, and pictured Lyle's smile in her head. Of course, that smile soon faded, replaced by his usual condescending raised eyebrows and blank stare. She closed her eyes and tried to clear her mind. *Why do I always think about him every morning?* she thought.

Their breakup marked a very bad time in her life. She was working as a receptionist for his law firm and was promptly fired without cause. Winter knew it was wrongful termination, you can't fire someone for breaking up with you, but she just wanted to get away and not think about her ex again. Suing the firm would probably be a long battle that she was not ready to take on. Besides, there was no telling what Lyle was capable of after he confronted her that last night for merely going to a bar with her coworkers. That was the bitter icing on the poisonous cake that was their relationship. *Ugh! Stop thinking about him, Winter!* she screamed silently. *He's not worth your time.*

As she rinsed her cat bowl in the sink and put it in the dishwater, her thoughts had shifted to figuring out the next post she was going to put up.

Ooh oh oh oh
That's the way it goes
Ooh oh oh oh
Dancing on your toes

Winter's current favorite indie song woke her out of her

morning trance, and her phone vibrated as it displayed a gif of a blood-red glider butterfly fluttering its wings. She accepted the video call and a beautiful, oval-faced, pony-tailed redhead with Cupid's bow shaped lips, and a Snow White complexion, appeared on the screen. She was riding a stationary bike, and her head bobbed from side to side as she pedaled.

"Hey, girl. Saw the morning post. Breakfast looks goooood," said Mia, slightly out of breath, "Did you make me a bowl?"

"If you wanna stop by," said Winter, very well knowing the answer.

"You know I can't. But I miss you. You look like you're feeling better."

"Yeah, I think I—"

"Okay then," Mia seemed to pedal faster. "We're getting together tonight."

"Oh, I'd love to, Mia, but I have to work on my next post and—"

"Dude, I'm sorry I'm cutting you off a lot, but I already know the crap you're about to spew and I really don't want to hear it. Besides, your post last night was scorching, sweltering—no—*blistering* hot."

Winter laughed.

"If I didn't love you so much," Mia continued, "I'd be jealous of that freakin' post."

"Yeah, right. I envy *your* post feed," said Winter. "You have this cool, physical and mental health vibe going on. I mostly just have clothes and food and fake scenes I set up." She tried to mask the melancholy in her voice, symptoms of that bad taste in her mouth she got whenever she let thoughts about Lyle creep in.

"You're so clueless and smart at the same time. It's so damn cute."

"Um, okay. I'll take that."

"So about tonight."

"Mia, honestly I'd love to hang but I have to start thinking about my next few promos and I'm already kinda stressing about it."

"Only you would stress about something like that." Mia breathed harder. "Look at me, I'm bombarded with people wanting to pay me more money," she said in a mocking tone.

Winter sighed. "Yeah, I guess you're right. I should be grateful, just like that quote you posted last week. I'm getting really sick of you being right all the time."

"So, what do you have? What kind of products?"

"Uh, I got a fake tan lotion."

"Not gonna work. Go on."

"And I have this detox system."

Mia made a buzzer sound. "What else you got?"

"I have this LED light-up skirt from this new designer."

"Ding ding dong! We have a winner! How much are you getting paid?"

"Oh, that one was a freebie. He's still in design school but he's so talented."

"'Kay cool. The LED skirt will be perfect for where we're going, and Jeremiah and I can help you take another *blistering* photo."

Winter's nose started to run again, and she blotted it with her breakfast napkin. "Blistering is a little too hot for my taste."

"Well, there's this new, upscale hipster bowling place that opened up at the top of the hill and you are going, girl."

"Bowling? In a skirt?"

"Hecccks, yeah. It'll show how classy Winter Smith can look, even in a bowling alley."

"I don't know."

"Do you want me and Jeremiah to give you an intervention? You've been more and more withdrawn since you left Lyle."

"Sorry about that," Winter said quietly.

"Don't be sorry, just be aware of it. You're so talented and gorgeous, you deserve to have a life too. You can't hide behind work forever." Mia stopped pedaling and wiped her face with a towel.

Winter thought for a second. She turned the phone away so she could put all her effort into stopping herself from crying, without an audience. Then she took another deep breath before turning the phone back.

"What did I ever do to deserve you as a friend, Mia? You're like a walking, talking, inspirational meme."

Mia stood up and shrugged. "You were born? I don't know." She put the phone close to her face for dramatic effect. "But what I do know is that you're going out with us tonight. And I'm gonna kick your butt on the lane. Like, I'm gonna get a lot of holes in one."

Winter chuckled. "Oh, yeah? Wait, don't you mean you'll get a lot of strikes?"

"You heard me," Mia said. "Meet us at the bottom of Tram 2 at 7:00 p.m., okay?"

"Okay."

With that, Mia winked, her naturally long, dark auburn eyelashes glistening with sweat. Then she morphed into the words: *Video Call Ended.*

Winter looked over at her mint green sofa. Sprawled across it were more packages she picked up from her P.O.

Box and a black skirt in a clear garment bag laying haphazardly across the sofa arm rest. She stared at it, trying to remember the last night she went out without Lyle. The last time she allowed herself to have fun. The last time she truly smiled. And she decided that *tonight is finally the night.*

CHAPTER TWO

It took Winter about thirty minutes to find a parking spot. Portland's downtown Southwest Waterfront district was under a lot of construction, and it seemed like two or three new luxury condo buildings had popped up since she had been down there last. *When was the actual last time I went to Portland?* she pondered.

As she bought her parking ticket, Lyle's face flashed in her head again and she remembered walking on the waterfront with him. It was one of their first dates and he had taken her hand after they sat down on a bench. They played the observation game, making funny comments about the path cyclists, runners, dog walkers, and even the poor, unsuspecting souls merely enjoying a nice stroll.

"Look at those two," Lyle had said, discreetly pointing to a thirty-something couple power-walking in matching black workout pants and white shirts. "That girl definitely talked him into wearing those horrible outfits. God, I hate soft pushovers like that. If he was trying to work for me and I saw a photo of him online dressed like that, I wouldn't even consider hiring him. No matter what his credentials were." Winter remembered finding Lyle's observations hilarious, only because she thought he was joking. After getting to know him over the next two years, however, she slowly realized he wasn't the "joking" type.

Winter walked down that same path to the Tram. The water sparkled under the setting sun, and in the distance, three small canoes floated next to each other toward the bridge. Winter remembered canoeing with a certain someone and —*No! That is the last time I think about him.*

The wind near the river was a little nippy, so she buttoned up her eggshell white trench coat, and wished she had worn a pair of socks over her sheer, black tights. She mentally patted herself on the back, however, for wearing the black suede ankle boots instead of something strappy and toe-exposing.

"Winnnnn-terrrrrr!" screamed a voice from across the street.

She turned and could see that oh-too-familiar flame of red hair bobbing in the wind, wearing a tan overcoat and standing next to her tall, golden-tanned companion wearing blue jeans, classic vans shoes, a black t-shirt (with an obscured graphic), and navy blue bomber jacket. The figures stood, statuesque, next to the lower tram entrance. Winter waved, waited for the green walk signal, and ran across the street to meet Mia and her boyfriend, Jeremiah.

"Well, fancy meeting you here," Winter said, hugging Mia.

"What's up, Wints'," Jeremiah said, taking his turn to embrace Winter. "I'm surprised Mia talked you into this."

"Yeah, I've been a little… focused, lately," Winter replied.

“I’ll say.” Mia rolled her hazel eyes, framed with army green eye shadow and forest green eyeliner.

Jeremiah looked back and forth at the girls, and scratched his beard, which was a few inches longer than the hair on his head. “Um… are you both sure you know where you’re going?”

“Bowling!” Winter and Mia said in unison, causing them to both break out in a fit of laughter.

Jeremiah shook his head. “Let me guess. I’m gonna be today’s photoshoot intern?”

“Probably,” Winter said.

“Yeah, I made sure not to tell him.” Mia put her arm around Jeremiah’s waist and looked up at him. “’Cuz I knew you wouldn’t have come. Besides, we all know you’re so much better at taking a photo than me.”

He averted his eyes from his girlfriend and nodded his head in defeatism. “And to think I thought this was actually gonna be a chill night.”

“Oh, sorry Jeremiah,” Winter said. “It doesn’t have to be anything complicated. I just gotta get my skirt in a fast, no-nonsense shot and we’ll be good to go.”

He looked at her skeptically.

“I promise. I actually wanna chill tonight, too,” Winter assured him, with an exaggerated, toothy, cheesy smile.

“Mmmhmm,” Jeremiah replied.

“Hey! I wanna see what you’re working with, gal!” Mia almost screamed. “Open that coat up and give it to me!”

“Geez,” said Jeremiah.

“Not yet. When the timing is right.” Winter gave a coy, devilish smile and wink.

“Fine, I won’t show you mine yet either,” Mia said. “Well, at least I can see your boots. They’re so *ice*.”

"Is that a good thing?" Jeremiah asked.

"Of course! They're so *ice*, they're *frigid.*" Mia pretended to freeze, shaking in her boots.

"Okay, but earlier you were saying everything was blistering hot, so—"

"So what?" Mia cocked her head to the side.

"So you could see why that's confus—" Jeremiah scratched his beard. "Ah, never mind."

There was an industrial creaking sound and they all looked up to see their transportation heading toward them. Winter once had to do a school report on the Portland Aerial Tram, and the facts have been seared into her mind ever since. The silver, round cabin could hold close to eighty people, travel approximately twenty miles per hour, rise upwards of 500 feet, and took only about four minutes to travel up or down the hill. The wind had picked up a little and as the cabin inched closer, it rocked back and forth. Winter suddenly felt her pulse in her ears.

Mia noticed her friend's expression. "Don't worry, Winter. It's as safe as traveling down a highway."

"But aren't highways, like, kinda dangerous?" Jeremiah asked, and Mia elbowed him to *shut it.*

"I'll be fine. I'll be fine. I'll be fine. I always am on the Tram," Winter said out loud, yet to herself, a stupid mantra she recited whenever she had to ride the contraption.

Jeremiah handed over the tickets as they walked around the corner to get in line. There were so many people in front of them, they had to wait three round trips before they could even get on the thing. The second the cabin doors closed, Winter thought happy thoughts to ease her anxiety; the forest, the coastline, the refreshing coolness of light rain, the *Life is*

Strange videogame. As more people piled in, the three were pushed from the seemingly protected center, all the way to a side window. Mia grabbed her nervous friend's hand and squeezed.

"I'm fine." Winter managed to produce a lopsided smile. "Piece of cake."

"Thatta girl." Mia matched her friend's enthusiasm and was happy to go along with whatever charade Winter required to deal with certain things.

The Tram vibrated forward, and the terminal looked smaller and smaller with every second that went by. The first time Winter watched that terminal shrink before her very eyes, was during her third date with Lyle. She had stepped on the platform and got in line, on the verge of tears, not just because she was afraid of heights, but because she thought she would let Lyle down if she were to chicken out. She had grown up suffering from *prisoner of shyness disorder* and he had the ability to push her beyond her limits—to the state of being constantly frazzled. "It's good for you," he would tell her. "There's no room in this world for the meek." *Perhaps he was right*, Winter thought. Still holding Mia's hand, she allowed herself to take in the scenery. The sun had already dipped below the horizon, and there was a luminous blanket of pinks and purples creating a nice safety hammock to cushion a plunging tram if the wires were to ever break. At least, that's what Winter told herself.

They passed over the bustling sidewalks, then the busy streets, then the presumably occupied houses. Though dim, she could see the outline of Mt. Hood in the distance, covered by white, cream cheese frosting. *Dang. I must be hungry*, she thought. Before long, the Tram slowed down to a jerky stop.

The doors opened to the booming sound of Synthpop, and a bouquet of melted cheese and grilled chicken. It dawned on her that the ride up the hill hadn't been that bad and she wasn't as afraid as she had anticipated. As they exited, Mia's hand slipped out of Winter's grasp and disappeared into the crowd, along with Jeremiah.

CHAPTER THREE

The pathway, lined with trees wrapped in firefly lights, sat under a bed of smoke, flowing out of hidden dry ice fog machines. Winter followed the group in front of her, and as they got closer to the entrance, the smoke swirled and pulsated to the music's bass. A large sign read *Blaine's Lanes*, and it cycled through every shade within the monographic blue color scheme. The sleek blue and yellow, square-shaped building boasted large circular windows that perfectly framed the view of its interior. Winter could see a massive, full dining section under a wood paneled ceiling, and directly behind it, a ten-lane bowling alley with large video screens playing what looked to be a montage of popular music videos from the last few years.

She walked in with a mission, trying to find Mia and Jeremiah, but was quickly sidetracked by something she somehow didn't notice from the outside. Behind the bowling lanes was a manmade, rocky mountain-like structure, split by an actual waterfall that flowed down and disappeared into a hidden drain. *Whoever this Blaine guy is,* Winter thought, *he must be riii-itch.*

"Ay yo ay yo!"

She thought she heard Mia's voice, but she just couldn't find that red rogue wave in the ocean of people.

"Ay yo, Winter!" shouted a deeper, louder voice, coming from the left.

It took a second, but she finally spotted Jeremiah waving her over to lane three.

"This place is incredible," said Winter after pushing her way through the crowd that looked like it stepped off a shoot for *Modern Hipster* magazine, if there was such a thing.

"I know, pretty interesting, huh?" Mia flipped her hair, and sat down in one of the six black recliner chairs that formed a crescent around a wood stump table that had a touch screen built in.

Winter nodded, looking around in awe.

"Yeah, this place is the shit," Jeremiah said, somehow already holding a beer. "Watch this - you guys want a Cosmo?"

"Sure," said Mia without looking up from her attempt to tie her brand new bowling shoes.

Winter nodded.

Jeremiah typed into his cell phone. After a few seconds, the screen on the wooden table slowly flipped over, replaced with a rising metal box that stopped at about two feet high. The side facing the seats slid open, displaying two cocktail glasses filled with the perfect translucently pink hue that made Winter's mouth water. Jeremiah nodded for her to grab the drinks, and she happily obliged, looking in the box for any kind of dispenser but only finding a slick, silvery surface instead. Once the drinks were removed, the box lowered and rotated back into obscurity, replaced again by the screen.

Dumbfounded, Winter handed Mia her drink and sat down in one of the recliners, which conveniently had cup—*and cocktail!*—holders built into the armrest.

"Am I in the future or something?" Winter asked.

Mia handed her a pair of shoes. "This is your size, right?"

"Uh, yeah," she replied, examining their sleekness. "When did you get—"

"Over there." Mia pointed toward another silver box built into a side table, slowly closing its silver sliding doors.

"Yep, this *is* the future," Winter whispered to herself.

"Yeah, pretty chill," Jeremiah replied.

Winter took a sip of her Cosmo. "Thanks so much for inviting me, guys."

Jeremiah nodded and Mia stood up to get a feel for her shoes, even running in place for about twenty seconds. Winter took a photo of her bowling shoes, realizing they would actually pair well with one of her dresses at home. Then she put them on and tucked her own boots behind her seat.

"Up," Mia said, motioning Winter to stand. "I wanna see the skirt."

Winter quickly tested the loops of her bowling shoe ties then stood up.

She took off her coat and Mia snatched it, throwing it on the farthest recliner. Winter's outfit looked modestly styled: a solid green crop top with a shin length pleated black skirt. Mia nodded approvingly, until Winter pushed a button on a small device hidden inside the back of her waistband. The skirt lit up, each pleat alternating magical blue and green. She twirled around and the colors blended into an absinthe-dream-like glow.

Mia stood there, jaw to the floor. And even Jeremiah looked stunned.

"I hate you," Mia said, and Winter stopped twirling. "This is like the coolest, most beautiful freakin' thing I've ever seen. I seriously hate you."

"I love you too," Winter said with a laugh. "By the way, you can borrow it if you want."

"I love you," Mia said.

"That is a pretty badass dress," said Jeremiah.

"Skirt," Mia corrected him. "Badass skirt."

The girls sat down, and Mia took a piece of the fabric for a closer inspection. "Wow," she said, over and over again.

"Okay, then. Let's start playing. I already entered our names." The annoyed tone in Jeremiah's voice went up a notch.

Winter looked at the name list on the screen. "It's so packed in here. How'd y'all snag a lane anyway?"

"Oh, I did some graphic work for the family that opened this place," Jeremiah said.

"Family? Is it like some kind of Oregon mob?" Winter joked.

Mia pretended to choke on her drink.

Jeremiah typed something into his phone again and within seconds, a large, fluffy, fabric cloud on wheels seemingly emerged from somewhere behind the chairs, rolling up to him. Three green bowling balls of varying sizes sat atop the cloud. He grabbed the largest one.

"Not a mob," he answered. "They're some kind of tech investors or something. And they're controlling owners of this huge company, FFS Industries. Owns that StyleSlap y'all care about so much."

Winter's eyes widened.

"No shit!" Mia said. "You hafta introduce us!"

"I mean, I've never actually met them in person. I kinda just interacted with their 'people'. Dang." He paused to think. "Maybe they *are* the Oregon mob."

"Well, that sucks," Mia said. Holding one of the smaller bowling balls, she playfully bumped her boyfriend out of the way, and rolled. "Let's play ball."

"That's not even the right—" Jeremiah shut up the second Mia knocked down every pin.

"Oh, my God!" Winter said, genuinely shocked.

Mia walked casually back to her seat. "Told you I'd whoop some booty today."

"Did you say that?" Winter asked.

"Something like that," Mia said, and downed the rest of her Cosmopolitan.

CHAPTER FOUR

Bo noticed her the moment she walked in. She was by herself and admiring the scenery so intently, she might as well have been visiting the Sistine Chapel. The entrance draft tousled her long, dark brown hair, and she casually tamed it with a hair flip and tucking any unruly strands behind her ears. It was one of the sexiest things he'd ever seen. He watched her float over to who he guessed were her friends, stationed at the other end of the bowling alley. Her guy friend was really tall and looked a lot like that mixed guy from Bo's ex-girlfriend's favorite soap opera, the one she promised she didn't have a crush on even though she had a habit of mentioning him randomly in conversation. Bo felt a sharp stab of jealousy on the side of his belly. Like he knew the girl across the alley and was expecting the tall, soap opera guy to hit on her. He breathed a sigh of relief when he saw the redheaded friend grab the guy's ass.

"Hey, man! Wake up!"

Bo felt a hand hit his chest with force, violently snapping him out of his stupor. He grabbed the perpetrator's hand and twisted it, maneuvering himself until he had the person in a solid headlock.

"Dude, what the fuck?" said the restrained man who sported a blonde man bun and lip ring. He tried wriggling his way out of his captor's grasp, but quickly gave up.

Bo finally let go, then pointed at Man Bun. "You know you deserved that."

"What the fu— No I fucking didn't."

Bo cocked his head to the side, displaying wide, crazy eyes.

"Okay, okay," Man Bun conceded with a smile, rubbing his arm. "Maybe I did."

Bo dropped his intimidation act and shook his head, smiling from only one side of his mouth. He looked at the wooden table monitor, grabbed the bowling ball from a large cloud floating near his feet, and kicked the fluffy device out of his way. Before he could make it up to the line, a girl in a short and tight, canary yellow spandex dress, drunkenly put her arm around his waist. Her twin, in matching spandex pants and halter top, stood behind her with eyes closed, swaying to the music.

"You've barely talked to me all night," Canary Girl said in a high-pitched, whiney squeak.

"Because you drank too much, Samantha," Bo said without looking at her. "You promised you wouldn't drink too much, but ya' did."

"Oh, whatever! I only had like…like one drink!" Samantha staggered back as Bo peeled her arm off of him. "Let's just go to your place and I'll show you how *not* drunk I am."

"Kevin, can you come get your girls. They can barely

stand," Bo said to a short man wearing a gray beanie and designer jeans.

"Sure thing," said Kevin.

"We're not his girls," said Samantha, over-dramatizing her hurt with an extra oomph of whininess. "You said *we* were together tonight, and you lied…again. You do—you do this every time!"

"Sam, hon,' you get too drunk every time. You're a cool chick but I'd basically be taking advantage of you at this point."

"Oh, whatever! That's just an excuse!" Samantha folded her arms angrily.

Kevin had helped the quiet twin to the closest recliner and gave her a water bottle, but Samantha wouldn't budge.

Her face flushed. "I've never been turned down, Bo Blaine. You're just a weirdo douche and everyone knows it. That's why your daddy is gonna sell the family company. 'Cuz you're such a fucking weirdo."

Samantha had gotten so worked up, she started foaming at the mouth. Well, at least that was what Bo imagined because he wasn't actually looking at her. He had his eyes set on that brunette across the alley whose skirt was glowing with blue and green lights, creating a kind of halo around her that highlighted her high cheek bones. It felt like a butterfly took a wrong turn and got trapped in his stomach, flapping like crazy for a way out. *Hmmm. That's...a weird feeling,* he thought.

He took a step forward, launched his ball down the lane, and knocked over every pin. He looked over at the brunette who was laughing with her friends. Her smile was a flame, and he was a moth that couldn't resist.

"Nice one, man!" shouted Kevin, sitting in his recliner and holding up a beer.

Bo grabbed a beer and sat down beside him. He repeatedly glanced across the lanes before realizing The Spandex Twins were gone. “Where’d the girls go?”

“Oh, they wanted to leave, so Matt walked them out to the car service.”

Bo blew air out of his nose. “Walked them out? Man, I don’t trust that guy. The only reason he’s here is ‘cuz my parents do business with his parents; and because he’s Olivia’s brother.”

“Yeah, I don’t trust him either. That’s why I watched him walk them out and he *did* try to get in the car with them, but they weren’t having it. He’s talking to some other girls now. That Samantha though…” Kevin adjusted his beanie. “She’s a feisty one.”

“Yeah,” Bo said flatly. “That’s a good way of putting it.”

They sat there for a while, drinking beers and bobbing their heads to the music. Bo couldn’t stop staring at the brunette, who was taking a lot of photos: Photos of her drink, of her shoes, of the bowling balls, of the waterfall backdrop. And the selfies. She took *so many* selfies. And almost every time she got up she had the redhead take a photo of her. If both girls got up, they got the tall dude to take the photos, and he clearly wasn’t happy with that role. The brunette in particular was really good at posing, she really knew how to accentuate her…assets. It was exhausting just watching it all.

“See something you like over there?” asked Kevin.

“Oh, yeah. That girl is fucking gorgeous.” Bo pointed to Winter who turned on her skirt again before bowling, knocking over half of the pins. Of course she was being filmed, and she did a funny curtsey move that almost made Bo laugh—almost.

“Damn, she is hot. That redhead too, man,” Kevin said.

"A lot of good-looking people here. I guess you could say opening night is a success."

Kevin chugged the rest of his beer then decided to take his turn to bowl, achieving a pocket 7-10 split. He tried again and the ball curved right, ending up in the gutter. Unaffected, he sat back down and cracked open another beer.

Bo leaned forward. "She looks kind of familiar, don't you think?"

"Maybe." Kevin squinted his eyes to try and get a better look. "Yeah, actually, she does."

After a few long seconds of staring, Winter briefly glanced up at them, as if she could feel the attention. The butterfly in Bo's stomach woke up and started flapping again. He shifted uncomfortably in his chair.

"Oh, shit, I know who that is!" Kevin took out his phone and opened Nanogram, then handed his phone to Bo. "She's that social media girl who has a ton of followers and shit. As you can see, *I'm* even following her."

Bo scrolled through her page and realized his stomach butterfly friend had duplicated to nearly a baker's dozen. "Gorgeous," he muttered.

He handed the phone back.

"Why don't you go talk to her?" Kevin asked, looking at his phone. "According to Google, she's single and ready to mingle."

"Nah. She's too into herself. I can't go for someone like that."

"Dude. You have an *in* though. Your family owns StyleSlap and she's like always trending on that shit."

Bo looked at him sideways. "How would you know?"

Kevin took a swig of beer. "I'm secure enough in my

manhood to admit I love that fucking app. Where do you think I get all my style pointers from?"

Bo raised his eyebrows, thought for a second, then lowered them. "Makes sense."

"Sure does."

"Damn, son! What the *fuck* did you say to Samantha? I've never seen a girl so pissed off." Man Bun Matt walked up holding a huge platter of nachos. He pushed the bowling balls off the cloud, and they fell to the ground with a thud. He then pulled the cloud up to his chair, using it as a makeshift coffee table.

"Oh, I just refuse to sleep with her because she's intoxicated," Bo said. "Fuck me, right?"

"Lame," said Matt and stuffed his mouth.

"Yeah, you are," said Kevin.

"What?" asked Matt.

"Nothing."

"Dude!" Matt's mouth was full, and cheese dribbled down his chin. "I heard Winter Smith and that Mia chick with the big tits are supposed to be here. They're so fucking hot. I'd do anything to get my dick even ten feet close to them."

Kevin rolled his eyes and Bo really considered taking Matt by the man bun and shoving his disgusting head into that damn nacho platter.

CHAPTER FIVE

Winter felt eyes on her but whenever she scanned the room, heads seemed to *turn* away. Eyes *averted.* Or was she just imagining it? Maybe somebody recognized her. Nah. She wasn't real-world famous, per say. More like, mildly internet famous. She'd gotten approached a few times and fans sometimes sent her things, or drew her, or blogged or vlogged about her, or made their own posts and videos trying out her styles, but that was basically the extent of it. No big deal. Winter finally rationalized that if she did get any looks her way, it was most definitely the result of her attention seeking light-up skirt. Therefore, she vowed to only turn it on when she needed to get another picture or video, which she had basically captured within the first fifteen minutes of arriving to the bowling alley. *It's all smooth sailing from here,* Winter thought.

"I can't believe Jeremiah is almost winning!" shouted Mia. "This is bullshiiiit!"

"You're doing amazing, though," Jeremiah said, unsuccessfully trying to hide his pleasure.

"Hey, you both should be happy. You're clobbering me," Winter chimed in.

"Of course!" said Mia. "You're the style girl. I'm supposed to be the athletic, good-at-anything-physical girl."

"I work out too, ya know," said Jeremiah.

"Yeah, but my boobs make it exponentially harder." Mia pointed to her chest. "So I win in that contest."

Jeremiah sat down, defeated. "Well, whatever. Let's just not play then."

Winter shook her head, watching the usual scene unfold. Mia sat on an annoyed and pouting Jeremiah. She kissed his cheek, then his lips. Then he tickled her, and all was good again in the world.

Winter tried desperately to not think about Lyle when her friends got like that. Lyle, at one time, was actually into public displays of affection. Well, at first he was. After a few months of being swept off her feet, Winter was knocked down by his constant nitpicking, his backhanded jabs, his affinity to embarrass her. Such instances would always put her in a bad mood, and he knew to never try to kiss her when she was like that. *Maybe I was too sensitive*, thought Winter. But she quickly remembered what her mother's psychiatrist friend, Dr. Ronda, once told her when she visited town: "Stop blaming yourself for everything that Lyle did to you." Winter had taken that advice with a grain of salt because right after, her mother sighed deeply and said "Yeah, but it takes two to tango."

Her mother was never really on her side about anything. Single Child Syndrome—referring to the stereotype that an only child can become spoiled, selfish, and entitled because they get too much attention—is a real thing. But that definitely was not a syndrome that Winter developed growing up in Cassandra Smith's household. Winter couldn't remember a whole lot from her early childhood, but she knew there had to have been good times. Her parents were vivacious and hopeful and free-spirited. And according to old family photos, they made time to do things together, like go to the pumpkin patch and corn maze every October.

Mother had so much to look forward to; she was attending a highly respected university for economics, modeling on the side, had a loving husband, and a little girl that looked up to her for guidance. She married and had a child right out of high school, but the marriage ultimately fizzled out after five years. Winter's father moved to Norway for a job opportunity. Her mother quit graduate school and moved down to Los Angeles, deciding she wanted to focus only on modeling and acting. Her depression soon caught up to her and though she was beautiful, and hasn't really ever stopped being beautiful, her entertainment career ended quickly. Lack of enthusiasm, maybe? Lack of dedication to the hustle? Lack of confidence? Cassandra then migrated up north to live back in her birth town and has lived off freelance writing work ever since. She did sell an economics eBook once that didn't do too badly. For years, especially living in Oregon, Winter had felt like a burden to her mother. Or a reminder of what her mother lost. *Thank God I was able to return her sweater before she noticed,* Winter thought. *It's not like she's going to see my posts or anything. She could care less about—*

"Hey, what's up? My name's Bo."

A deep voice snapped her out of muddled musings. Her eyes focused and a trim yet muscular physique towered over her, holding out a hand. He had light brown hair styled into a high fade and a hard side part. She couldn't help but glance at the stunning picture. He wore polished, brown, wing-tipped brogue shoes, black chino trouser pants rolled up at the ankle, a brown belt, and a white, buttoned up dress shirt rolled up at the sleeves and tucked in. His gentleman-like attire was juxtaposed with tattoos that covered his exposed skin, including his ankles, arms, hands, and chest. Thankfully, his neck and sharp, angular face were untouched by any semblance of permanent ink. *Covering up that face would be a travesty*, she thought. Winter's stomach tightened but she tried not to show her impression in her countenance.

"Oh, um. Hi," Winter said and shook his hand. He gripped firmly and a bolt of electricity shot through her whole body. *Am I shaking a taser?* she joked to herself.

"What's your name?" he asked.

"Her name is Winter Smith!" Mia answered. "Isn't that a badass name?"

The Bo guy smiled, flashing beautiful white teeth.

"Oh, yeah. Sorry. I was kind of zoning out," Winter said as she scrambled to her feet. "Yeah, my name's Winter. It's nice to meet you, Bo."

"Well, I just wanted to thank you all for attending opening night," he said. "This place was something I thought up when I was a kid and somehow we were able to finally make it work. It's pretty surreal."

Winter nodded a little too fast.

"And I hope you spread the word so the building's not immediately replaced by another marijuana dispensary," he added.

Jeremiah and Mia laughed. Winter smiled, but she was briefly distracted by the waterfall slowing its cascade of water intensity to match the slower tempo coming out of the speakers.

"It's like art," Winter said, quieter than she intended.

"What was that?" Bo asked.

"It's like art," Winter said louder. "The always changing neon color scheme, the clouds, all this new tech stuff, the waterfall, I feel like I'm in some kind of enchanted, futuristic land."

Bo looked at her, intently, with piercing green, deep set eyes. For a few seconds it felt like they were locked into each other and would be stuck like that forever. She couldn't help but feel a warmness inside her, and a subsequent embarrassment that someone might detect it.

"That's exactly what I was going for," Bo said, still holding her gaze.

His presence, his unwavering confidence, was so strong that it seemed to rub off on the people around him. When he looked at Winter, she felt interesting, *important*, even.

"Yeah, this place is legit," added Jeremiah, slicing the connection between Winter and Bo like a machete to rope. "And anytime FFS needs graphic design work, I'm your man."

"Oh, yeah," said Bo, scratching his head. "You said you did some work for the family, right?"

"Yeah, man. I really enjoyed it."

"Well, unfortunately I don't really have a lot to do with that kind of stuff. I'm more, like, the face, I guess." Bo stopped and thought for a second, before clapping his hands together. "According to my dad I'm just an aimless, wayfaring Earth wanderer with no future, so…"

Jeremiah's eyes widened as big as his girlfriend's.

"Oh, fuck. I'm sorry, guys." Bo shook his head. "You didn't need to hear that."

"No worries," said Mia with a courtesy smile.

Jeremiah kind of just grunted and nodded in support.

But Winter… Bo's words hit her like a blow to the heart. She didn't know if she related because of her mother or because of Lyle or because everything just sounded more intense coming from *him*. Without realizing it, she was sitting back on a recliner, feeling dizzy.

"You okay?" Bo asked. He crouched down, concerned. "Do you need me to call somebody?"

"Oh, no. Just feeling a little lightheaded." Winter forced a laugh. "Getting over a cold, you know."

He nodded but squinted his eyes as if to analyze if she was lying or not.

Mia was already sitting next to Winter, opening a water bottle. "Oh, this happens from time to time."

And Mia wasn't lying. Winter often had things wrong with her. Phantom colds. Dizzy spells. Random sharp pains in random spots of her body. It usually happened when she was under some kind of pressure, though. Like the time she had a video diary due for a local magazine's website at the same time she found out her father had a whole other family on the other side of the world. Or the day she decided she wasn't going to college and had to tell her mother. Or, of course, the time she had to accept her father was dead. That was a particularly bad one, in which she broke out in a rash, got vertigo, and contracted the flu, all at once. Dr. Ronda diagnosed Winter with a mild form of "somatic amplification disorder," triggered by stress. In other words, she was a hypochondriac.

"Oh, don't worry, man. We can take it from here," Jeremiah assured Bo. "I'm sure you have other people to meet."

Bo gently took Winter's hand in both of his. That initial jolt of electricity morphed into a steadfast, soothing current that flowed back and forth between them. Somehow, the room had stopped spinning the moment she realized how warm and comforting, and sturdy, his hands felt.

"If you need anything, Winter," he said earnestly, "don't hesitate to ask."

Though the music changed, blasting another bass-heavy track, Winter could not only hear him clearly, she examined each word and syllable formed on his lips. Lips she wished she could press to her own. His green eyes, framed by his brooding, dark eyebrows, seemed to shimmer with the changing brightness of the video screens. Winter was convinced she was dreaming.

Maybe this isn't some techy-artsy bowling alley, she told herself, *but instead some temporary, imagined, wonderland that's gonna disappear the second I wake up*.

Bo finally stood up and let go of her hand, and Winter could do nothing but look away. Mia rubbed her back and encouraged her to drink from the water bottle.

"Ay, man," Winter heard Bo say. "You got a card? Cuz I can still talk you up to my old man."

"Oh, yeah. For sure," Winter heard Jeremiah say. "I'd really appreciate that."

When she finally looked up, Bo was gone. And yes, she *knew* it was crazy, but it felt like a piece of her had gone with him.

CHAPTER SIX

"Let's get the hell out of here," Bo said, firmly.

Kevin had just bowled a turn, fist-pumping the air as the last pin fell over. He spun around in good spirits, until he saw Bo's anxious expression. "You okay, man?"

There were two unfamiliar, pretty girls sitting at their lane. At least, Bo guessed they were pretty, since he was too foggy-headed to understand what 'pretty' even meant. He was consumed by *her*. The dark-haired brunette with the light-up skirt. The sweet, beautiful woman he'd just met and felt a tinge of nervousness around, like he would say the wrong thing. Which of course he did. The girl with a cold hand that trembled when he held it, that looked straight into his soul when he allowed himself to look back.

Who the fuck was I back there? he thought. *That person back there should get his ass handed to him by someone like me. 'Someone like me?' Who the fuck am I anyway?* He tried to shake her off, like he would shake off his raincoat before hanging it up to dry. But he couldn't. She stuck to him. Seeped into him. It didn't make sense. Nothing made sense.

Winter Smith. Winter Smith. He said her name over and over in his head like a mantra. *Gorgeous... Winter...Smith.*

He imagined telling his parents about her. He could see the vacancy in their eyes. His dad slapping him on the back on the way to locking himself in his office all day. "Okay, playboy," his dad would say to him, in that condescending, snarky, don't-give-a-shit tone.

"So, how was meeting Winter Smith? Was she as cool as she seems?" Kevin asked.

"What the fuck? You met Winter Smith?" Matt walked away from his ball as it crawled down the lane. "Where is she?"

One of the new girls, the one in the tightest jeans Bo had ever seen, pointed to the other side of the alley. Matt jerked his head to look.

"Yeah," said the other girl wearing a long black and white striped dress, "Winter and Mia are in lane two or three or whatever. We were gonna say howdy, but they don't look so, I don't know, howdy-able, I guess?"

Bo closed his eyes and took deep breaths and tried to defrag his mind. Shotgun meditation was one of the only coping mechanisms that his mom taught him as a child, when she first realized he had anger issues. Meditation usually worked, but that night, it didn't make a dent on his ever increasing uneasiness.

"Hell, yeah! Come on! Now is always the best time!" said Matt, giddily.

The two girls stood up, happy to have an escort to meet their social influencer idols.

Bo watched the three practically skip toward their victims. He wanted to run after them and act as bodyguard in his own place of business. But he knew that'd be a bad idea. His mom told him that if he ever wanted to prove he could run a business, he had to avoid fights, stay away from scandals, and overall, just not embarrass the family name. Then conceivably, maybe, *possibly*, he'd be given a controlling stake of FFS Industries. "It's your last chance," Mom reminded him, only a week before. "Your siblings have their own things going for them and are willing to hand over the reins to their baby brother. Don't. Mess. This. Up."

His ma always got right to the point.

Instead, Bo just stood there witnessing the horror show unfold (yep, he was being a little dramatic) before his very eyes. Matt, the oblivious asshole that he was, interrupting Winter and Mia's conversation, spouting something out of his punchable face.

"Man, maybe we should go over there," Kevin said.

Bo cracked his knuckles, one by one, as he watched Winter and Mia feigning happiness to greet such obnoxious miscreants. *Okay, maybe they weren't that bad,* Bo thought, not wanting to revert to his old self. That angry-at-the-world bloke he had become after his dad sent him away to boarding school, in England, for God's sake! Bo took another deeeeeeeeeeep breath. An acoustic song had started playing over the speakers, allowing Matt's loud horn of a voice and the sound of the giggling girls to permeate through the crowd.

"I don't think I should go over there, man," Bo said, who was done with knuckle popping, and had transitioned to repeated fist squeezing and shuffling from side to side.

Kevin recognized the state his friend was in. "Okay, I'll go over there then. Don't worry, I won't get in a fight. Just as long as Matt doesn't step on these shoes, I'm good."

Bo looked down and realized Kevin was wearing a replica of the 1989 Nike MAGs from *Back to the Future*.

"Holy sh— How did I not notice you were wearing those?" Bo was genuinely shocked.

"See, that's how you know you're in your head, man. You don't even notice your friend is Marty Mcfly."

Bo laughed, releasing harbored tension. He looked again at lane three and could feel Jeremiah's palpable annoyance, especially anytime Matt talked.

"No, I'll wait sixty seconds," Bo said, "and if they don't leave them alone, I'll get security."

"Good idea."

Bo and Kevin stood silently, arms crossed, for exactly one minute, indicated by the alarm on Kevin's digital watch, which Bo noticed had a red band made out of the same material of Marty McFly's signature red vest.

"Now that's a damn fine watch," said Bo.

Kevin silenced the alarm. "Oh, thanks man."

Winter and Mia were still getting harassed by The Annoyancers (aptly named by Bo as he waited), so he went off to find security. He was deterred by two men in suits that he didn't recognize, who said they used to work with his dad, so he had to shake their hands and talk to them. He nod-signaled to Kevin to finish the job, and Kevin gave the two-finger salute that he would do just that, before getting swallowed up by the crowd.

As The Suits spoke about their new company's potential future partnership with FFS Industries, Bo saw a wondrous event unfold in his peripheral: Two running-back sized security men and one security woman of equal size, telling Matt and his two friends to "take a hike." At least, that's what it seemed like they said. They pointed, and when Matt didn't oblige, they pushed. Like a toddler, he got more and more upset the farther they moved him away from the seemingly relieved Gorgeous Winter, Mia and Jeremiah. Even Matt's two friends had scattered, wanting nothing more to do with him.

"Do you know who my father is? Who my mother—who—who my sister is?" Matt was beyond irate, and despite the low light aesthetic in the place, his face was beet red. Especially after one of the security guards seemed to say, "We don't care, sir!" And even more so when Matt saw one of the security guards shake Jeremiah's hand, apologetically.

"Bo! Bo!" Matt shouted. "Where the hell are you?"

Where the hell am I? Well... I'm right here.

Bo smiled and gave the suited men his full attention, and for the first time in a long time, he felt the comfort of being calm and collected and right where he needed to be.

CHAPTER SEVEN

"Oh, my God!" Mia laughed. "That guy was a trip!"

"And what really sucks is how he left us hanging. Do we know his father?" Jeremiah said, mocking Matt's inflections. "And his mother? And his sister?"

Winter laughed. "Yeah, but those girls were sweet."

"If by 'sweet' you mean heads full of air," Mia said, and Winter shot her a look. "Okay, okay." Mia held up her hands. "They were kind of sweet. Like a candy, one of those sweet, sour candies."

"I guess I can live with that." Winter put on her coat and looked around for—

"You're looking for that Bo guy, huh?" Mia smiled and wiggled her eyebrows up and down for effect.

"Um, yeah, kind of."

"Now *he* was a big hunk of man candy if there ever was one."

"What the?" said Jeremiah.

"Oh, my God, everyone knows you're my chocolate vanilla swirl ice cream," Mia said in a baby voice.

"Ew," said Winter.

"And you're my angel food cake covered in cream cheese frosting," Jeremiah said.

Winter looked horrified. She covered her ears and turned her back to her friends who started making out. "La la la! Make it stop! La la la! Make it stop!" she sang. "And I'm still trying to figure out if what you both said was racist! La la la!"

"Okay, okay! We're done!" Mia yelled.

"I don't believe you. You've done me dirty before."

Mia playfully scuffled with her friend, trying to get her hands away from her ears. Before long, she succeeded triumphantly.

"I hate you," said Winter with a smile.

"I love you more," Mia said, blowing a kiss.

"And I can, sometimes, tolerate you both," said Jeremiah. "So, what?"

They packed their things up and threw away trash. Mia had lost her cell phone so she started searching under the clouds, in recliner seat crevices, and behind the wooden table. Drained, she looked over at her man, who was holding her phone up.

"What the hell, where'd you find it?" she asked.

"It was in the damn 3D printer thing," said Jeremiah. "I mean, how does that even happen?"

Mia smiled and grabbed it. "I'm not giving you the satisfaction of an answer."

They all took one final look at the waterfall backdrop, watching the mist change colors as it reflected all of the lights. Then they headed for the door. Winter scanned as many faces as she could, holding Mia's hand to keep from running into people.

At the exit, Mia stopped abruptly, and grabbed Winter by

the shoulders. "You *have* to talk to him again before we leave."

A sexy R&B song by the band THEY had started up, and for some reason it made Winter want to flee. She shook her head.

"Yes," Mia continued with a slow nod. "I've never seen such obvious sparks between two people."

"What are you guys doing?" Jeremiah sighed, then moved the girls over so they weren't blocking the door.

"But I don't even know what I would say," Winter said. "He—he probably does that to lots of girls. Like one of those charmer types."

Mia rolled her eyes, then stood on her tiptoes and looked around. Finally, she spotted Bo talking with a group of people near a side bar, and not-so-discreetly pointed.

"Come on, gals. It's getting close to my bedtime," Jeremiah said.

"Okay, Grandpa." Mia rolled her eyes even harder, provoking another long sigh out of Jeremiah, who then took his phone out to pass the time. "Winter!" Mia screamed. "Bo is hot as hell. And he's so into you. I honestly thought he was gonna pick you up like a bride and take you directly to the altar."

"Oh, my, geez, you're so ridiculous," Winter said.

"Okay, then. Well, you see how he keeps looking around as he talks to people? I'm guessing he's looking for *the* Winter Smith."

Winter shook her head vigorously until the palm of Mia's hand lightly slapped her across the face.

"Hey!" said Winter, in exaggerated shock. Her reaction caused them to both smile.

"I'm not letting your stupid insecurities stop you. I have a good feeling about this. Take your coat off."

"What? Why?"

"Just do it."

Winter followed orders, handing her coat to Mia, who shoved it into Jeremiah's free hand. He looked as if he was going to say something but decided against it, looking back down at his phone.

Mia stepped behind Winter and fiddled with the back of her skirt. Before long, the garment lit up at full brightness. Winter felt like a firefly signal-flashing in order to attract a potential mate. She remembered that tidbit from a David Attenborough documentary on bioluminescence.

"Mia. Let's just go," she whined. "What's the—"

"1…2…3…" Mia sang.

"Mia!"

"4…5…"

The firefly turned around, only to see Mia leaning casually against Jeremiah.

"Oh, heyyy, Bo!" shouted Mia.

"Hey, man!" Jeremiah said.

"Hi, guys. Leaving already?" asked a familiar, low voice.

Winter's stomach tied into a strong knot. She slowly turned back around to see Bo, who immediately locked into her eyes again.

"Yeah, we're leaving 'cuz Jeremiah's an old man," Mia said.

Bo smiled, but still didn't move his eyes from Winter. "Is that so?" he asked.

Winter nodded.

"No, I'm not," said Jeremiah, in a serious, almost pouting tone. "I'm like five months younger than Mia, for goodness sake."

"I was hoping I got to talk to you again." Bo leaned closer to Winter as the beat seemed to get louder. "My buddy filled me in on some stuff. I looked at your StyleSlap page. You got real talent for styles and putting scenes together."

"That's nice of you to say. Thanks." Winter began twirling her hair but stopped when she realized how gross and cliché that must have looked. "What do you do, besides opening amazing Portland night spots?"

"I'm into tech. Apps, video games...that kinda stuff."

"Hey, take your time. We'll be right outside," Mia drive-by whispered.

Realizing she and Bo were alone, Winter's heart started to race. "So…um…what kind of apps and video games…and stuff?"

"Like VR experiences and—ah, I don't want to bore you to death."

Bo ran his hands through his hair, inadvertently showing off his tattoo covered muscles. On his left forearm, she noticed he had a vivid depiction of a Vincent van Gogh painting.

"*Self-Portrait with Bandaged Ear*," she said.

"What?" he asked, visibly confused. Winter pointed at the image on his arm. "Oh, yeah. Wow, you're a fan?"

"Yeah. Me and Vincent. We go way back," she teased. "It's an impressively accurate tattoo."

"What was that?" He took a step closer to hear her better…or maybe just to *be* closer.

"It's an impressively accurate tattoo," she repeated louder, "but I only see two problems."

"You do, do you?" He raised his eyebrows, amused, and held out his arm for her to analyze.

She pointed at Van Gogh's right eye. "That eye should

wander to the side a little and the pupil should be just a tad bit wider."

He mulled over her words, then flexed and turned his arm slightly. "You mean like that?"

Sure enough, the eye changed shape, though it exaggerated the rest of the portraits' features.

Delighted, Winter laughed. "Oh my, wow. That's perfect. Really captures the verge of insanity."

Bo held up his right wrist, palm side up. "What about this one? How much could I get this appraised for?"

His wrist displayed a small, yet detailed, sunflower, mimicking Van Gogh's *Sunflowers* painting.

"Hmmm," she teased. "The colors look pretty good, except the yellow—"

"Hey, I just got it retouched. The yellow is *spot on*."

"Yeah. You're right. The yellow is vivid and really captures the rare happiness the artist felt during that time in his life."

"What else do you see? And please, don't hold back."

She put her finger on his skin and traced the flower petals. "I think we'll be able to sell this one to the Louvre for millions. Maybe even trillions."

"You should be an art dealer. Got a real knack for it."

In one smooth motion, Bo moved his *Sunflowers* wrist and lightly grabbed onto Winter's tracing hand. Before she could even think about what was happening, their hands were loosely interlocked. It all felt so…natural. They didn't move for a few seconds, before he slowly pulled her closer to him.

"Where'd you come from?" he asked.

She reminded herself to breathe, all the while realizing where she was. The music, banter, and various bowling sounds, which had been pushed to the background of her awareness, were suddenly back at full volume. It vibrated through her bones. She bit her lip a little too hard and looked up at those piercing green eyes. Eyes that she detected held some kind of pain.

"Tell me if I'm being too forward," he said. "I just—I feel like I'm under some kind of trance around you."

She nodded slowly.

Suddenly, a small, sharp pain passed through Winter's chest just as Lyle's face flashed in her head. The face he got when he was really mad. The face that truly scared her. *What am I doing?* she thought. *Slut,* Lyle said. She winced and briefly closed her eyes, catching herself before she surrendered to her backstabbing mind.

"I…I…um…should probably catch up with my friends," she said and stepped back, letting go of Bo's hand.

"Did I do something?"

She realized her skirt was still cycling through a variety of colors and she felt so exposed.

"No. I…I have to go."

She crossed her arms and started walking away. Winter could hear people saying Bo's name, trying to get a piece of his time before another firefly distracted him.

"Winter, how can I get a hold of you?" he yelled after her.

She could see Mia and Jeremiah through the window, nonchalant, like they hadn't just watched their crazy friend standing in a bowling alley, practically throwing herself on some guy she'd just met.

"Social media!" Winter answered him, without looking back.

She pushed the door open and was met with crisp evening autumn air. The kind of air that bit. That stung. That warned Winter when heavy rain was coming.

CHAPTER EIGHT

The bowling alley had only a few stragglers and a third of the staff left. Bo shook hands and exchanged parting words with Lisa Schlesinger, the editor for the *Food & Liquid* section of *Portland Life* magazine. She had wanted him to know that she was very impressed with the whole experience and adored the food. The wine menu, she added, could use an overhaul, but she was still going to write a positive review and recommendation.

Talked out, Bo sat down at the printer bar in the back. He pushed a few buttons and out popped a whiskey on the rocks.

"I'm heading home, my guy," Kevin said, putting his coat on as he walked up. "I have work in the morning."

"Oh, shit, the DeLorean's here?"

"Yeah. I wish."

They bro-hugged.

"Anyway, I really appreciate you showing up for me tonight," Bo said.

"Are you kidding? You're gonna be the next big tech mogul. I'm riding those coattails to the moon, son!" Kevin pretended he was on a surfboard—scratch that—a flying hoverboard.

"Says a man who sold his first million-dollar website when he was two years old." Bo shook his drink, then took a swig.

"Actually, I was seventeen years old and all I got was a measly $850,000. I'm still bitter about that deal."

Kevin patted Bo on the back and walked away.

Bo sat there, for who knows how long, as various staff members finished up and waved tired goodbyes. The last group of guests left, just as he finished his last gulp of his second glass. He couldn't stop thinking about Winter. Imagining her face. That sparkle in her eyes that held a touch of sadness. The happy shock when their skin touched. *What the hell is wrong with me?* Bo didn't dare allow himself to think of an answer. He finally got up to greet the nightly cleaning crew and when he realized there was nothing else he needed to stay for, he put on his coat and went out the side exit to meet his car service in the designated car pickup/dropoff area. The temperature had gotten exponentially colder in the last two or three nights, brought on with force by the strong wind.

"Get the fuck out!"

Bo heard a voice but couldn't see who or where it was coming from.

A black car pulled up. Through an open window, a gentleman in his late fifties, with a weathered face, and long gray beard said, "Hello, Bo."

"Hey, Steve."

"No! No, you get the hell out or I'll get you out myself!" screamed the mystery voice.

"Just a second, man," Bo said. "I'm going to check on something."

"Sure thing," said Steve.

Bo walked around the corner to the employee parking lot and saw Matt, *the mother fucker*, drunkenly trying to open the driver side door of a silver Mercedes AMG. He could faintly hear a woman's voice screaming from inside it.

"Hey, man," Bo said. "What's going on? You all right?"

Matt turned to him with narrow eyes, clenching his jaw. It took him a minute to recognize Bo, and his demeanor changed so drastically that he might as well have been impersonating the DC Comics' Joker.

"Bo! Wadddup!" Matt slurred his words, but somehow made it over to Bo to shake his hand. "So, today was a fucking success! Congratulations!"

"Oh, yeah. Thanks, man. I hope you had a good time."

"Would have been better if I went home with one of those social media girls, but whatever."

A window slowly rolled down revealing a distressed looking woman with runny mascara.

"You know, you got some real punk ass bitches for security," Matt continued.

"Hmmm. I didn't know that."

"Yeah. I'd highly recommend you fire their asses." He staggered closer to Bo, then said quietly, "That Winter chick was soooo going to suck my—"

"Hey, man, maybe you should get home, drink some water. Say a few prayers while you're at it."

Matt looked puzzled. "Dude, I'm fine. I barely even drink—drank."

"Come on, Matt. I'll drive you home," said the woman, her voice wavering.

"No, it's my fucking car! And no gold-digging wife of mine is gonna stop me from driving it home!" he yelled.

The woman turned her head away.

"Hey, come on man," Bo said. He tried to sound as calm as possible, despite his threshold meter about to hit its limit.

"What?" Matt laughed. "I spent a lot of my inherit-inheritance on that thing and I'm going to drive it."

"I'm afraid I can't let you do that."

"Oh, yeah? Well, I might have to report back to my father about this. You know…he was really interested to see if you were going to crash and burn after Olivia dumped you. And I —man—I was the only one that stuck up for you 'cuz my sister can be a real bitch sometimes." Matt smiled, but his eyes were dead.

Does he even know what planet he's on right now? Bo wondered.

"Well, thanks for that." Bo put up his hands in defeat. "But how about we let your wife drive you home. I just want to make sure everyone is safe. I mean, hell, even I'm getting dropped off tonight. It's not a big deal."

Matt nodded his head. "Cool, cool. Okay, yeah. Sure."

"Okay, man. I'm happy to hear that."

They shook hands again, but Matt squeezed way too hard. Bo could feel a vein throbbing in his neck. He wanted to clobber the douche, but he pushed it way, way down to the pit of his stomach, assuring himself that it was all going to be over and good in a couple seconds.

"See you on the flip-side," Matt said.

Bo felt eyes on him as he walked away. He looked back once before turning the corner, and Matt was still standing in the same place, smiling. It sent a shiver up his spine.

Just as Bo was about to open his service car door and put

everything behind him, he heard a blood curdling scream. He ran back to the parking lot to see Matt attempting to pull his hysterical wife out the window, by her hair.

"What the fuck!" Bo shouted.

Before Bo could even get to him, Matt struck her in the cheek with an elbow and she cried in pain. The men wrestled to the ground, both landing a few blows before Bo was able to pin Matt down. Steve the driver jogged up and stood over them.

"Should I call the police?" Steve asked.

"No! I'm fine! I'm fine. It's over," Matt insisted. "I'm cool. I'll be cool."

Bo hesitated for a moment before letting him go. Matt sprung to his feet and wiped blood from his mouth, breathing heavily. Steve helped Bo up.

"You're not going anywhere with her tonight," Bo said to Matt, catching his breath. "You need time to calm down."

Matt looked at the ground and nodded. "Yeah, okay."

"Steve, can you drive him to a hotel?"

"Yeah, of course. I'll dispatch another car out here for you." Steve started walking away. "Let's go."

Matt followed, but looked back a few times at his wife, who seemed relieved to see him go. When they were far enough away, she rolled the window up and pulled off before Bo could get a chance to talk to her and see if she was okay.

Bo found himself standing alone in the middle of an empty parking lot, on the opening night of a business that was supposed to mark a change in his life.

And all he could think about was Winter's kind eyes and the nagging feeling that he didn't deserve someone like her.

CHAPTER NINE

Winter could barely remember driving home. Couldn't recall drawing the iridescent pastel shower curtain, running the bath, pouring in vanilla scented bubble soap, or even lighting various LED candles. In autopilot mode, she turned on a Joji playlist, undressed, stepped into the warm, soothing, water, and lay down. *His eyes.* Winter took a deep breath. *The way he pulled me closer to him.* She just couldn't stop replaying the whole scene in her mind.

Winter was told at a young age that she had a photographic memory, but after the years went by, she realized that it only pertained to things she actually cared about, so it wasn't that impressive. His tattoos, however… when she closed her eyes, she could see them so vividly it was like he was standing right in front of her.

She remembered: a realistic eighties TV set with an 8-bit scene from *Super Mario Bros.*; characters from *The Nightmare Before Christmas*; Edgar Allen Poe on the front of a vintage style opium bottle; cedar trees, maple trees, fir trees; storm clouds; a variety of distorted, melted clocks from

Salvador Dali's *The Persistence of Memory* painting; Calvin & Hobbes reading a book together. *How much did it all cost?* she wondered. *And each tattoo was so bright, colorful, and detailed, he must have to get them touched up all the time.* She also imagined what he was hiding under his clothes. And she wasn't just thinking about the tattoos anymore.

Winter tried to think about something else...but she had to know who he really was. *Need to go online.* She sat up, wiped off her bubble-soaked hands, and grabbed her tablet in its frog-shaped, waterproof case. She searched for him on all the social media sites, but he didn't have any profiles. He was featured under a lot of hashtags, though. There were videos of him at parties, working out in gyms, hanging out at the beach, attending concerts. Sometimes it seemed like he knew he was being photographed or recorded, other times he didn't seem to notice, and it made Winter feel...dirty. Almost voyeuristic. Even so, Winter scrolled through a myriad of posts, mostly featuring females, young to old, posing in photos with him, using hashtags like *BoBlaine* or *WeMetBoBlaine* or *BoBlaineSelfie*.

Winter watched one particular video over and over and over again. It had an excited college-aged girl and her equally enthusiastic mother, asking Bo for a hug. He said, "Of course. But I'm not sure why you would want a photo with me." And the mother said, "Because you're a cutie." And that seemed to take him off guard, and then he said, "You're too kind but I'd suggest you make an appointment for the eye doctor." And the mother playfully swatted him away and everyone laughed, including some voices off camera.

Winter hesitated, but couldn't resist clicking on #BoBlaineTattoos, which showed her a few new ones. For instance, in a faraway shot of him with his shirt off, Winter recognized the old town Portland neon white stag sign, near the middle of his…chiseled back.

Realizing she was basically cyberstalking the poor guy, Winter turned off her tablet and lightly tossed it on her bathroom mat, out of reach. She kept looking at the device. It just sat there. Taunting her. She tried to relax, but the bubbles had already dissipated, the water wasn't that hot anymore, her playlist had stopped, and she probably needed to go to sleep. If only she knew what time it was… After a few seconds, she reached for the tablet, almost having to crawl out of the damn tub. By the time she got it in her grasp, she had splashed a little water on the floor but didn't care. The clock said: 2:16 a.m. Winter thought about that number for a second and decided she had a few more minutes to kill.

She typed "Bo Blaine" into the search engine browser and couldn't believe how many articles it brought up. Apparently, Bo used to have close to 3.5 million followers across all of his social media pages. *Wowsers!* But he deleted his accounts, for no apparent reason, after he and some Hollywood actress—and daughter to a high-profile Pacific Northwest real estate investment firm—broke up a year ago.

Winter skimmed through an article titled: *Will All of the Blaine Siblings Inherit Family Business?* She found out Bo's mother thought up the idea for StyleSlap. Trischa Blaine grew up poor but found strength in her own mother's dedication to fashion, discovering firsthand that fashion was an artistic expression, projected specific messages, and had the power to inspire. Bo's dad, Noah, grew up wealthy, and had a string of successful businesses before FFS Industries took off. For reasons unlisted, it said that Bo's dad was close with his children, except for Bo. They had some kind of falling out and Bo was in the process of "earning back his father's respect" after years of "anger issues."

The term "anger issues" both confused Winter and disappointed her. Until that moment, Bo seemed like a gentle soul. He was welcoming and grateful and genuine. Throughout the night, she would catch glimpses of him conversing with people—they seemed so comfortable and happy in his presence. *This article has to be bogus,* she assured herself. *I'm sure it's based on some stupid, unverified gossip.* She was about to do more research, when she noticed the goose bumps all over her body, and the fact that half of the *freezing* water had drained out. Annoyed, Winter pushed herself to get out of the tub, and start her nightly beauty regimen so she wouldn't wake up looking like a gremlin.

Winter's mind raced as she brushed and flossed her teeth. She had a real connection with someone, and it may have all been based on a façade. *He was one of those evil charmers, wasn't he? One of those liars.* She decided she wasn't being fair as she washed her face and applied her beauty creams. Shouldn't she trust her gut instead of some random clickbait journalism? Physically and mentally drained, she turned her bedroom light off and flopped down on her bed, putting on a relaxing Matt Corby song to calm her nerves. But all it did was make her sad. A sad that she didn't want to escape for some psychotic reason. So she played another song. And another. Finally, she was ready to face the truth.

She pulled the covers up and typed his name again into her phone, pairing it with "trouble" and "anger." The search results hit her like a baseball bat to the temple, and she had to remind herself to keep breathing.

She read an article that chronicled Bo Blaine's troubles over the years: Fights in boarding school, excessive partying, addiction to pills, rehab, and women. Lots of women. When he was twenty-six, he got in a physical altercation with his father and was subsequently arrested, though his father never pressed charges.

He did attend college, pursuing a double major for Computer Science and Software Engineering, and earned high marks for two years. But he decided to take a year break, helping his family develop and improve their tech apps and services, and was subsequently set up with actress Olivia Graham, the daughter of his father's friend. Things were going great for a while, until another altercation at a business meeting, though the article didn't say with whom. But it did say Bo was arrested again. And that time the charges stuck. His relationship with Olivia ended and his family somehow got him out of jail after a month and a half. The last headline Winter saw before throwing her phone across the bed was: *Bad Boy Bo Blaine Attempts to Erase Reputation with Upscale Bowling Alley.*

It was too good to be true. Of course it was. Winter vowed to never think about him again. It didn't matter that he was a creative person who respected and admired the art in the world. It didn't matter that his eyes pierced through her. That she felt something when they touched each other or that he made her feel special. He could put on a really convincing show when he needed to. He was obviously just trying the good-guy persona out for a while, laughing behind the backs of the gullible and the oblivious. She was mad that she fell for it…*again.*

She tried to sleep but could only toss and turn, trying so very hard to not think about the roller coaster ride she'd just been on. Trying not to remember that fluttery, warmness in her—*Ugh!*

But he won. In her mind, Bo looked at her again and whispered in her ear, "Where'd you come from?" Then he started kissing her neck. Then her lips. Then he put his warm hands under her shirt. And slowly unzipped her light-up skirt....

Getting hot, Winter pushed the covers off her, pulled up her navy floral velvet tank top, and pulled down her matching navy shorts....

She slowly slipped her hand into her panties and imagined his tattoo covered muscles moving and flexing as he touched her, kissed her, caressed her.

If she wasn't ever going to see him again...at least she'd make the night count.

CHAPTER TEN

Bo walked sluggishly toward the enormous silver box that reflected its surroundings and all of the night lights like a distorted mirror. The valet and guard were lounging comfortably near the front, under one of the new heated terrace awnings added to the building last winter. When the valet saw him, he nervously jumped up.

"Need your car parked, sir?"

"I got dropped off. Thanks, though," Bo answered.

The lobby greeted Bo with one of his favorite orchestral pieces: "Dance and Angela" by Franz Waxman.

Sarah, the brunette and blonde haired nighttime concierge desk manager was on her phone, but put it away and sat up straighter as he walked by. She was about five years older than him and divorced—she wasn't looking for anything serious. But she was attractive and nice to him and -

"Good evening, Mr. Blaine," she said, cordially.

He stopped in front of the elevator. "How's your night been going, Sarah?"

She blushed. "Oh, not bad."

"Well, that's good to hear."

"I heard opening night went well."

"Yeah, it went surprisingly well, actually. Let me know if any staff wants to check it out. Bowling, dinner, and drinks on the house," he said and pushed the elevator button.

By the time the elevator opened, she was standing next to him, examining his face. "Oh, my God. Are you okay, Bo? Can I can send a first aid kit up with you?"

"No, that won't be necessary. Probably looks worse than it is." He stepped into the elevator and feigned a smile. She attempted to hide the disturbed look in her eyes but failed. "You're sweet, Sarah," he continued. "But I promise I'm okay…everything is okay." He winked and the doors closed.

"Um, okay. But don't forget to put ice on…" Her voice trailed off as the elevator went up, stopping at the top floor.

Bo glanced at his reflection as he walked down the hallway, stopping in front of a large, rectangular mirror framed with golden faux flowers and what his mom described as "hand cast in pecan shell resin." This design was one of Mom's favorites and found its way into a lot of the decoration elements in their family properties, especially the luxury apartments. Bo's right eye was already black and though his cheek was only slightly swollen, he hardly recognized himself. He pulled out his phone and called the front desk.

"Hi, Sarah. If my dad asks about me or the condition of my face, could you just—"

"I'll say you and your face looked handsome as always."

"Well, you don't have to lie."

"Goodnight, Bo." Sarah laughed and hung up.

Bo looked at himself one more time, shook his head, and continued down the hall.

He walked listlessly into the kitchen, pushed buttons on the fridge and the same Franz Waxman song from the lobby started playing. He grabbed a bag of frozen peas and lifted himself on the dark bamboo island counter. He could see his swollen face in the reflective paneling on the huge stainless steel fridge and wondered how he never noticed how many damn mirrors there were in the world. He stared at the ground for a few seconds before closing his eyes and wincingly pressing the peas against his skin, pulling the cold bag away only when he couldn't stand it anymore.

Her eyes...sometimes they looked dark chestnut brown, sometimes they looked a lighter amber hue. Everything about Winter was an enigma. She seemed shy or flustered at times but held herself confidently, like she was comfortable in her own...beautiful skin. She tried to be unreadable, but on a dime her emotions were as blatant as a Vegas casino sign. And his tattoos. Winter looked so interested in his tattoos and at the same time it was like she understood *why* he got them, even though he didn't really know himself. Bo and Winter had an obvious connection, yet she seemed ashamed of it. She was like an art piece, changing and morphing based on light or perspective. And he was so drawn to the lines, shadow, shape...*Oh, God, the shape...* The whole fucking composition captivated him.

He forced open his eyes, jumped down, threw the peas back in the freezer, and turned off the orchestral music. He had some work to do and that music was going to put him to sleep. He realized just how dark and empty the apartment was. He had barely been there in the last year. Olivia had broken up with him, but she still had most of her stuff there until just a few weeks prior.

Every time they saw each other, she would somehow bring up the cheating and somehow blame him for it. *Pfft,* Bo thought, *like I was the one who pushed her into the arms of her co-star when she was shooting for two months up in Canada.* When Bo and Olivia reiterated those same old spats, he'd usually word-vomit up the fact that she was jealous and controlling and couldn't even handle him on social media—to the point where she'd go after girls that left comments on his photos—to the point that he had to delete his social media all together. She'd retaliate by throwing things or accusing him of being full of himself or mentioning how her father said Bo was a "rich deadbeat" and though she didn't believe "daddy" at first, she slowly figured "daddy was right." But what really got her mad, what made her blood boil and her ears produce a thick plume of smoke (or was that the joint he was always hitting back then, knowing it would make her mad?) was when the last time he saw her he said, "To tell the truth, the cheating doesn't bother me. It all comes down to us not being compatible, Olivia." He still didn't understand why those were the words that set her off. Maybe she was taken aback by the idea that someone wouldn't think that she was right for them. Maybe she wanted him to fight for her. Maybe she wanted him to grovel, show mercy, or sadness, or something other than calm acceptance to the demise of their relationship. What he really wanted to say was that she was an amazing actress because for a while, she was able to hide all of her horrible traits from him. Disgusting traits that she shared with *those* people—the people he hated more than anything in the world. People like her family. People like his dad.

Bo turned on the electric fireplace in the living room and

wrapped a gray knit throw blanket around him that his mom made by hand.

He pulled the curtains open and stood at the glass windows that overlooked the waterfront. The water looked calm, but the surrounding trees were bending back and forth under a grumpy sky. He hoped it rained. He always loved rain at night—something Olivia hated. In fact, she hated Oregon. Said it was "too dreary," and preferred to work and stay in Los Angeles or "literally anywhere else." The first time she said that shit, Bo almost choked on his peanut butter and jelly sandwich. He remembered the day clearly because it was so traumatic for him. That also sparked one of their first arguments. He shook his head just thinking about it and checked the battery on his phone, which flashed red, coincidentally just like Olivia's eyes whenever she was mad at him, which was often.

He attempted to imagine Olivia's *mad* face to verify his thoughts, but he could only see Winter looking up at him when they first met. He closed the curtains and plopped down on the navy blue sectional, putting his feet up on the big matching ottoman. He opened up the sofa armrest and threw his dead phone in it.

"Projector," he said, and a gigantic projector screen slowly came down from the ceiling. Behind him, a framed *The Goonies* film screenshot of Haystack Rock in Cannon Beach, Oregon, slid over, revealing a built-in wall projector. "Play the album *Carrie and Lowell* by Sufjan Stevens at volume level 3. No, level 4."

The music started up and Bo took a deep breath, sinking lower into the sofa. In a quieter voice, he said, "Google Winter Smith." The screen lit up, displaying a list of results.

"Top one," he said quickly, and the screen changed to Winter's StyleSlap page.

He remembered a lot of the posts from Kevin's brief Winter Smith tutorial at the bowling alley, but he was distracted by a lot of things, mostly *her,* standing only lanes away, in real life.

Sitting in his home, alone, however, he was able to admire the work Winter must have put in to create such intriguing images: In one photo, she wore a loose-fitting black t-shirt with the word "Tang," tucked into mint-green jeans. She sat in front of a crumbling brick building, on a white cruiser bike with a basket full of matching mint-green and pink flowers, looking off into the distance; in another photo she seemed to be mid-laugh, standing in the middle of a busy outdoor shopping mall, wearing a light blue jean jacket, with a tight, tan mini dress underneath; in a gif, she twirled around and around, wearing a flowing white, silhouette see-through skirt with a cartoon cat belt and a black bandana style crop top that showed off her sexy midriff.

Bo was a big proponent of those kind of shirts, after sitting in on many fashion line development meetings with his mother right after he graduated from high school. Of course, his mother kicked him out when she found out he had hooked up with two of the ten models she was working with. And both of his parents had the audacity to get mad at *him*, without taking into account he was an impressionable eighteen year old that basically just got out of an all-male school jail and those models were years older than him anyway and taking advantage of his innocence. His mother ended up scrapping her fashion line aspirations, despite having some great ideas. She insisted Bo wasn't the reason for it, though, said it had something to do with his dad, but she never elaborated any further.

Bo went through each post, then read some blogs and articles Winter was featured in. One headline read *How to Look Like an Extra on Saved by the Bell.* It showed Winter wearing a nineties inspired outfit—denim overalls, a fanny pack, "Jelly shoes," a "daisy choker," a "Scrunchie," and hoop earrings, and revealed her thoughts on each piece. A caption under the earrings said, "I wore hoops all the time in high school and if they were too big I'd get in trouble for them. Made me feel mature. In fact, I'm going to start incorporating them into my style again."

Some posts and articles also featured Winter performing workout routines, making DIY projects, or demonstrating healthy recipes, referring to her as a "Fashion and Lifestyle It Girl." He couldn't find a lot of in-depth information about her background, besides a blurb that mentioned her father died a few years back and that she didn't have the best relationship with her mother, an economics author and former model.

"Google Winter Smith Images," Bo said, and the screen morphed into a collage of images pulled from her profiles and article features.

She was so gorgeous it hurt. *Her hair.* It didn't matter how she wore it—whether in a ponytail or worn down, straight, wavy, curled, or messy—it all complimented her features perfectly. *Her body.* It was obvious she worked out, but she had those beautiful curves. *Her face.* She had a heart-shaped face with full, pouty lips and high cheek bones. *And those big round eyes.* Bo realized a part of him was waking up, and he looked down to see the tent pitched in his pants. He had the urge to relieve himself, but he had something more important to do.

"Direct message Winter Smith," he said loudly.

The screen displayed the text: *How would you like to direct message Winter Smith?*

"Text."

No phone number available online.

"Okay then, Nanogram or Styleslap."

I'm sorry, sir. You do not have active accounts set up with either.

He stared into space for a while, biting his nail.

"Okay, okay," he finally said with a sigh. "Reactivate my Nanogram and turn off notification alerts."

In a few seconds, his page was up and running, and the notification heart icon at the top listed 2,396, going up with every second gone by.

"Message Winter Smith," he said. "Greet her and tell her that I loved meeting her and would like to take her out."

Just then there was a knock at the door, which was extremely odd since no one was allowed on the floor unless he gave them permission or cleared it with the concierge.

He got up and glanced at the screen: ***Winter Smith's messaging is blocked.***

"What do you mean it's blocked?"

Winter Smith has blocked the following username: 'BoBlaineBoBlaine'

"What the fuck!" he exclaimed and threw the blanket off of him.

The knock got louder. His heartbeat doubled and he felt as if he were just splashed with a bucket of ice water. *There has to be some kind of mistake,* he thought, just as there was another loud, long knock.

"I'll be right there!" he shouted, without even trying to mask the annoyance and anger.

"Direct message Winter Smith through email. Tell her this is Bo and I loved meeting her and would love to take her out. At the end of the message, list my phone number."

His email popped up on the screen and asked him if the email composition was ready to send.

"Yes. Send," Bo demanded.

A second later the screen displayed the words: ***Message Sent Failed. Email blocked by recipient.***

He stood there, staring at the text, reading it over and over again. Another knock slapped him out of it. And a woman's voice...

"Bo. Bo, are you okay?" asked Sarah.

He had to unclench his fists to open the door, and Sarah was standing in the hallway holding an oversized first aid kit.

"Hi," he said, trying as hard as he could to soften his scowl.

"I don't care what you say. You need this stuff." She held the kit out to him, and he caught her glancing down at the bulge in his pants.

He took the kit and scratched the back of his neck. "When are you on a break?"

She smiled coyly. "I'm actually off now. Thanks for asking."

He nodded for her to come inside and she pretended to think about it for a second before entering.

He was confused and sick all at once. They started to kiss, and he felt a sharp pang of guilt, though he knew he shouldn't. He guided her into his room and when they undressed each other he avoided any more kissing on the lips.

He ran his hand over her naked body and imagined Winter's skin. *For fuck's sake!*

He turned Sarah around and admired her backside and realized he had been excited for over an hour—it wasn't fair to his body to not address it any longer. He remembered Winter's perfect ass in one of the bikini posts on her StyleSlap page. Winter's ass was spectac—

Damnit! Stop thinking about her! He bent Sarah over and she put her hands on the bed to steady herself. He put on a condom and looked at the temptation standing in front of him, but hesitated.

"Are you okay back there?" she asked. When there was no answer, she turned around. "You had a long day, Bo. How about I take care of you?"

She put her arms around him, and he felt another sting of guilt, hoping she wasn't expecting another kiss.

"You sure you want this?" she asked, then looked down and smiled. "It sure looks like you do."

He nodded. They got on the bed, Bo laying on his back. Though the curtains were closed, Bo could see a diffused reflection of light from the water moving in waves over the room. She climbed on top of him, settled in, and started moving her hips. When he put his hands on Winter's—*shit!*—on Sarah's waist, she moaned. It felt great, but something was off and the faster she moved, and the louder she moaned, he knew he wasn't going to be able to finish.

She suddenly stopped. "What's going on? I feel like you're somewhere else."

"No, I'm here, I promise," he assured her. "I really need this right now."

She got off of him, laying on her side. "Usually you're much more into this. Who is it?"

"What do you mean?"

"Come on. Who is it?"

"Someone I met at the opening, but—"

"Shh," she interrupted. "Say no more. I want you to keep thinking about her."

"What?"

"Think about her as we fuck. I don't care. I need this too, remember?"

He smiled slightly but shook his head. "That wouldn't be fair to you. And it's weird."

"What do you mean? How do you not know I'm not thinking about Jason Momoa or Ryan Gosling or one of my exes?" She rubbed his stomach.

"Touché."

"But hurry up and decide because I have a meeting with a new grow house in the morning. If all goes well, I probably won't be working here as often..." She sits up. "So do you want to use each other or not?"

"Use."

She climbed on top of him again, slowly moved her hips and started to moan. He moved with her. He put his hands on her breasts. She moved faster and leaned over and started kissing his collarbone, and he moved his hands to her waist. Then after a minute, she leaned back and felt her own breasts, pulled her own hair, was losing herself in her own world. *She definitely knows what she wants,* he thought.

He closed his eyes and let himself drift away too. He remembered that smile in the bowling alley and couldn't believe how much that girl made an impression on him.

"I'm almost there," he heard Sarah say.

He kissed Winter's lips. He grabbed her ass and squeezed and moved her up and down on top of him. And after a while he couldn't help but call out her name, knowing very well that she wouldn't respond back…

Bo woke up early and Sarah was gone. He made a cup of coffee, pulled back the living room curtain and stared at the different sets of people walking down the waterfront pathway, recognizing a couple and their Irish Wolfhound that lived in the building. He had a full day ahead—*Blaine's Lanes'* first day open to the public. After getting his workout clothes on, he grabbed a small gym bag and was heading out the door when he remembered his uncharged phone was in the sofa armrest. He was in the middle of plugging it in a kitchen charge port when his front door slowly opened.

"Really, son? The fucking concierge?"

Bo almost jumped out of his skin when he realized his dad was standing in his apartment—his dad—*The* Noah Blaine—had never visited him at any place he'd ever lived, including Parent Weekends at boarding school.

"Dad, what—what are you—"

"Sarah. The fucking staff," Noah stated incredulously.

"How do you know?" Bo asked. "You were watching me?"

"I have a right to do that, son. I own the building."

Bo wanted to take long, deep, meditative breaths but could never allow himself to show that kind of weakness in front of his dad, who always thought his anger coping mechanisms were "embarrassing."

Instead, Bo nodded and sat down at the kitchen counter. "So, what's up?"

Noah sighed. "I take it you haven't gone online this morning."

Bo's dad took off his gloves and threw them on the counter. He pushed his rectangular wire-framed black glasses—which looked eerily similar to Bill Gates' signature specs—up on his short, white mane. He pulled out a slick, black, caseless phone out of a hidden pocket in his mid-length, gray trench coat, typed something into it, and handed it over.

Displayed on the screen was the headline *Matt Graham Threatens to Call Police on Bo Blaine.*

"Wait, what?"

"Take your time." Noah's tone was flat.

Noah unbuttoned his coat before sitting down on the blue and white striped armchair, catty-corner to the sectional. He then took a wallet case out of a hidden pocket, opening it up to reveal another phone.

Bo started reading the article to himself, in disbelief, when his father cleared his throat.

"Out loud, son. You know the rules."

Bo hated when Noah treated him like a misbehaving child, which, ironically made him want to behave badly. *Instead, how about I throw this coffee maker at you?* Bo thought. After a few seconds of silent opposition, he gave in.

"In a bizarre late night rant posted to his Twitter page and deleted twenty minutes later," Bo read quickly, "Matt Graham, brother of Olivia Graham and heir to the real estate investment firm Graham Property Group, vowed to 'ruin' and 'pulverize' bad boy Bo Blaine of FFS Industries. As claimed by the visibly inebriated husband and father of two, Matt was 'sucker punched' by Bo Blaine, in front of his own wife. Allegedly, Bo then stopped Mr. Graham from leaving by pinning his arms behind his back and only letting him go when someone else showed up to the scene."

Bo's stomach dropped. He clicked on a highlighted video in the middle of the article, and watched as Matt, sporting a fat lip, scrapes and bruises on mostly one side of his face, and a swollen shut eye, screamed through gritted teeth. He was slurring his speech and kept pointing into the camera, addressing his threats to Bo directly.

Bo watched until he couldn't take anymore, pausing the video in disgust. "Man, this little punk is lying. That's not even close to what went down."

"You think it matters that he's lying?" Noah glanced over and put down his phone.

"I had to step in for a reason."

"I saw the parking lot security footage." Noah took a piece of cleaning cloth out of another hidden pocket and began buffering out his glasses.

"Wait a sec…how would you see that?" When he realized he wasn't going to get an answer, Bo continued. "Okay, then… If he goes to the police, we'll just show them the tape."

Noah pressed his lips together.

Bo sat back, shocked at all that had gone down during the night. "So…?"

Noah put his glasses back on and looked sternly at his son, as if he already knew the reaction he was about to get. "I need you to publicly say you're sorry to Matthew."

Bo shook his head. "Are you kidding me? No, I'm not doing that."

"It's important that you do this. In fact, the board voted, and we demand you make a public apology within twenty-four hours."

"Or what?"

"Or you'll be less involved in the company. Or we won't approve projects. Or we'll stop bailing you out of shit."

Bo's muscles tensed up. His dad acted like he was some lionhearted businessman but whenever he had to punish Bo growing up, he sent his mom to do his bidding. Luckily, she would usually go easy on Bo and make him vow to not tell his dad. Since Bo had become more involved in the business, however, Noah's dad used the Board of Directors as his shield. *Coward,* Bo thought. They didn't say anything for a while, then Noah stretched and walked casually to the kitchen. He helped himself to a small Perrier from the fridge before walking back over to the window and staring out.

Noah sipped his drink. "Nice view."

"He was hurting his wife, Dad." Bo looked at the floor, realizing anything he said was not only futile but also information his dad already knew. "I am so sick of that family. I thought I'd get a break from them after Olivia left."

Noah turned around, his salt and peppered brows furrowed, the lines in his forehead deepened. "Do you understand how much we owe that family?"

Bo thought about that for a second. "So, you want me to apologize to Matt because of his father's investment into FFS Industries?"

"It's more than that. His father got me into—" Noah chugged the rest of his drink, then put the empty bottle on a side table. He took a wide stance and crossed his arms, and that's when Bo realized his old man wasn't wearing his usual business suit—he wore a light green sweater under his coat and...*jeans!* "Never mind," Noah continued. "Just know that if it wasn't for the Grahams, I'd probably be in prison and you and your brother and sister and your mother would be—I don't know—up shit's creek somewhere."

"What are you talking about?"

"Apologize. Say there was some misunderstanding between both of you. Don't mention that his wife was there."

Bo clasped his hands behind his head. "I just don't think—"

"Your mom would be so devastated if you were thrown out of the company," Noah mumbled to himself

He took one last look out the window, made a sucking sound with his teeth, then, out of nowhere, turned and charged toward the kitchen. Bo braced himself, sighing inwardly with relief when his dad grabbed his gloves and put his phones back in their secret compartments. He was spooked by the whole encounter: his dad stopping by out of the blue, demanding he apologize to that crap of a human, threatening the family business, bringing his mom into it all. The energy emanating from the asshole visitor was causing a static feeling in Bo's chest.

As his dad headed for the door, Bo got a surge of courage. "Instead of an apology, I think I'll just call the cops on that piece of shit myself."

"No need. He's already had a firm talking to."

Bo shrugged. "He still shouldn't get away with that."

Noah Blaine turned around and leaned against the kitchen counter, only a few feet from his son. His eyes were in that pointed feral mode that made Bo feel like prey. The eyes that reminded Bo where he got his own anger issues from. Reminding him who he never wanted to become.

"If you call the police…" His dad talked plainly, like he was merely conveying a sensible and realistic fact. "Well… then you're a goner."

Bo's heart stopped. He swallowed. "What?" he managed to croak out.

Noah smiled but there was still a hint of wild behind the eyes. He had cigar smoke on his breath and tiny white patches on his chin and neck that a shaver missed. These details unnerved Bo the most since his dad was a hygiene and grooming perfectionist.

Noah slapped the counter. When Bo flinched, the ogre chuckled all the way out the door, which closed with a thud behind him.

Bo slumped against the counter, relieved the meeting was over, and convincing himself that his dad was only fucking with him. His dad did crap like that; said things like that, his whole life. He liked to scare Bo. Put him in his place. But that was usually the extent of it. *This time, something's different*, Bo admitted. There seemed to be a threat in not only his dad's words, but also his expression. And his body language. And his movements.

Bo unplugged his phone and sat down on the couch. He stared at the device for a long time. He put his head down in defeat, then lifted his head back up and slowly sat up straight. He typed into his phone and after a few seconds the screen flashed: ***Selfie mode: On. Recording mode: On. Post to enabled social media accounts: On. You will go live in 3… 2…1…*** The phone beeped and Bo held the phone out in front of him.

"Hey…um… Some of you may have seen a video or read some stuff online regarding an altercation between Matt Graham and me. All I can say is that there was an unfortunate misunderstanding between both of us and I'm sorry to anyone I let down…"

Bo looked away for a second, before pulling himself back.

"And Matt…if you're watching this. No hard feelings. As you can see…" He points to his face, "We both got roughed up and it never should have happened. And...and I am sorry. Okay, man? I'm sorry."

He clicked the phone off and set it to silent. He closed his eyes, took three deep inhales and three forceful exhales. Then he went to his kitchen junk drawer and moved items around before pulling out Jeremiah's business card. He looked at it, taking three more deep breaths. Then he threw his phone and the card in his gym bag and headed out the door.

CHAPTER ELEVEN

Winter fished her keys from under the driver side seat. The sun was shining but it had also been sprinkling all morning, so she had no idea what to wear. She decided on a pink camo raincoat over a black tank top and workout tights but every other minute she got too hot or too cold. She finally grabbed onto and pulled out her pesky keys when a bead of sweat rolled down her forehead. She dramatically tore her jacket off, tied it around her waist, and leaned her head on the steering wheel to collect herself.

Over the years, she'd gotten more and more stressed out whenever she had to visit her mother. And it had gotten especially bad since her and Lyle broke up. Last month, Cassandra had said a random, inappropriate, and just plain weird remark about Winter during a local wine tasting. One of the tasters said a certain wine tasted a little "astringent," to which the host agreed that there was indeed a "harshness, a roughness—provoking a puckering feeling on the tongue."

"My daughter's ex-boyfriend knows the meaning of the word *astringent*, all too well," said Cassandra with a laugh.

Aunt Sherry, Cassandra's sister, shot a look at her.

Winter just shook her head, blaming the wine for her mother's behavior. By the end of the night, though, the comment had gotten to her. She asked her mother to explain what it meant as the plates of fresh artisan food were being set on the tables.

"Oh, honey, it was an inside joke," Cassandra answered. "Nobody even knew what I was talking about."

"Yeah, including me."

Cassandra sighed. "I just meant you were kind of harsh and rough on Lyle and he probably—"

Winter couldn't hear anymore because she was already leaving the winery. She stood outside in the chilly evening air, in the middle of nowhere with no cell reception, for about fifteen minutes, before realizing she was gonna have to wait for the winery car to take her home with everyone else. She reluctantly went back inside, pulled her chair to sit on the other side of Sherry, and ignored her mother for the rest of the night.

The phone vibrated on the dashboard, displaying Mia's red winged butterfly gif. Winter accepted the video call and propped the phone in the car mount. Mia was in a blue, gray, and white workout bra, and her hair was in two low and loose pigtails.

"Hey girl! You're finally answering your freakin' phone. It's been like four days. I thought you died. I mean, not really, because you were still posting. Oh, and those light skirt bowling posts were fucking amaze-balls. But Holy Schnikes—what's wrong? You look disheveled?"

"Thanks," Winter said sarcastically, looking through her purse.

"You're about to see your mom, aren't you?"

"Yep, she wanted to talk to me about something." Winter pulled out a brush and quickly attempted to subdue her mane.

"Well, I can feel the stress through the phone. Is there any way you can just, I don't know, postpone meeting her? Like…indefinitely?" Mia sipped on a cup that Winter recognized was from a protein drink shop near the local gym.

"Please don't tell me you got a Peanut Butter Jelly Jammer without me."

"Well, if you would pick up your damn phone," Mia said. "Oh, yeah and start going to the gym again with me instead of doing your hermit workouts at home."

Winter sighed. "Yeah, I just need a little more time."

"So…"

"So…?"

"His video I forwarded to you. Did you watch it?"

Winter put her brush down. "Yeah, I did."

"And…what do you think?"

"I think that I dodged a bullet."

"No, he seems like a good guy." Mia took another sip. "I'm good at reading people."

"Mia, he's obviously troubled. You can look online and see what I mean."

"I did, and oh, my God, I can't believe how many followers he has. Ask Jeremiah, I almost got a social media orgasm."

Winter exhaled sharply through her nose. "You're so weird."

"I know, but hey. He's a good guy, I'm telling you."

"Oh, right. He's a good guy, yet he gets in fist fights all the time and has gone to jail."

Mia rolled her eyes, then got up. "He said the fight was a misunderstanding."

"The same excuse Lyle used all the time."

"He's nothing like Lyle, Winter."

"How do you know?"

"Because I just do."

Winter could hear Jeremiah's voice through the phone but couldn't make out what he was saying. "Hey, Jeremiah," she said closer to the mic.

Half of Jeremiah's face popped onto the screen. "Bo is the shit," he said. "Like…the good kind."

"Mmm-hmm," Winter replied.

She couldn't help but remember Bo's face in the apology video. How swollen it was. How he didn't seem genuine. How he seemed to be hiding something. She really wished he was what she had initially thought he was, but—*God, even in my mind, why does he have to be so hot?*

Mia pushed Jeremiah aside, and turned her phone around briefly as she opened a sliding door and sat down on her white backyard porch swing.

"Can't you stay still for more than two seconds?" Winter asked, watching her friend move back and forth on the swing. "I'm starting to feel queasy."

"I have a proposal to ask you," Mia said, picking up her swinging pace.

"Okay, just know that I might not be able to look at you the whole time."

"No problem."

Winter looked up at her mother's small yellow house. The once plush green and mowed grass was overgrown and browning, and a new set of dark brown curtains covered the large window.

"Okay, Mia continued. I have some exciting news."

"What is it?" Winter noticed a mist forming on her car

window. "Ope—it's about to rain again. I guess you're gonna have to get off that swing."

"Nah. I love swinging in the rain." Mia stuck her tongue out to capture falling droplets, but lucky for Winter, also stopped swinging. "So, this weekend, Jeremiah and I are going up to Seattle because I'm being featured in a fitness magazine."

"No way! That's awesome, Mia!"

"It's so awesome. And they're paying for the full trip."

"You deserve it."

"Thanky, thanky. But...that brings me to something I wanted to ask you. Kind of a favor...but also something I think would really benefit you."

Winter's face fell. Mia's favors were never easy. When they first met, Mia asked her to attend an after school aerobics class. When Winter arrived to the flagpole where the class was allegedly being held, it ended up being a dang 5k run—that she was somehow already registered for!

"What is it?" Winter asked grumpily.

"There's this organization I've been involved in called The VP. Stands for The Volunteer Program. Remember, I tried to get you to sign up with me?"

"I think so."

"Since you're feeling better, and since I have to go out of town this weekend, I was wondering..."

"Yes?"

"I was wondering if you'd fill in for me, just for this weekend. After that you don't ever have to do it again...or maybe you'll like it and we can start doing it with each other. Whatever, you know?"

"Um...what would I be doing?"

"Well, VP places you in whatever place needs a volunteer.

You just put your availability in their app, and they match you with a place. I had literally just been placed in a local animal shelter when I got the call about the magazine."

"Okay…yeah, I guess I can do that."

"I know you're not the best with animals but…"

"No, I'm good with animals, I just never really grew up with them. My mother never liked animals."

Winter wiped the fog off of her window and looked out. Of course her mother wasn't worried that she was late. She probably wouldn't even notice if Winter went missing for, like…a year.

"You're such a sweetheart, Winter. I think the animals will love you."

"Thanks, Mia."

"Okay, I'll let them know you're filling in for me. I know the organizers so they'll be cool with it."

"Okay," Winter said quietly.

"I think this will be really good for you. The internet gets a piece of you but you're depriving the rest of the world of how special you are."

Winter looked away, her eyes starting to water. She saw the curtain move in her mother's window. "I think I should get this mother visit over."

"Yeah," Mia said softly. "But call me if she acts like a butt. No one hurts my bishhh."

Winter smiled. "Love you. Bye."

"Okay, love you. I'll send you the details. Thanks again!"

Winter could hear Jeremiah's distant, muffled voice again as she ended the call.

She took one last look in the visor mirror, put her raincoat back on, grabbed her purse, took a long, deep breath, and opened her car door.

As she walked up to her mother's home, something she hadn't done in a while, she realized her anxiety had dissipated a little. Mia always seemed to know when Winter wasn't feeling well and just what to say, or what to distract her with. It was like she had a sixth sense for that kind of stuff. The rain had already stopped, and the clouds were glowing with light, as if they had swallowed the sun. Winter stopped to admire the rainbow that arched from behind the row of houses to beyond the horizon.

"Head is always in the clouds," Cassandra Smith said, standing at the door in a robe, wine glass in her hand.

But for once, Winter didn't get defensive. In fact, she surprised them both by initiating a hug. "Good to see you, Mother."

CHAPTER TWELVE

Bo sipped his staple morning drug of choice: Café con Leche with almond milk. It went down smooth, and by the time the cup was empty, he felt fully awake and ready for the day. Folk music played at a low volume but was overpowered by coffee shop chitter-chatter and constant door opening from the morning rush.

Bo zipped up his thick, green and black fleece sweater, and rubbed his hands together to warm them. He was about to take out his phone when he realized he'd never noticed the craftsmanship of the shop tables. They were beautiful slabs of oak wood shaped into the state of Oregon, with a thin layer of clear glass over blueprints of Portland. In the small table in front of him, Bo inspected an old and worn down map titled *Portland Street Map – 1938*.

"Excuse me, sir," said a timid voice.

Bo looked up to see a young—maybe even still in her teens—blue hair-dyed girl in a black apron.

"Um," she continued. "Would you like another drink? Or anything else?"

"You know what, I probably shouldn't but…. Yeah," Bo said as he got up.

She waved her hands to stop him. "Oh, no, let me get that for you."

"I don't want you to have to wait on me. I'll just get in line."

Bo noticed the people in line were glancing over at them.

"Well, actually…" She ran over to the counter, and carefully brought back another Café con Leche. "I thought you might want another one, so here you go."

"Wow." Bo took the drink and smiled. "That's really nice of you. I'm here so often I have a tab, so please just add it to that." He sat down. "I haven't seen you here before, are you new?"

The girl nodded, giddily. "And I um… I follow you on Nanogram and Instagram and Twitter and TikTok and Tumblr and Facebook."

Bo raised his eyebrows. "I didn't realize I was on all of those."

"Some of them are run by fans. Like my friend, she—"

"Ashley, can you come over here?" The assistant manager, Tanner, with his black Mohawk and sideburns, looked beyond annoyed.

Ashley went back behind the counter and he gave her an inaudible, yet obviously stern lecturing.

"You got a good worker on your hands, Tanner!" Bo said loudly, hoping that might take a little of the heat off of her. "She deserves a tip!"

Tanner gave him an unenthusiastic thumbs up.

For some reason, Bo was portrayed in the media as hating recognition, when in reality he usually found "fans" or "Stans" to be nice and interesting to talk to. It was all the other people Bo had to deal with that got under his skin. *Like Matt, that little weasel.* Of course, not everyone else was bad. *Winter...she was one of the good ones. And Mia and Jeremiah. They were cool too.*

He sat back and drank his drink slowly, wrapping his hand around the cup to warm his cold fingers. After a few seconds, he finally pulled out his cell phone and started scrolling.

Winter's recent posts tagged *Blaine's Lanes*' Nanogram, not Bo's personal account. He didn't dare *like* or leave a comment for three reasons: he might be blocked from liking or commenting and that would crush him; she might just ignore the comments and likes all together, and that would also crush him; or God forbid, it might compel her to change her page to private, and that would kill him. There had to be an explanation as to why she didn't want him contacting her, but it was her choice and he needed to respect that. Looking at her photos and posts, however, couldn't hurt anyone. Well… except him, that is.

He spent some time on her StyleSlap page, and noted that within the last three days, her followers had gone up about by about 20,000. The comments under her posts said stuff like: **"Beauty!"** or **"You're my inspiration, Winter! 😊 "** or **"wifey"** or **"I want that outfit"** or **"Gorgeous smile."**

He visited his own Nanogram page—something he hadn't done in a while—and looked at the apology video posted to his feed. He was shocked to see it was almost at a million views, despite his mom calling him and telling him how well the video was being received and how happy she was that he was back online. His dad never called him, but who cares? Bo was even asked to do various interviews and local radio spots but had declined it all. Under the Nanogram video, the top comment, from username

MattTheLizardGramGraham, read: ***No hard feelings, dude. Let bygones be bygonned. Put me on the list for next weekend!***

Bo realized he was shaking his knee, bumping it repeatedly into the table. His coffee spilled and Ashley the blue-haired girl came out of nowhere and wiped it up for him.

"Would you like a refill?" she asked.

"Oh, no thank you. *There's* still a little left…and I probably don't need any more caffeine."

She smiled and turned bright red and went back behind the counter before her boss figured out she was gone.

Jeremiah walked in just as Bo noticed a young couple whispering and looking at him. He waved at them, causing them to retreat and look away, then said loudly, "Hey, Jeremiah. I'm over here!"

"I'll be right there!" Jeremiah said, getting in line. "Gotta get my fix!"

Bo nodded. He looked back down at his phone, thought for a second, clicked *reply* under Matt's comment, and wrote *Sure, douchebag*. He smiled then deleted *douchebag* and just posted *Sure* and a thumbs up emoji. In less than five seconds, MattTheLizardGramGraham had liked his comment.

"Hey, what's up, man?" Jeremiah set a small paper bag on the table.

Bo jumped up to greet him. "I'm glad you could make it, Jeremiah."

"Are you kidding me? I'm stoked."

They shook hands and sat down opposite each other. Jeremiah wore a thin pullover hoodie and track pants and had his hood up over a trucker hat with what looked like an 8-bit illustration of a sunset.

"Okay, so, I'll just cut to the chase." Bo slapped the table, rattling his already half spilt coffee cup. "Your work is fucking amazing. Your illustrations and flyers and the way you edit videos—you just have this really eye-catching design style that I've never seen before."

"Sweet. Thanks, dude. But before we get into all that..." Jeremiah smiled from the corner of his mouth as he opened up his brown paper bag. He grabbed a napkin and used it to pull out a golden baked square, sprinkled with gooey chocolate chips. He held the glorious treat out in front of them.

Bo suddenly realized he hadn't eaten breakfast.

"This, my man," Jeremiah continued, "is the best thing you will taste all day. It's called Chipped Squared and it will blow your mouth. Pun intended."

Bo tried to resist. He really did. But he didn't want to be rude. After Jeremiah handed it to him, he inspected every side, every delectable crevice, like it was the Holy Grail, or something. Finally, Bo took a bite of the baked good and almost collapsed out of his chair. He could see the blue-haired girl briefly stopping her task and watching him, before realizing he was okay.

"Yeah, no shit," chuckled Jeremiah, who was already half done with his square.

"I was just gonna have a bite, but damn."

Jeremiah stuffed the last bite in his mouth and showed Bo the remaining contents of his bag: four more squares. "Don't judge me. I've barely had any sugar since I met my girl. She broke up with me once when she found a family fun-sized Snickers wrapper in my car trunk."

Bo laughed. "Oh, that sucks man. Hey, at least she cares about you, right?"

"If sugar is evil," Jeremiah sat back. "Well, then…call me the Illuminati."

Bo finished his last bite and wiped a dab of chocolate off of his thumb. "You're hired, man."

"What?"

"I mean, I want your energy, your creativity, your… Chipped Squared. Okay that was dumb, but I'd love to pay you a salary to be my go-to design guy."

"No fucking way," Jeremiah said.

"Yes fucking way. If you're down, of course."

"So, what would my job entail?"

"I'd need you to periodically make flyers and you know, the kind of advertising stuff that you did for opening night…"

"And I'm sorry," said Jeremiah, "but the *Blaine's Lanes* social media presence is seriously lacking. I can take care of that for you—I mean, I help Mia and Winter out all the time. My buddy has a production house, and I can work with him to make some marketing videos."

Bo swallowed and tried not to change his expression, picturing Winter's big beautiful eyes in his mind. "Um, yeah, that'd be great." *Get ahold of yourself, man,* he thought.

Jeremiah's phone vibrated from his hoodie pouch. He quickly pulled it out to look at the caller, then put it back.

"But I also have some other ideas I'd like to run by you," Bo continued. "Some apps and whatnot—have you tried virtual reality, or do you play video games?"

Jeremiah closed his eyes for a second. "I'm so glad Mia's not here to shame me…but yes and yes."

"Favorite games?" Bo asked.

"Of all time?

"Sure."

"Ah, I guess…" Jeremiah counted them out on his fingers. "Red Dead Redemption, GTA Five, and Skyrim. Oh, and Days Gone"

"No shit, you play Days Gone? You know what's up!"

The two high-fived each other.

"Hell yeah, dude. That game was made in Oregon. I gotta have love for it, right?"

"It's such an amazing, underrated game."

"So damn true. So, what are your favs?" Jeremiah asked, excitedly.

"The Last of Us, number 1."

"Legit."

"Also, all the games you listed. And throw in The Witcher and Horizon Zero Dawn."

Jeremiah nodded and stared into space, his eyes reddening.

Bo looked at him, perplexed. "Are…are you about to cry?"

"No, no. Of course not." Jeremiah smiled and stretched his arms. He pulled his hoodie off his head and turned his hat backwards. "It's just—I appreciate others who appreciate the beauty of games. That's all."

Bo laughed. "I get it man. I get it."

"Dude, I am all for this," Jeremiah said. "That fucking bowling alley was so different and weird, and I felt this numbing pain of jealousy when I left the place—like fuuuuuck I wish I came up with this. I'd be so stoked, dude, to help you with any projects you think up."

"Thanks man. I have some good feelings about this."

Jeremiah's phone vibrated and he rolled his eyes. He

asked Bo quickly, "Do you mind if I get this?" without waiting for an answer, then went outside to talk.

"Oh, yeah, no problem," Bo said to himself.

He stood up to stretch and looked around to see the café was mostly empty, other than one person in line and one person waiting for their order. He admired the lights above him that were made out of industrial, steampunk pipes contorted in different shapes and thought about getting something similar for his apartment…or maybe he could just buy one of the shop lights straight from Tanner. Slip him a couple bills. Although the only worker behind the counter was an unrecognizable rail thin man with a goatee. Outside, Jeremiah was pacing back and forth and talking passionately into his phone.

"Excuse me, Bo. Can we get a picture?" said the blue-haired Ashley, who had changed into off-work, plain clothes.

She was accompanied by an Asian girl with long, blonde dyed-hair and black roots. They both held matching blue-tinted, clear backpacks, carrying what looked like papers that had the Portland Community College logo on them.

"You wanna picture with *me*?" Bo asked.

"Yeah. Please," Ashley said.

"Okay, yeah, sure."

The girls giggled. Bo stood in the middle with his arms crossed. Ashley struggled to hold her arm out long enough to capture all three of them in the selfie, when Jeremiah walked in.

"Let me try," said Jeremiah, grabbing her phone. "This moment deserves to be captured right." Jeremiah held up the phone, stifling a smile as Bo's eyes seemingly flatlined. "Okay, on three. One, two…" Then he froze in place. Everyone uncomfortably laughed waiting for him to say *three*, and that's when the shutter sound went off. "Okay, we got it," Jeremiah said and handed the phone back.

"Wait, but we weren't ready," said Ashley's friend.

"Yeah, I was laughing," said Ashley.

"Exactly. I got a candid moment of y'all," Jeremiah said proudly. "Now you can look back at your time with Bo Blaine with a fondness that you would have never had otherwise."

Bo couldn't help but laugh. He was only able to stop himself by taking a sip from his cold coffee. "Did it come out okay?" he was finally able to ask.

Ashley looked at the photo on her phone and showed her friend. They both giggled. "It's actually really good. Thank you." She looked up at Bo, happily. "I'll tag you in the photo, Bo. It was nice meeting you."

"Nice meeting you. And let me know if Tanner gets on your case again. I'll have a word with him."

Ashley turned red again and ran over to a surprised Bo and hugged him really fast before running out the door with her friend. Bo sat down with a daze.

"Fuck, does this happen all the time?" Jeremiah asked. "You sure have a way with these females, man. I've noticed how they all look at you. Must be exhausting."

"What do you mean, how they look at me?"

"I mean, damn, man. They were a little young, but earlier I saw a grandma giving you the googly eyes. Of course, she was chugging a blended drink, so she may been suffering from brain freeze."

Bo laughed heartily and threw a napkin at Jeremiah, which he smoothly dodged. "You're a trip, man."

Jeremiah looked at his phone. "I'm gonna have to leave in a second, but please email me any information or paperwork."

"For sure. And we'll definitely set normal hours so you don't feel like you're on call twenty-four hours a day."

"Okay, but I love living life dangerously like that. If I'm out of town or whatever, I can still work. In fact, it keeps me sane to have something to always do. So…"

Bo slapped his leg. "Okay, then."

"Uh, there is something I wanted to spring on you, though. Something Mia is pressuring me to ask and I'm not usually a pushover, but she just won't stop. She like. Won't. Stop."

"Sure, what is it?"

"So, we're going to Seattle over the weekend to do this magazine shoot." Jeremiah spoke fast. "And she's involved in this volunteering app thing that plugs people into different places that need volunteers. Blah blah. I do it sometimes too. And we committed to this weekend before Mia was booked. So…she got someone to cover her spot. And we're wondering if you'd be interested or available in covering *my* spot…maybe?"

Bo raised his eyebrows and scratched his lower back. "Uh…"

"I totally understand if you can't. I just sprung this on you and Mia—she's my girl but you know what? She's kind of a coward. There. I said it… Shit, is my phone on?" Jeremiah looked at his phone. "Okay. Phew." He looked back at Bo. "She had the nerve to say that 'volunteering could help Bo's reputation.' That's what a…a brat she is sometimes."

"No, actually that's a good idea." Bo clasped his hands behind his neck. "My mom wants me to do something about my 'image.' I wouldn't mind helping out the community while I do that."

"Well, I don't see why you would need to improve

anything. What? 'Cuz you have some tattoos and beat up some big mouth?"

"If you only knew." Bo shook his head. "Just text me the info." He stood up and wiped off the table, put his coffee cup in the dirty bin, threw his trash away.

Jeremiah stuffed his used napkin in his pants pocket, and stayed sitting, staring into space.

"Okay, man. This meeting went fucking amazing. I'm looking forward to working with you." Bo held out his hand.

Lost in thought, Jeremiah stood up and shook Bo's hand slowly. "Yeah, man."

They waved at Mr. Goatee Barista and Bo opened the door for a group of people walking in. When they got outside into the cold air, they said their goodbyes, and headed off in opposite directions. Bo was about to open his street-parked car door when he heard a distant shout.

"Aye, Bo!" Jeremiah was already across the busy street.

"What's up?" Bo shouted back.

"I'm not supposed to tell you this—" A loud motorcycle cut him off.

"What was that?"

"I'm not supposed to tell you this," Jeremiah shouted louder, "but Winter blocked you because she doesn'—" A line of cars passed between them.

Bo went a little up the street to hear him.

When there was a small break in the traffic, Jeremiah continued, "Winter blocked you because she doesn't trust herself with you. Whatever that means. And she's filling in for Mia—she's gonna be at the volunteer job with you."

Another car passed between them. Bo couldn't remember saying thank you or goodbye or acknowledging he heard Jeremiah's words, but he could hear an echo of a memory of it. He floated to his car. Didn't take one breath. Probably didn't blink either. *I'm actually going to see her this weekend. I'm actually going to see her again.* He pushed the horn a few times in celebration, hoping that no one would think he was nuts and call the cops and have him committed before he got to see *her* again. Just then, his phone chimed with text alerts from Jeremiah.

The first text: **Mums the word, dude.**

The second text, arriving one minute later: **Oh, and Winter doesn't know you're volunteering. I thought you should know because boys before Helen of Troys. You know what I'm saying? But from now on, I'm staying out of my girl's schemes and drama.**

Then Jeremiah sent a gif of a character from the show *Breaking Bad* saying: **"I'll never make that mistake again."**

Bo texted back: ***Thanks for the heads up. I owe you one.***

Jeremiah replied: **You don't owe me shit.**

At that moment, Bo knew he had made a friend for life.

CHAPTER THIRTEEN

Winter pulled into a visitor's parking spot at Beaverton Animal Rescue, a massive shelter tucked away behind a park, only two miles from her cottage. The rain poured down—ironically, like cats and dogs—and her windows fogged up the second she turned the ignition off. She breathed hard and felt the first signs of dizziness creep up the back of her head. *Am I going to be able to do this?* she thought. At the very least, when it came to appropriate attire, Winter was ready: She wore brown, over the ankle, men's logger boots; oatmeal colored, shin high socks; thick, stretchy tights designed to look like black jeans, complete with faux pockets; a long, burnt umber knit sweater, and a white raincoat.

Her morning mirror selfie, titled "What rain?" and hashtagged *fallstyle, October, Rain,* and *Oregon* was doing really well, and so was the streetlights-in-fog photo she took on a late night frozen yogurt run and uploaded before she went to bed.

She had spent so much time choosing her outfit, she forgot to think about the fact that she was going to be immersed in a new, uncomfortable environment, with animals that she probably wouldn't be able to control. She never had a pet. When she was really little she asked for a puppy in a Christmas letter addressed to The North Pole, but her mother told her she was too easily distracted and obviously wouldn't be able to take care of an animal, so it was out of the question.

She had wondered why Santa let "mommy" open up her private letter to him and from that day on she wasn't as trusting, especially to jolly, bearded men that wore red clothes. One time, a Target store employee asked her if she needed help finding a toy, and she ran away crying.

Winter turned on music. Then she tried a podcast. Then she put on an audiobook. Nothing stopped her mind from racing. Would the shelter animals sense that she didn't grow up with pets? Would they bite her? *Maul* her? They could have rabies for all she knew! Winter had a few minutes to think of the horrible consequences of taking Mia's shift, and leaned her seat back a little to really take it all in.

The rain started to slow down, and the world shifted into a brighter tint as the clouds moved across the sky, allowing the sun some breathing room. Suddenly, there was a knock at her driver's side window. She lowered the window slightly to see Bo's green eyes under a black beanie. Her stomach dropped and she couldn't get a word out. She just stared up at him like a dummy. *He's so handsome.*

The light hit the rain just right, forming a nimbus around Bo. He put the hood up on his blue raincoat before stuffing his hands in his coat pockets. Her heart was beating so fast it didn't seem healthy.

"Hi, Winter. I'm filling in for Jeremiah." His face remained serious. "I wanted to let you know but I couldn't—I couldn't contact you online. So, if you feel uncomfortable, one of my friends said he could fill in for me."

Oh, Mia, she thought. *I see what you did here.* She lowered the window down all the way.

"No, that's okay. It was nice of you to cover for Jeremiah," Winter said quietly.

He smiled and his stance softened, as if he had been balancing a weight on his shoulders and just let it fall.

"It's good to see you again," he said.

Winter watched him jog back to the shelter, and realized some rain was getting in her car. She quickly rolled the window up. Then the anxiety and panic set in… She had to leave. She couldn't stay because she knew—she knew she wouldn't be able to resist him. *His eyes. His lips. His nose. His ears. His- Aargh!* Was that a ship wheel wrapped in rope on his left wrist, peeking out from under his raincoat? She wanted to ask him the stories behind each and every tattoo on his body. And it was an urge she knew she shouldn't have. She couldn't afford to fall for another so-called "bad boy"—as the headlines referred to him. For goodness sake, he got into a fist fight literally hours after they met! And all the other fights with his father and the jail and—he put on a good front but she wasn't stupid.

Lyle did the same thing. Maybe Lyle was a blessing because he kept her more vigilant, warned her by example. Maybe the piece of crud, Lyle, knew what he was doing when he forbade her from going out with her friends, accused her of cheating—even after just running to the drugstore—and when he…

She felt nauseous and promised herself that she would

stay away from Bo during her shift, no matter what charm he tried to pull. She was already there. She didn't want to quit or make a scene. But the second she got off, Winter vowed she would call Mia and ask her the following question, "What kind of friend are you?"

CHAPTER FOURTEEN

The three volunteers stood in a half circle in the staff break room, facing a hippie, middle-aged man that could stunt double for The Dude in *The Big Lebowski.* He introduced himself—his name was Gilbert and he was the Lead Animal Care Technician—and explained that Beaverton Animal Shelter was a no-kill shelter that placed many of their animals in temporary homes until they were adopted in their "forever homes." Dogs sporadically barked in the distance, and the sound of rattling cages echoed and reverberated through the room.

"Most of our adoptions happen through our website, so every two weeks we take photos and videos of our animals and create a profile for them," Gilbert explained.

He talked with his hands, and took turns looking each volunteer in the eyes for an uncomfortable fourteen seconds. Bo knew that because he counted.

"So, it's kind of like that Tinder app…but for animals?" asked a high pitched, forty-year-old woman, wearing black cat-eye glasses.

"Not sure what Tinder is so I couldn't answer that question," Gilbert replied.

"It's more like Facebook for animals," said a large, red-bearded, early thirty-something man, wearing camo from head to toe. He laughed. "Unless Beaverton Animal Shelter is trying to get their animals laid."

Bo smiled and shook his head. Camo Man laughed again.

"I can assure you that is not what we're doing here," said Gilbert.

Just then, Winter walked in, took her rain coat off and hung it up on the coat rack near the door. She walked sheepishly over to the volunteers and stood as far away from Bo as she could, at least that's what it seemed like.

"Ah yes, I thought we had another one." Gilbert smiled at the newcomer.

"Sorry I'm late… My name's Winter." She did a little wave to everyone, strategically not making eye contact with Bo.

"Winter, that's a pretty name," said Gilbert, obviously smitten with her. "Nice to meet you."

"Likewise." Winter smiled but when Gilbert looked away to continue his monologue, her face dropped.

She stared at the floor and bit her bottom lip. She wore her dark hair in a high, neat ponytail. And her face glowed despite wearing minimal makeup: lipstick a few shades darker than her natural, pink lip color, and a thin line of eyeliner on her eyelids. He started paying attention to stuff like that after working with the models on his mom's fashion line. He tried not to look at Winter. Really tried to nod and pay attention to the Lead Animal Care Technician. But how could he stay focused when *she* was standing only feet away from him?

During a lull in Gilbert's speech, Cat-Eye Glasses turned to Winter. "You look so familiar. Are you famous or something?"

Winter looked shocked, as if she were just jolted awake. "No, I'm just nobody."

Cat Eyes laughed. "Aren't we all?"

Bo ran his hands through his hair. *This is gonna be torture,* he thought. And when he glanced, involuntarily, again, over at Winter, she was looking at him, then quickly looked at the ground.

Gilbert continued, "So, we need someone helping with photos and transporting our adoptees to and from the kennels or cages to the back patio where we're taking the photos. And two people cleaning out the empty kennels."

"I'll clean," said Bo, raising his hand.

"Wow, that's a first. I don't usually have people itching to do cleaning duty. It's going to be a difficult task. Let's just say, some of our current residents aren't exactly potty-trained."

"Well, I'm prepared. Wore my hazmat gear." Bo stuck out a foot and displayed his tall, yellow boots.

"So you did. Very good," Gilbert said, impressed.

"Uh-oh. I forgot my boots," Camo Man shrugged his shoulders, giving an *aw-shucks* look. "I guess I'll be a photographer and animal transporter today."

Cat Eyes squinted and adjusted her glasses. "I swear… you look familiar too," she said to Bo. "Are you…hmmm… are you…"

"I'm nobody," said Bo.

He glanced at Winter and to his surprise she was half-smiling.

"I'll clean," Winter said.

"What was that?" asked Gilbert.

"I don't mind cleaning, too." Winter pursed her lips together, but her eyes were bright.

"Oh, good. I was getting worried," said Cat Eyes.

Bo raised his eyebrows, and realized his mouth was open. He chose the cleaning gig because he was sure Winter was going to choose something else. *Who was this girl?* He barely knew her, besides the magical night they met and any information he could find online, but she somehow surprised him about a million times in the span of a few days.

"Okay, that settles it," Gilbert said, then yelled, "John!"

A teenage boy walked in the room, holding a box of t-shirts. He looked like a mini version of Gilbert—same long, hippie hair, same unkempt eyebrows.

"This is my son, John. He'll hook you all up with volunteer t-shirts. We ask you to wear them under your coats or sweaters—helps with teamwork and moral. And don't forget to spread the word about us—post us on Nanogram and Twitter and all the other ones, tacking Beaverton Animal Shelter or BAC."

John rolled his eyes. "It's tagging, dad. Not tacking."

"*Tagging*," Gilbert exaggerated the word to annoy his son even further. "*Tag* us and don't forget to use the pound sign."

"Hashtag," John corrected him, provoking chuckles from the room.

"Well, in my day, it was called a pound sign."

John gave out teal t-shirts with large white block "VOLUNTEER" lettering on the front, guessing the sizes for each person. The shelter's name and logo, complete with a silhouette of a dog and cat sitting side by side, made up the back of the shirt.

Winter and Cat Eyes conversed as they removed their

sweaters and put on their volunteer shirts. Camo Man tried on a few different sizes *over* his camo jacket, before settling with the largest one, which fit snuggly. Bo gave them all some space and went off to the corner. He took off his black workout shirt and pulled off the tag of the volunteer shirt—tags always made him itchy.

"Holy shit!" said Camo Man. "I've never seen anyone with that many tattoos. Must have taken forever." He went over to Bo and got really close, trying to get a better look. "Man, that Gandalf back tattoo is incredible." His voice shifted up a tone. "The details! Gandalf's pipe and his skin and nose." He laughed happily. "It looks so realistic."

"Thanks, man," Bo said. "Yeah, I had to get Gandalf. He's a legend."

Camo Man pulled up his long camo sleeves, revealing a few, nondescript tattoos. He pointed to a faded tattoo on his left arm. "I got this Smaug tattoo like twenty years ago."

Bo and Camo Man talked about tattoos for a few minutes and the whole time, Bo could feel eyes on him. *Winter's eyes.* And he made a point to keep the conversation going…just hoping it would make her squirm.

CHAPTER FIFTEEN

Winter was mesmerized. She liked Mora and keenly sat down at a table with her to go over the paper handout that listed all of the rules, tips, and tricks that went into volunteering at the shelter. But Mora didn't have her full attention. Bo's breathtakingly sculpted body did.

Winter felt guilty that she was happy when Mora said she had myopia and had to take her glasses off to read. It meant that Winter could look at Bo without explaining herself. Without Mora asking questions or making observations or acknowledging what a gorgeous man Bo was. For a few moments, he was all hers.

Gilbert and his son had excused themselves to get everything prepped and ready to go. And even though the guy in camo was there, he only seemed to care about tattoos. Winter was in awe of Bo's perfectly shaped biceps. She was slapped in the face by his abs. She was wonderstruck by his broad shoulders. He had a slender build, like a professional soccer player. His muscles weren't big, but they weren't small by any means. *They're just right*, she thought. *I'm*

Goldilocks in Goldilocks and the Three Volunteers, and I want that one. She pointed at Bo in her mind. Then Winter put her head in her hands. *What is wrong with me? I've seriously lost it.*

"Are you okay?" Mora asked, putting down the volunteer sheet.

Winter shook it off. "Yeah. The tired just hit me for a second."

"Oh, tell me about it. I had to work all morning because my husband accidently ran into my rose bushes and—"

Mora's words floated away as Winter watched Bo put the teal shirt on. It juxtaposed his tan skin and colorful tattoos so drastically that he looked like a walking, talking, art installation.

Just then, Bo locked eyes with her. Then—she would bet her life on it—he gave a little smirk. The butterflies wreaked havoc in her stomach, as if they were in protest to what she was feeling, waking her up, reminding her who he was. *Bad Boy Bo*—it was phrase she saw over and over again when she read articles about him. He didn't seem troubled, or, as his father referred to him, "problematic." He seemed so nice to everyone. And he was so confident, but not in a vain way…*oddly enough, even when he has his shirt off in a public place.* And would a bad person be volunteering at an animal shelter?

Mora was back to reading the handout and she pointed to something on the list. "That's interesting, it says they also have rabbits and birds here."

"That's cool. I've only heard barking and meowing since I got here," said Winter. "They must keep the other animals in another section."

"Yeah, I sure hope they're not all crammed together. I

don't think a cat would be too happy to be across the cage from a bird, but you—"

Mora's words trailed off again, disappearing into the ether. Bo nodded his head, putting on a black hoodie, as the camo man talked his ear off. But Bo never looked annoyed, even for a second. He was so kind—*No! He was not to be trusted.* But his eyes. Those green eyes. The way he put his eyebrows together to show he was interested.

He was so inviting. So accepting. *Nope, nope, nope. Bo probably set this whole thing up. Maybe he duped Mia and Jeremiah. Concocted a weird volunteering scheme. It probably bothers him that he can't conquer me like he does every other female and he's not gonna stop until he wins some sick, twisted game he created with his other playboy friends.*

"Okay." Gilbert walked in, winded. "Time to get to business."

Mora and the camo guy followed Gilbert out the door. Winter stayed sitting, and put her knit sweater back on, making sure her phone was still buttoned inside the pocket. Bo walked over to her. She didn't want to look up. Didn't want to give him the satisfaction of looking up.

"Winter," Bo said.

She looked up.

He flashed a disarming smile, but he still furrowed his eyebrows in that concerned way. He towered over her, holding out his perfect hand to help her up, and though she knew she would regret it in the long run…

She took it.

CHAPTER SIXTEEN

They followed Gilbert down the long, cement corridor. A female staff member was walking toward them with two leashed dogs: a calm, uninterested Yorkshire terrier puppy, and a hyper, yapping dog that looked like a mix of Husky and Australian Shepard.

"Bay 2?" Gilbert asked as they passed him.

"Bay 2," the staff member confirmed.

Winter kept her hands in her sweater pockets and Bo in his jeans. He wanted to talk to her, but he didn't want an audience... so he just looked ahead. From his peripheral she kept doing the same.

"Okay, here we are," said Gilbert.

They entered a large room that smelled like wet dog and urine, comprised of a walkway and what Gilbert referred to as "Home Suites." In reality, the "suites" were two rows of compartment rooms—five on each side. Each room had a small cement recliner with cushion, a fake television, a rug, a small bed fit inside of a small cement bed frame, viewing windows, large ventilation panels, and large doors. The row of suites on the left also had doggy doors that opened to personal, fenced-in grass areas for bathroom needs.

"The Home Suites provide our animals with a relaxing, calm, stress free environment that mimics a real home," said Gilbert.

"These are great," said Winter.

"Who gets the luxury of staying in here?" asked Bo.

"Well, we also have crates, and actually some of our animals prefer to be in smaller spaces or don't get along with others, but we try to give most of our *guests* as much time in here or outside, as possible." Gilbert started opening the compartment room doors, one by one, down the line. "It's kind of like our idea of rehabilitation, you know? We wanna get our dogs and cats ready for adoption."

"It's a great idea," said Bo.

"Yeah. Actually, it's more like a rehab halfway house." Gilbert laughed and went to the other side to start opening doors. "You'd know about that. Wouldn't you, Bo?"

Winter stopped looking into the compartments.

"What was that?" Bo asked, squinting.

"Oh, my son filled me in on who you are. He said he uses the FFS Industries' sports app or something." Gilbert laughed again. "All I can say is I envy your life."

"Um, thank you but I was never in a halfway house. I'm not sure where he heard that."

"We read it. You know, there's no privacy these days—even when your family tries to scrub it from the internet."

Bo stood there, in the middle of an animal shelter, feeling like he was the one in a viewing room—the one being caged up. He squeezed his fists and watched Gilbert open the last door, oblivious to Bo's increasing heart rate. When Bo glanced over at Winter, he realized she almost looked...

scared. Of him? Of the tension in the room? He wasn't sure. She crossed her arms and took a step back and he felt himself unclench, well…everything. It was like her very presence calmed him.

"I had probation but not rehab," Bo finally said. "You know what, it's not a big deal. I just want to help in any way I can and escape my family business for a little while."

"I get it," said Gilbert, his hands on his hips. "There's a reason I sent my son outside. When he realized who you were, he tried calling his friends and—but don't worry, I didn't let him." He pulled a cell phone out of his back pocket and waved it in the air. "He ain't calling anyone or posting anything for the whole weekend."

"Oh, man, I kind of feel bad about that," Bo said. "But at the same time, I don't want to distract from what everyone is here for."

"Slumming it with the lowly people. Am I right?" Gilbert laughed hard.

He really amused himself.

Bo was about to say something, but Winter saved the day.

"So, what're we doing in here?" she asked.

Gilbert encouraged Bo and Winter to put their sweaters in the far closet, then had them put on clear, plastic aprons to cover the rest of their clothes from any bleach. He then pulled out the bed pillow, rug and any other washing machine abled items from Suite 1 and stacked it in the hallway for staff to pick up.

He pulled out a long, stretchy hose from a panel and sprayed down the whole compartment. Then he brought out a cart of cleaning supplies and demonstrated how to disinfect the room before rinsing it all off again with the hose. The walkway and each compartment had a drain, but Gilbert provided them with two push brooms to guide the water if they wanted to move the draining process along. After Bo and Winter got the gist of it, they were left alone. The dogs that were barking in the distance, had stopped. And the room was eerily quiet. As they put on gloves, the sound of latex stretching and snapping echoed.

"You were mad back there, weren't you?" Winter asked quietly, picking up the chair cushion and rug from Suite 2."

"How could you tell?" Bo picked up the bed mattress.

She cleared her throat. "The vein on your left temple. It kind of throbs."

"It throbs?" Bo smiled. "You're shitting me."

"I promise. And it went away the second you said, 'it's no big deal.' I'll take a video of it next time."

They hauled the contents of Room 2 to the corridor and started on Room 3.

"So, why'd you volunteer for cleaning? I'd think you would be all for the photography and the whole 'Facebook for animals' thing."

Winter's ponytail swung back and forth. Her body language was so closed off at first, but it seemed to loosen with every passing second.

"Nah," she said. "I need a break from all of that."

"I know what you mean. I had to take a break from it too."

She stopped in the walkway, holding the rug with one hand. "Then why'd you go back?"

Bo stopped in front of her, setting a smelly bed full of cat hair on the ground. "Do you really wanna know?"

"Yes."

"Because I wanted to contact you."

Winter did an irresistible turn-away smile.

They continued their work making casual conversation, then as they cleared out the last compartment of the first row, Bo finally got enough courage to ask, "I, uh…I was wondering why you blocked me."

Winter bit her lip and Bo could barely take it.

"You just remind me of my ex," she said, and there was a hint of irritation in her tone.

"What about me reminds you—"

"Your anger issues."

Bo felt like he could implode. "A lot of that stuff online, Winter—it's either misunderstanding or—or its exaggerated. And yes, I used to have a hard time controlling my emotions and I handled things in ways that I—" He shook his head. "But I've changed."

Winter nodded but her eyes were downcast. Bo almost jumped out of his skin when Gilbert stuck his head in the room entrance.

"Hey guys!" Gilbert shouted. "How's it going?"

"It's going well," said Winter.

"That's great, *Winter*. Great time of the year, by the way." Gilbert did one of those annoying finger point and mouth clicking maneuvers.

Thank God Gilbert didn't add a wink to that lame move, Bo thought, *or I wouldn't be able to restrain myself. Fuck… this guy really rubs me the wrong way.*

"Oh, yeah, man," said Bo, unable to hide the sarcasm in his voice. "Gotta love the dreary days and nights, freezing your ass off whenever you go outside, scraping ice off your window and waiting for the defrost to kick in before you can drive anywhere."

"Okay, then." Gilbert slapped the wall. "You're making good progress. I'll check on you two soon."

Once Gilbert fled the scene, Winter seemingly couldn't hold it in any longer—she giggled uncontrollably. "Wow. You really don't like winter, do you?"

"It's not that bad," Bo said, amused with himself.

"Honestly, I kind of love everything you listed. It might be annoying but it's so—so *Oregon*."

"I went a little overboard there. I actually really like…*winter*."

She stared at him for a few seconds and he was convinced she was about to roll her eyes, but she didn't.

Instead, she smiled and looked up and to the left, as if reminiscing: "I love wearing sweaters and the blankets and fireplaces and driving up the mountain to pick a Christmas tree, and when it snows, it's so magical, and drinking cocoa and taking warm baths."

"Well, you make it sound enticing," Bo said, and then he thought, *With you. I want to do all that stuff with you.*

They started clearing out the opposite row of suites. A puff of dog hair clung to the back of Bo's arm and since they were wearing soiled gloves, Winter helped him get it off with the end of a broom handle. Bo took off his glove to help Winter get a ponytail-escaped strand of hair out of her eye. He had to look for another glove from the closet, but it was worth it. Especially how she looked up at him. Especially how she said, "thank you," in that embarrassed, sweet way.

When they were done hauling, they began the disinfectant process, starting with Suite 2.

"Do you mind if I put on some music?" Bo asked. "I'll just put on a playlist or something."

"I'd love that."

Bo put his phone on the cleaning cart. At full volume, an electropop song played, and it reverberating off of the walls.

Bo bobbed his head along to the beat, grabbed a mop and dunked it in the bleach bucket. Winter mimicked him with her own mop, and they both went into different compartments. They worked for some time and when Winter was halfway through, Bo stood at the door of Suite 8, waiting for her to turn around.

"Do you know how talented you are?" he asked.

"Talented? At disinfecting?"

"Well, that too." He pretended to inspect her work. "But also your posts. You have an eye for aesthetics—the composition of your shots, the creative settings. And you probably have the best style I've ever seen. It makes sense you have so many people who follow you."

Winter leaned her mop against the wall and put her gloved hands behind her back.

"You're—you don't have to say that," she said and her face flushed. "But you should talk! You have millions of followers."

"Yeah, but that's because people know me through my family business. It's not like I curated followers through my own efforts…" He scratched his chin with the back of his forearm. "Your mom must be really proud of you."

Winter sucked on her bottom lip. A hip hop song started playing on the phone, and it caught Winter's attention. "Is this 'This Is Halloween' from *The Nightmare Before Christmas*?"

"Good ear. It's a remix. Do you like it?"

"It's pretty good."

"I got a few Halloween themed songs in this playlist."

She smiled, grabbed her mop and continued working on her compartment. After a few seconds, she realized he was still standing there, watching her.

"I wish I could say my mother is proud of me," she said,

"but sometimes I think that she'd be happier if I wasn't around."

"Why do you say that?"

"Because she tries to make my life miserable. But I won't let her, and it drives her crazy."

"Good," he said, matter-of-factly. "Um, about the not letting her part."

"Yeah…good," she said, lifting up her chin slightly.

They locked eyes and his skin had more goosebumps than a Scholastic Book Fair. *How could anyone be so beautiful?* he thought.

"Hi, guys," said John. He was walking up the suite walkway. "Have you seen my dad anywhere?"

"Oh, hey man." Bo said. "He stopped by about thirty minutes ago."

Winter stuck her head out of the compartment door. "Hi."

"Um, okay," said the teenager. "Hey, I was just wondering —it's Bo Blaine, right?" He fidgeted with a piece of rubber sticking out of the cart and kept moving his eyes from Bo's tattoos to Winter.

"Yeah, I'm Bo Blaine."

"Um… Well, I was just thinking…like…what made you come here? It's really weird. This place kinda sucks."

"Oh, um," Bo chuckled. "This place isn't that bad, actually."

"Are you like, obsessed with animals or something? Cuz that'd make sense. Cuz, you know, you're rich and shit."

"You know what? I do love me some animals, John. You're right on the money with that."

John awkwardly laughed, then pointed at Winter. "And who is she? I just can't figure it out."

"Hey! I told you not to come in here!" Gilbert shouted from the entrance.

John rolled his eyes. "What the eff," he mumbled, pulling his baggy pants up and sulking past his dad.

Gilbert held up his hand. "Sorry about that guys! Carry on. You're working faster than my own staff."

"No problem," said Bo.

Winter waived and when Gilbert and John were out of sight, she whispered, "They're funny."

"A real hoot."

They finished disinfecting the rest of their compartments and moved the cart to the side. Bo got the hose and brought it over to Suite 2, handing it to Winter.

"Would you like to do the honors?" he asked.

"Why, thank you."

They both took a few steps back and Winter turned on the hose. With delight, she sprayed every crevice of the compartment. Bo watched her. Briefly glanced at how her formfitting pants accentuated her tone thighs, and her round, tight behind...but the guilt of her not knowing he was admiring her, made him look away. He'd never felt guilt when looking at a woman before.

"Your turn," she said and handed him the hose.

They took turns spraying down each suite and laughed when Winter wasn't able to turn the water off after finishing up the first row. She lost her grip on the hose and it flailed around like a rabid snake. It sent water in the air, landing on its victims like heavy rain. After a few seconds, they were both soaked. They laughed and laughed and finally when they realized they wouldn't be able to wrangle the damn hose, Bo ran over to the valve and turned it off. A slow acoustic song was streaming out of his phone, contrasting the frenetic energy that had just passed through the room.

"You saved us from that sadistic monster," Winter said teasingly, in her best damsel voice. "How can I ever repay you?"

"It was my pleasure, miss. No need for repayment," he said in an old-timey western accent.

He was stunned when she wrapped her arms around him.

"A hug is the least I can do," she said softly.

CHAPTER SEVENTEEN

He slowly put his arms around her, and she put her head on his chest. She could swear his heart was beating just as fast as hers, and she had to remind herself, more than once, to breathe. He smelled like sandalwood and bergamot and she closed her eyes to sink into it. *Why am I so attracted to him?* she thought. He was like this magnet and no matter how much she wanted him to repel her away, he did the opposite. It was her fault. She knew what was going to happen. Maybe she was masochistic? Maybe she was certifiable? Why else would she put herself through that again? She had finally gotten over Lyle. Finally took enough showers and scrubbed hard enough to get Lyle off of her. Finally could go out. Could interact with the world. Could finally be herself. *Of course this would happen.* It was nothing but a disgustingly cruel test put upon her by the universe. She wasn't dumb. And it didn't matter how happy she felt around him. How beautiful she felt when he looked at her. It was all a part of the test. And she wasn't going to fail it. Not again.

"You're trembling," Bo said.

She looked up. *His lips*. More magnets trying to reel her in. Trying to trick her. She almost gave in. *Almost.* Almost put her lips on his. Felt his tongue caress hers. *Almost*. She pulled away from him, their wet aprons were stuck together and slowly separated.

"I can't—I can't—" she stammered.

"What is it?" He looked so perplexed that she almost felt bad.

"I'm not feeling well. I think I'm gonna go home a little early."

He shook his head. "What? What did I do?"

"I'm just not feeling well, okay? I'm so sorry. I won't be able to help rinse the last row."

"That's okay, Winter. Just—just please tell me what I did. Or what I can do."

Winter took off her apron and gloves and threw them in the bin. She opened the closet to get her sweater, standing in a shallow puddle that was slowly flowing toward the drain in the center of the walkway. She wanted to explain. She really did. But she couldn't talk. Her throat was dry, and she fought her body to keep producing enough saliva to even swallow.

Suddenly, Gilbert strolled in, completely oblivious. "Whoa, whoa. Looking good." He looked in the first few compartments, then noticed Winter putting on her sweater. "Done already?"

Bo's pointed eyebrows relaxed a little. "We only have a couple suites to rinse out. Winter's not feeling well so I'll finish the rest myself."

Winter couldn't look at Bo anymore. She wasn't strong enough.

"Oh, that's too bad," Gilbert said, disappointment in his

voice. "Do we need to get someone to take your Saturday and Sunday shifts?"

"Oh, no," Winter said. "I just—I think I'll need to do a different job. Maybe photography or something."

"Absolutely. That's my forte so I'll teach you the tips and tricks of the trade."

Gilbert smiled and winked at her, but she pretended not to notice.

Winter realized John was leaning against the side wall, just as deep, booming barks emanated from the vents connected to the patio outside. Everything seemed to scare her, and she couldn't get out of the room fast enough.

"Winter," Bo called after her.

But she couldn't answer him. She needed to get as far away from him as possible, at least until she could catch her breath. Until she could get rid of the anxious knots imbedded in her lungs. In her rib cage. In her heart.

John pointed at her.

"Oh, I know who you are. You're that fashion girl." John looked at his dad. "Dad, she's that fashion style girl!"

The sun was bright and made the oil on the wet streets sparkle. Winter clenched the steering wheel, vowing not to crash. She only had one more mile to go. No big deal. At the last stoplight, she wiped a small stream of tears with the sleeve of her sweater. Maybe she couldn't volunteer tomorrow. Maybe she could get someone to cover for her. *Or —or—*she pushed the gas for a second then realized it was still red, and abruptly stopped. *I might have to leave my car* *right here*, she thought. *Just turn the car off, get out, and walk home.*

When the light turned green she was breathing hard. By the time she was pulling into her cottage driveway, she was hyperventilating. Somehow, in a daze, she was able to unlock her front door, lock all of the locks behind her, take off her clothes, and lay herself in the empty bathtub. After ten minutes, she was able to turn the bath water on. And her breathing slowed. The knots unwound. The frantic prayers for mercy quieted. *I'm not going to die*, she thought. *Today, I'm not going to die.*

Sitting on her couch, knees to her chest and wrapped in a pink and gray faux fur throw blanket, Winter looked at her morning selfie, which was getting a surprising amount of likes on all her accounts.

Thankfully, she already did her ads for the week, but she also didn't have any ideas for the weekend—which would usually feature her in a public or social setting, or some interesting (hopefully) photo she took around the city or found online (always giving credit, of course). She was definitely going to post about Beaverton Animal Shelter and encourage her followers to adopt, but she also thought it'd be tacky to post photos of herself volunteering. After some debating, Winter decided she would take a few videos of the animals and of the shelter building, then post it all on Monday with direct links to the BAS website and app. If she posted anything on the weekend, someone may have put two and two together and figured out where they could find her.

She typed *Bo Blaine* into the Nanogram search bar and

clicked on his profile. Under his name a button said "Blocked." Winter clicked it and a popup asked her "Do you wish to unblock this user? Yes / No." She hesitated before clicking "No."

She scrolled down and noticed he hadn't posted anything since his apology video to Matt Graham. In person, any semblance of the fight had already vanished, but Bo's video really highlighted how bad that fight was: his cheek puffed out, his eye was black and bruised, and to top it off, his hair was uncharacteristically disheveled.

Watching Matt's ranting videos, though, anyone could see who won the fight. Matt had a huge fat lip, his eye was so swollen he couldn't open it, and it was obvious that half of his bloody face had met either a fist or the ground. *They were hanging out all night*, she thought. *Why did they get in such a horrible fight? Did Bo hit on Matt's wife, or something?* Bo didn't really give an explanation in his apology video, other than there had been a "misunderstanding." Winter had never misunderstood someone so badly that it resulted in a fistfight.

Heck, when Mia and Winter fought, they usually just avoided each other for a day or two until they cooled off. Then one of them would like or comment something frivolous on the other's post—in a sense, throwing up a digital white flag to signal the end of battle. Violence was not a way to solve conflicts—at least, not a healthy way. Violence was the coward's way out. Violence–

Winter threw her phone to the other end of the couch. She closed her eyes and saw Bo, laughing, soaked, wrestling the hose. She smiled. Then opened her eyes. Then grasped the remote, then turned on the TV.

A rerun of *Keeping Up with the Kardashians* had just

started, and she watched half of the episode before turning it off.

She wished she could call Mia and tell her everything that happened, everything that she was feeling…but Mia was to blame for all of it. Her so-called best friend would probably just repeat what she had been saying since they all met—that Bo was a good guy, that he and Winter were meant for each other, that she should give him another chance to get to know him.

Winter's living room sliding doors provided a beautiful frame to the trees outside, and though the sun was going down, she could see two squirrels chasing each other, hopping from branch to branch. They looked so carefree. Like they'd never heard of the concept of anxiety disorder or PTSD, which Dr. Ronda recently suggested to her over the phone. Dr. Ronda asked her to come in to her office for a free session, but Winter declined. *What would be the point of dredging up old news, anyway?*

On Saturday, Winter barely saw Bo. He stayed on cleaning duty, with an obviously annoyed Camo Guy—whose name was apparently Stanley—something she found out after Gilbert gave everyone name tag stickers to wear. Winter was disappointed that Mora and her cute cat-eye glasses wasn't going to be there for the rest of the weekend. She had apparently gotten sick the night before, blaming it on a bad batch of corner store sushi, but was going to rest for a few days to make sure she wasn't actually coming down with the flu.

Luckily, the self-assured, loud, and very talkative Camilla, was filling in. She was apparently a cousin of John, on his mother's side. Instead of scraggly blonde hair like her cousin or her uncle Gilbert, Camilla had silky black hair she put in a bun, bestowed upon her by her Latino father. She was a self-proclaimed "Thicc bitch," and blamed it on her lifelong salt addiction. She also got pregnant "the second she lost her virginity," but was blessed with a beautiful five-year-old son because of it. Winter found out all that information within the span of moving the outdoor camera setup indoors, due to the ever-worsening Saturday wind and hailstorm.

The room was used for animal training purposes. It had light hardwood floors, big, blue walls, red cones and folding chairs lined up on each side, and large, sliding door closets and cabinets. The smell of chlorine and soap, mixed with the constant stream of heat flowing out of the vents, and the steadfast pattering of sound on the roof, was making Winter dizzy. After taking a few photos of the first dog—a friendly border collie—she had to sit down.

"I love this dog, man," Camilla said, scratching the happy canine behind the ears. "If I could, I would totally take him home. But my job is a bitch, man. There's no way I'd be able to give him enough attention."

A staff member walked in and greeted the girls, then untethered the Border collie's leash from around a chair leg. On the way out, the dog stopped at Winter and looked up at her, panting. She pet him and immediately felt better. *Aint that something?* Winter thought.

"Be back soon." The staff member lightly tugged the dog away and out the door.

"So, what do you do?" Winter asked Camilla.

"I work as a receptionist for a video game company." Camilla spoke with her hands and for a few seconds she fervently played what looked like an invisible video game controller. "It's pretty cool but damn those developers are needy. Do you understand how many sandwiches I have to make and how many different snacks I have to keep stocked in the kitchen? Do you even understand, Winter?"

"No, I don't," Winter said, amused, happy for Camilla's entertaining distraction.

"I swear, they're all on the reefer because they all—and I mean every single one of them—have the munchies, twenty-four hours a day."

"On the reefer?"

"Petting the skunk. Juicing the green."

Winter laughed and shook her head. "That'd be a pretty cool job, though. Getting high, making video games, and eating junk food."

"I mean, I can't judge. I moonwalk the dragon whenever I'm home alone, but that's neither here nor there."

Winter laughed again. "Okay, I really hope that was another euphemism for weed."

Camilla wiggles her eyebrows.

"So, are you interested in making games, too?" Winter asked.

"Nah. My uncle is one of the developers. I'm just working there for the money." She cleared her throat and started to sing with one of the most soulful voices Winter had ever heard in real life: *"I'm a singer. Thanks for asking. What do you doooooooo?"*

Winter's mouth dropped open. "Oh, my God, Camilla. You're amazing."

"Oh, stop." Camilla waved her away.

"I'm sorry, but why are you working as a receptionist with a voice like that?"

"Ohhhhhh stoppppp," Camilla sang, drawing out each word with long, runs and impressive breath control. Her voice had perfect pitch, perfect tone, and a thick, raspy quality that made Winter think she had been through some things.

"I—I'm blown away."

Just then, Bo entered the room and walked over to a row of cabinets next to a stack of red cones. He bent down and looked through each cabinet, until he pulled out a black bucket full of cleaning supplies. Winter held her breath and looked away, then looked back at him, then looked away again. *Be casual,* she thought. *Just, be casual.*

He stood up and looked over at them. "Hello."

"Oh, hey, dude," Camilla said.

"How's the photoshoot going? Able to keep the furry models in frame?"

"You know, it's really not that bad." Camilla leaned back. "We were worried the storm was gonna spook 'em but our first dog was really chill, actually. He jumped a little when the thunder—remember when that big thunder hit like twenty minutes ago?"

Winter couldn't help herself; she looked up at Bo and exhaled.

"Yeah. I remember," he answered, nodding slowly, but keeping his eyes on Winter.

"Well, he—" Camilla sat up. "Winter, tell him what you said."

Winter didn't say anything.

"Winter," Camilla chuckled, "You have to tell him what you said the dog looked like."

"When the thunder hit," Winter said reluctantly, "the dog looked like one of those bad guys whose masks get ripped off by Scooby Doo and the Gang." Then she said under her breath. "It's stupid."

"Oh, she's too much," Camilla said laughing, then she mimicked the dog's shocked expression.

Winter averted her eyes from Bo's enchanting smile. The smile was a façade. His eyes, his jawline, his body—a freakin' Venus flytrap. He wore his volunteer shirt, but his sleeves were rolled up to reveal even more of his tattoos. Displayed on his left bicep was a realistic wolf howling under a full, purple moon. An old pirate ship was on his right arm.

"That's a vivid description," he said.

"I know, huh?" Camilla snorted.

Winter swallowed hard and closed her eyes, wishing he'd go away…hoping he wouldn't. Another staff member walked in holding a young Maltese, barking incessantly.

"Well, I'll see you around," Bo said.

Winter waited until she heard him leave to open her eyes again.

Camilla looked confused. "What was that all about?"

"What do you mean?"

"There's some weird tension between you two."

Winter scoffed. She jumped up and pulled a chair in front of the tripod before the staff member handed over the dog wearing a "Bear" nametag.

Bear wiggled and shook in Winter's arms and she pet him, saying, "It's okay," quietly, over and over until he calmed down.

"Damn, girl. You're the dog whisperer," said Camilla.

"You really think so?"

"Alright. How's it going in here, girls?" Gilbert walked hastily into the room.

Bear started to shake, and Winter started her dog calming routine again.

"We're doing fine, Uncle Gilb," Camilla said, clearly annoyed by him.

He put his hands up. "Okay, okay. I'll be leaving in just a second."

The rain fell heavier on the roof.

Gilbert pet Bear. "We have someone interested in this little guy. But I thought we should still put him online just in case his adoption falls through."

"Oh, that's so good to hear," said Winter. "He's a sweetheart."

Gilbert crossed his arms, smiling at Winter. "Well, I'm glad to see you're feeling better."

"Yeah. I'm feeling a lot better. Thank you."

"Okay then, I'm off. You can take turns taking a break. If you need me I'll be in my office." He saluted himself away.

Camilla rolled her eyes. "He's always checking on me. Like I'm some ignoramus who can't take pictures."

They continued their photo shoot—mostly dogs and a few cats. And Winter didn't see Bo for the rest of the day.

On Sunday, Winter parked on the street because the shelter parking lot was full. The sun was out and the red and golden trees almost glowed. As she walked, she found comfort in the sound of dry leaves crunching under her brown and black, fake leather Bean boots, and right before she arrived at the entrance, she took first-person POV video of the experience to post later.

"Ohhhh, shit, I'm so glad you're here." Camilla ran up

behind Winter and gave her such a big hug she lifted her off the ground.

"Wow, you're in a very good mood today," Winter said.

With her feet back on the ground, Winter readjusted her light blue jeans and her rose patterned, flared shawl collar wool coat. Then she quickly patted down her ironed straight hair that she decided at the last second to wear down.

"Damn," Camilla looked her over. "You really be dressing like that in real life."

"What do you—"

"I followed you on StyleSlap this morning. Come on, style girl. Today is going to be fucking crazy. I brought some Hank the Dank if you want a hit."

"Hank the Dank?" Winter asked, and Camilla shot her a look. "Oh, you mean weed."

Winter noticed Camilla was wearing the same black sweats and pouch sweatshirt she wore the day before—or at least, a duplicate of the same. Her hair was in a low, loose ponytail and she wore virtually no makeup. In grade school, Camilla would have been labeled a "Pretty Tom Boy"—and not the kind that posts themselves working out on social media, like Mia—the kind that really just doesn't care about female social expectations. *She could wear a paper bag and still be more confident and cool than me*, Winter thought.

Inside, they were faced with organized chaos. The sounds of meowing, barking, screeching, and howling all conglomerated into a giant buzz that echoed through the halls. Inhabited cages and crates spilled out of each room and the break room was so full of staff and volunteers, Winter and Camilla had to stand outside its entrance. Winter stood on her tippy-toes and looked around for no one in particular…but she couldn't see who she wasn't even looking for. *Is Bo even here today?* she thought and got mad at herself for even caring.

"He's next to the window," Camilla said.

Sure enough, Bo was leaning against the back window, an orange tree behind him shedding tired leaves. Winter felt her cheeks redden.

"How'd you know who I was looking for?" she asked Camilla.

"Well, I know Gilbert's not making you hot under the collar."

Winter smiled and tried to shush her new friend up. They play-chased each other.

"Oh, good, everyone's here," Gilbert said loudly. "Please, everyone make room for Winter and Cammy." He waved for them to come in.

The crowd simultaneously looked at them and parted. Winter wondered if all her blood had gone to her cheeks, and if that was even safe, as she and Camilla settled in the back where, thankfully, she couldn't see Bo, even if she tried. Which she didn't.

Gilbert stepped onto a wooden crate and it creaked under his weight. "Okay. So, here's the deal." He cupped his hands in front of him. "If we called you to work or to volunteer last minute, I am truly sorry, but we need all the help we can get. Our sister shelter, Lake Oswego Rescue, had a fire caused by a fallen tree and powerline."

The room filled with gasps and murmurs.

"Luckily," Gilbert shouted over the noise, "we don't think any of the animals were hurt but it's not safe to keep them there while the area is being cleaned up and the shelter is being rebuilt. As you could tell when you walked in, we're now over capacity. So, Toye and I have come up with a few ideas so we don't have to resort to handing over our animals to a traditional shelter. Toye, you wanted to take it from here?"

Gilbert stepped down and lent a hand to a petite, dark-skinned woman in her forties, with her hair elegantly tied up in a light green scarf, and who looked like she hadn't slept all night.

"Hello, I'm Toye from Lake Oswego Rescue. We had a hell of a night and I want to thank everyone who has helped or that is going to help. Our plan is to contact all of the no-kill shelters in Northern Oregon, maybe even some cities in Washington, to see if they have any room. We also want to get photos of our animals online, and in the BAS system. I'm personally asking you all to make a call out to your friends or your followers through social media, asking anyone and everyone if they would be willing to adopt or temporarily foster. Our fundraiser is already up and running, and you can find that link on our website. And lastly, if any of you could foster one of our animals, at least until we can find alternative homes—it would help us so much."

Her voice started to break, and she stepped down, a tear rolling down her cheek. John was standing next to his dad, looking forlorn, and immediately hugged her. *He's a good kid*, Winter thought.

Gilbert stepped back on the box. "So, we have volunteers and staff that are willing to drive animals to a small list of foster homes or shelters that we managed to gather in the last few hours. I need my usual staff to run the front desk, process papers and fees. Um…" Gilbert looked around, as if unfolding his plan off the cuff. "Okay, Camilla, Bo, Stanley, and Winter, please go to the training room. We're going to take more photos and John will be in there with his laptop so we can put them online immediately."

Winter's stomach knotted up, right on cue. Camilla saluted her uncle.

"And as Toye mentioned, we ask everyone to look at what we post on our pages and do the same—"

"Repost, reblog, retweet," John said loudly.

"Yes, what my son said." Gilbert looked at Winter and winked. "Especially from the two famous people we have in our midst."

Winter smiled, embarrassed by the constant looks she was pretending not to notice. Somehow, John was more affected by his father's words, shaking his head with obvious mortification.

"Okay then," Gilbert clapped. "Please go to your stations. And talk to me if I haven't assigned you something yet."

Gilbert jumped off of the box and was seemingly engulfed by a small crowd of confused or concerned helpers. Camilla took Winter's hand and pulled her out of the room before they got trampled, and yes, Winter was being dramatic about almost getting trampled.

"What happens if we can't find enough homes for all the animals?" Winter asked.

"Well, they'll have to send them to one of those shelters that don't mind killing beautiful, defenseless creatures."

Winter stopped in the middle of the hallway. "No freaking way."

"I agree," Camilla smiled, empathetically. "No freaking way."

CHAPTER EIGHTEEN

Bo sat at a small plastic table in the training room, next to John and his friend, a tall, gangly redhead named Anders, complaining that the universe owed him one for taking time out of his birthday weekend to help. The teenagers argued about that, then argued about how Anders kept using John's Netflix login to watch "weird shit." Bo kept glancing at the door and his stomach flipped when someone finally walked through, but it was only a staff member and volunteer he didn't recognize setting up the camera.

"What kind of weird shit," Bo asked, curious, and hoping to get his mind off of certain things.

"Dude." John turned to Bo. "He watches like *Hallmark* crap."

"Whatever," Anders said. "You're such a liar."

"Why else would it be recommending all these stupid movies, then? And most of them are Christmas movies. I mean, what the hell? It's almost Halloween."

Anders leaned his chair back. "Whatever, man. Christmas is cool."

"I'm with you," Bo said with a laugh. "I fucking love Christmas."

He and Anders fist bumped. John shook his head.

Bo's heart started beating faster the louder it got in the hallway. *Any minute now.* He felt like a kid in grade school waiting for his crush to walk by or sit next to him during lunch. He heard Camo Stan laughing loudly, then he entered the room wearing his signature pants, but surprisingly, rocked a green, camo-free, sweatshirt.

"All-righty. What can I do, boss?" Stan said to John.

"Oh, um," John sat up straight and tried to sound as professional as he could for a teenager with a randomly cracking voice. "I'll let everyone know what my dad wants when the girls get here. Do you know where they are?"

"Last I saw them they were putting on BAC sweatshirts. I asked for one, but Camilla told me they didn't have anymore. You think there are any in the back or something?"

"Dude? What is this—the Gap or something?" Anders snapped.

Stan threw up his hands.

"Sorry," Anders continued, shamefully. "I haven't eaten yet and this is my birthday weekend."

"Yeah, mind my friend, Anders. He can be a grumpy old man sometimes."

"No problem." Stan pulled up a chair next to Bo. "Tell your friend, happy eightieth birthday."

John snorted. Bo smiled and realized the staff member was gone and the whole photo area had been set up; a chair behind a camera sitting on a low tripod, two side lights on tall stands, a small, square platform, and a white backdrop. It was a lot more elaborate than what he remembered from the previous set up.

"Yeah, yeah," muttered Anders.

Time slowed down when she walked through the door…

Winter wore boots, light blue jeans, and a teal Beaverton Animal Shelter sweatshirt, but she might as well have been walking down the runway in a designer outfit. Somehow her clothes accentuated every curve. And her skin was flawless. And though her hair swayed with her movement, it kept settling back in its rightful place. Whenever he saw her it was like being slapped in the face with her beauty. And he could tell the teenagers in the room felt the same—they stopped talking the moment they realized she was there. John fidgeted with his seat and Anders sat up straight—but they both just stared. They all stared. It took Bo awhile to realize she held a calm tuxedo kitten in her arms.

"Need any help?" Stan asked Winter.

"Oh, thanks Stanley, but I think I got this little guy," Winter said. "Camilla's bringing his sister. Their mom passed away so Gilbert thinks we should try to get them adopted together."

"That's a good idea," Stan said.

Winter went over to the chairs and shifted the kitten to one side, holding him with one hand. She went over to the corner of the room and started pulling a chair over. Bo jumped up and helped her with the chair, setting it on the opposite side of the table.

"Thank you," she said quietly.

"My pleasure," he said and wanted to punch himself the second it came out of his mouth.

"Um. Winter," John's voice cracked again. "When Camilla's here I'll go over everything we need—um, we need to do."

"Yep," said Anders, seemingly trying to sound confident but failing.

"Sounds good," she said as she sat down.

A group of people swiftly walked down the hall, scaring the kitten. She set him in her lap and pet him slowly, carefully.

After a long silence, Bo said. "Do you have any pets, Winter?"

Still petting the cat, Winter bit her lip and shook her head. She avoided eye contact with him like usual, but he knew it'd only be a matter of time before her curiosity would get the better of her and she'd look at him. At least, that was usually how it went.

"I had some pets growing up but for some reason I haven't had any as an adult," Bo said. He leaned forward and felt a slight smirk forming. "Probably because I'm selfish and irresponsible."

Winter looked up and they locked eyes for a few seconds before she looked back down at her purring lap creature. *Gotcha!* he thought.

Stan laughed. "Oh, man. I know what you mean." He patted Bo on the back and for once Bo didn't feel rage at the blatant violation of personal space.

"If y'all like animals so much," said Anders, "then maybe you should adopt one." John stopped typing on his laptop to shoot his friend a look. "What?" Anders smiled. "I'm just trying to help."

Winter raised her eyebrows then tucked a strand of hair behind her ear. Her beautiful ears—the perfect size, with the kind of earlobes that are attached to the side of her head. And they were pierced. And she wore small, silver studded rose shaped earrings. Bo realized he was being weird and turned his chair slightly.

"You know, I think I actually would adopt but unfortunately my landlord wouldn't allow it," Winter said. The kitten stood up and stretched—funnily enough—into the Cat yoga pose. Then he curled up, swooping his tail around him. Winter pet him for a few seconds and the purring started up again. Then she said, "What about you, Bo? Are you going to adopt today?"

Bo rubbed his chin. "You think I should?"

Winter nodded. "I think you should… But it's not up to me."

"Well, maybe I will, Winter," Bo said.

He smiled and as if it were contagious, she smiled too.

Camilla walked in holding the sister tuxedo kitten, but instead of being mostly black with spots of white on the face, underbelly, and paws, like her brother, she was mostly white with black spots around the ears, back, and tail.

"Sorry, guys," Camilla said. "Gilbert is freaking out and I'm the bitch who has to calm him down."

"You're not a bitch," said Winter.

Bo jumped up and set up a chair for Camilla, who sat down with the hyper kitten. "Damn, chivalry isn't dead. Thanks, man," Camilla said.

"Well, you have a handful." Bo laughed.

The cat climbed her like a rock wall, finally perching on her shoulder.

"Owe, damn. You can put the knives away." Camilla pried the kitten's claws off of her, eliciting chuckles from the room.

Winter's eyes lit up and she cupped her mouth. She was the cutest damn—

"Okay." John closed his laptop and cleared his throat a

few times. "Um, now I'll fill you in on what my dad said. Um..."

"Speak up, dude," said Anders.

"Fuck off," said John.

More chuckles from the room.

John continued but did speak louder. "We need Stan and Anders to transport animals—take them out of their cages and put their leashes on or just pick up the whole damn cage, whatever works for you. And bring them here for photos and video and take them back or whatever."

Stan said, "Sure."

Anders looked annoyed.

"I'll keep track of the photos or videos that we take and I'll um, I'll upload them into the system too," John continued. "And Camilla, you can take the photos. Um, Bo and Winter can you—my dad wants to know if you can, like, post on your platforms and email any local people you've worked with or whatever." John's eyes got red. "You know, get the word out and stuff. He's really—we're really scared we're going to have to turn animals away and it's just—anything will help, you know."

"Yes, of course." Winter looked concerned, seemingly realizing the severity of the situation.

"I'll do anything I can," Bo said.

John showed them the link to share, he answered any questions, and didn't take the bait when Anders threatened to leave early because it was his birthday weekend. It was obvious that John cared deeply about his dad and the shelter and the animals, and Bo was determined to not let him down. Anders grabbed a backpack from behind John's seat and pulled out a laptop, setting it up in front of Bo. Winter hesitatingly woke her kitten up, kissed the little furball on the head, and handed him to Stan.

"What are the kittens' names?" Bo asked.

"I'm not sure. I don't think they have any names." Winter sat down next to him.

She smelled intoxicatingly floral and Bo wondered if she had intentionally coordinated flower-scented perfume with the rose patterned coat she wore earlier.

"You want to make up some names, just in case we see them again?"

Winter bit her nail. "Okay," she finally said.

"You go first."

She looked at him and he tried to read her but couldn't. She was either attracted to him… or repulsed.

"Edgar," she said.

"Like *the* Edgar?"

"Like *the* Edgar."

"Why, may I ask?"

"Because he's one of my favorite writers."

"What do you like about him?"

She crinkled her brows. "Are you kidding? What's not to like?"

"He's one of my favorites too. I was just asking."

"Oh, okay, I'm sorry. I just get very defensive when it comes to my Poe."

"*Your* Poe?"

She nodded.

"Okay, I'll be careful what I say about him," he said with a smile.

"He usually wrote blitzed out of his mind on opium and morphine," she spoke fast, "and alcohol and he suffered from recurrent depression. I have a theory that Poe was every narrator—like he was so messed up that he—at least emotionally—experienced each story as he wrote them."

"I wouldn't be surprised, because a lot of his narrations were in the voice of someone fucked up."

"Yeah," she perked up, "like in *The Black Cat*—the narrator says he's 'mad indeed,' and his words are confusing and affected by alcohol."

"I always thought that story was cool because you almost didn't know to believe the guy or not."

"I love that. *The Fall House of Usher* is like that too. It's told by this person with no name, who's suffering from paranoid schizophrenia."

He smiled and just stared at her.

"Your opium Poe tattoo is really nice," she added.

He cocked his head to the side. "You saw that."

She bit her lip then said, "Can I see it again?"

Without hesitation, he rolled up the left black sleeve he wore under his volunteer shirt, revealing the opium bottle with the portrait of Edgar. Winter shook her head.

"It's fantastic. Who does these?" She looked closer.

"It's this guy I met in Spain. Whenever he's in the U.S. I go wherever he is and get something new done. I usually get my touchups done in Portland though."

"When did you start?"

"When I was sixteen. I tried to hide it from my parents, but my roommate told his mom who told my mom, and it was this whole ordeal."

"Do they care now?"

He rolled his sleeve back down. "My mom doesn't care and my dad's just a dick head."

Winter nodded and her eyes wandered as if something had just jumped into her head. She folded her arms.

"Okay, my turn," Bo said, getting her attention again. "I'll name the other kitten. I'm thinking Elmira, after Sarah Elmira Royster Shelton."

"Edgar's first love," she said quietly.

Bo looked around, dumbfounded by the commotion that he didn't even notice mere seconds before. John was on the phone in the hallway, pacing back and forth. Across the room, Camilla and Anders and Stanley were making jokes with each other and having a hell of a time trying to make a large dog stand still or at least not have his backside to the camera. He heard the sound of distant barking, cages clanking, people shouting. Outside the window, cars pulled in and out of the parking lot.

Winter scooted closer. "We probably should start posting."

"Please. You first." He gestured to the laptop and she obliged by pulling the laptop in front of her. "I can do a few things on my phone," he added.

He took his phone out of his pocket, went to the Beaverton Animal Center's Twitter page and retweeted its recent posts. Then he copied the adoption catalog system link and the fundraiser link and posted them to his Nanogram account, tagging as many people as he could think of, hashtagging with words and phrases like *animal shelter*, *animal rescue*, *dogs*, *cats*, and *PortlandOregon*. He also emailed most of his contact list, explaining the situation, and asking nicely if they could adopt, foster, or give to the fundraiser. He glanced up at the laptop and Winter was doing the same—posting to all of her accounts and emailing individual people for help. When she was done, she sat back and pushed the laptop back to Bo.

"You know what, I was actually able to do everything on my phone," he said. "You have any other ideas?"

She thought about it for a second, then moved even closer, her chair touching his. She knew what she was doing to him. Why else would she suck her bottom lip? Or flip her hair?

"Uh…I don't know…I guess I could message some bloggers. Since you're way more connected than me maybe you could DM some people that have big platforms. Maybe that Matt guy?"

"Ah, I can't. I hate him."

"Oh, really?" Her tone was sarcastic but amiable. "Why would anyone think that?"

He smiled. "Very funny."

She giggled and their lips were only a few feet apart. Just something Bo noticed. Something he felt in a certain part of his body.

"But you know what, I'll do it for the cause." He started typing. "Hell, I'll even DM my ex. She has a big fanbase."

"The actress."

"Yeah," he looked at her. "How did you know?"

"Um…google."

"You googled me?"

She didn't say anything.

"It's okay," he continued. "I googled you too."

Her laugh was punctuated by a tinge of embarrassment.

"How's it going, guys?" John slumped into his chair. It looked like he'd been crying.

"Fine. How about you, man?" Bo asked.

"Apparently, a few Lake Oswego animals died of smoke inhalation. The firefighters found them in the rubble. And there could be more."

Winter gasped.

"Oh, fuck, man. I'm so sorry," said Bo.

"Toye wants me to break it to Dad." John sighed. "He's already overwhelmed as it is."

Bo put his arms behind his neck. "But it will probably be better coming from family."

Winter reached over and took John's hand. "Just know, you and your dad do so much. You're saving so many lives and we're going to help you."

John quickly wiped tears away. "Thanks."

John slowly started typing into his laptop. Winter started contacting bloggers and Bo worked on his phone.

After about ten minutes of quiet work, John blurted out, "Holy Shit!"

"What is it?" Winter asked.

"Check out the fundraiser page. Holy shit, no way!"

Winter brought up the page and it displayed the words *Fundraising Goal Met!* across the top.

"John, my man," Bo said. "At least your dad doesn't have to worry about this."

John said loudly. "It has to be a joke. I mean—what? How?"

"What're you hootin' and hollerin' about?" Camilla walked over to the table, a leashed dog trailing behind her.

"Someone just donated $30,000!"

"No way." Camilla knelt down to take a look.

"I'm gonna go tell Dad!" John got up shaking with excitement and ran out of the room.

"Wait up!" Anders followed him out.

"Damn, some rich ass dude or dudette just decided to give $30,000," Camilla said.

Stan sat down for a moment to catch his breath. "Let me guess, the head of Nike or something?"

Camilla sat in John's seat, scrolled and clicked. "No information. It's just some anonymous donor." The dog lay down at her feet.

Bo took out his phone again, leaned his chair back. His Nanogram already had 100s of new notifications. Some of the replies asked him what the BAC shelter address was and though he wanted to type, *I posted the link to the website*, he found the address in google and copied it. Before he could even reply back, however, he noticed Winter was looking through the donor list. *Anonymous* and an empty avatar box was attached to the $30,000 donation amount. She clicked on it and Bo's heart started racing again. Another page popped up displaying *No Profile Available.* The only information connected to the anonymous benefactor was the—Bo held his breath—was the stupid fundraiser site username: *Edgar123*. Winter snapped her head toward Bo, and for once, Bo avoided eye contact with her.

CHAPTER NINETEEN

Winter squinted her eyes and shook her head. "Can you afford this?" she whispered.

He closed his eyes for a second then exhaled. "What do you mean?"

She gave him a look like *Come on, I'm not stupid.*

"Well," he leaned close to her ear, "Let's just keep this between us."

She noticed Stan and Camilla get back up and commence the dog photo shoot, but the room was quieter than usual. Winter brought up the notepad on the laptop.

She typed: ***That was incredibly nice of you.***

He smiled and typed: ***Thanks, but it's no big deal.***

Her eyebrows raised and she typed: ***Are you kidding me? That's a lot of money.***

He typed: ***My family has a lot of money so it's really no big deal.***

She typed: ***You should tell people. It could help your reputation.***

He typed: ***People will believe what they want to believe, no matter what I do.***

She typed: ***I don't believe that.***

He hesitated, then typed: ***Well, you think I'm an asshole. You judged me from stuff you read about me. Stuff from my past. And a lot of it wasn't even true. So…***

Winter was about to type something but stopped herself. She noticed Camilla glance over at them before handing the leashed dog over to Stan. Camilla then put a cage on the table and tried to coax a scared cat out.

Winter stood up. "I'll help you, Cammy."

"Winter." Bo took her hand gently.

A wave of warmth…of comfort…swept through her body. He looked serious, like they were never going to see each other again. She slowly pulled her hand away and typed the following words into the computer:

I don't think you're an asshole. I just didn't trust you before. Now I do. She turned away briefly before quickly adding: ***And I came to that conclusion before you gave the money.***

She went over to help Camilla who was talking in a baby voice to the cat. "Damn, I'm probably scaring the poor thing," Cammy said and stood up to adjust her sagging sweatpants.

Winter laughed, savoring the rare moment of feeling anxiety-free. She could hear people talking loudly in the hallway and realized Bo had moved over to John's chair and laptop. When they were finally able to get the cat out and sitting on a table—thanks to a lot of treats—Winter got a text from an unknown number.

It read: **Forgive me, but I got your phone number from John's unsecure computer. Are you free this evening? (This is Bo Blaine, by the way).**

Winter looked up and Bo was smiling but his eyebrows brooded.

She texted back: **Yes I'm free. Why do you ask?**

He read the text and immediately replied: **Can I take you on a date?**

Winter's heart skipped a beat. Their eyes locked and everything felt right. After a few long seconds, she nodded.

His face relaxed with relief and when he clasped his hands behind his head, his sleeves rolled down showing a canvas of vivid colors, lines, and shapes. *Art*, Winter thought. *He is art.*

Most of the staff and volunteers stayed late to post, get all the animals in the system, arrange adoptions, meet with interested adoptees or foster parents, and anything else they could think of to help both shelters. Bo and Winter made a point of being around each other when they could and would text each other when they couldn't.

Things like:

Bo: Have any ideas for what we should do?

Winter: I'm up for whatever…to an extent. No skydiving, please.

Bo: Now I got to take skydiving off the list. How about nighttime mountain climbing?

Winter: Sounds good. Bring the climbing gear, I'll bring the beer?

Bo: Hell yeah. But, honestly, I just want to be next to you.

. . .

By sunset, less than half of the helpers remained. Gilbert ordered pizza and summoned everyone to the break room to eat and have a final meeting. Camilla took hot sauce out of her purse and poured it over her pepperoni pizza slices.

"Of course you would bring that," Winter chuckled.

"Biootttch, I come prepared," Camilla laughed, then realized her uncle had heard her from across the room "Oh, sorry, I meant to say, *splendid female*, I come prepared."

As Bo pulled up a chair and set his plated slice next to the girls, his phone started to buzz in his pants.

He pulled out his phone and his face dropped. "I'll be right back," he said and left the room.

He still wasn't back by the time everyone was basically done with their food, save for Anders still scarfing down his sixth or seventh slice.

"I just want to say," Gilbert wiped his mouth off with a napkin, "I can barely put into words how grateful I am for all of your help. Toye had to leave because she hasn't slept in God knows how many hours, but she wanted me to thank all of you. She's been through a lot but," his voice wavered, "she thanks each and every one of you."

He paused and a few people clapped. A few more joined in. Winter noticed Bo walking back and forth outside the door, talking fervently on his cell phone.

"As you may have heard, we have more than met our fundraising goal. And we have managed to find forever or temporary homes for almost all of our displaced animals. We have a few more dogs to go—a lot more cats, but I may be able to squeeze them into the suites…maybe." He looked at John, dejected. "We'll figure something out, right?"

John nodded, unconvincingly. Just then, Bo sat down. His

face was red, and he stared into the middle distance, rubbing his hands.

"Are you okay?" Winter asked.

He didn't respond.

"Bo, are you okay?" she asked again a little louder.

After a few seconds his rigidity softened, and he looked at her. "Now I am."

She smiled shyly. He rolled his sleeves up and began eating his cold pizza.

"Um…you know what, I think I can take a cat home," said Stanley.

"Are you sure?" Gilbert asked. "Because that would really help us, Stan."

Stanley nodded as he gulped down soda.

"My mom said I can foster a cat for a few weeks," a young volunteer said, wearing a black, collared Lake Oswego Rescue shirt.

Gilbert clapped his hands together. "Oh, good, Martha." He looked at his son again.

"See, Dad," said John, "it's gonna be okay."

Anders stuffed the last bite of his pizza in his mouth. "Yeah, Mr. Caldwell. You can chill."

"Oh, Anders. I haven't *chilled* since The Great Portland Snow Storm of 1950, the year I was born."

Anders and John looked at each other with that kind of embarrassment that only a teenager could feel when a dad makes a dad joke in front of an audience.

"Hey, that joke would have actually worked if I was really born in 1950," Gilbert said.

Anders shook his head, disappointedly. "I don't think so, Mr. Caldwell."

Everyone in the room was amused by the scene playing

out before them, and Camilla almost passed out from laughing so hard. Winter couldn't stop laughing at Camilla laughing, and Bo smiled watching them both.

"Okay, okay." Gilbert waved his hands to command the room to calm down. It took close to a minute for people to get their bearings.

"Gilb," said Camilla, "just, please warn me when you drop your next zinger. It's—I just can't handle it."

"Very funny, no pun intended," Gilbert said, adding to the teens' embarrassment. "After all the work we did today, we needed that cathartic release. So, again, I just want to say thank you from the bottom of my heart. Martha and Stanley, please stop at the adoption office before you leave. And if anybody else could-"

"Were those tuxedo kittens adopted yet?" Bo tossed his pizza crust on his plate.

"Oh, um," Gilbert looked over at a sweet older lady with a rounded back, drowning in an oversized BAC staff shirt. "Janice, do you remember if those kittens were adopted? The ones Toye and I wanted to be adopted together?"

Janice thought for a second, then talked slowly. "No. We had some interest, but they couldn't adopt two," she shakily held up two fingers, "cats at once."

"Well, I'll take them," Bo said.

"Both of them?" Janice asked, surprised.

"Both of them," he said, matter-of-factly. "They've been through enough. They deserve to have a good life."

Winter looked around the room, stopping at a framed photo of the BAC staff posing in front of the shelter. Her mind raced. *Who is this guy? This could all be a ruse. Maybe he does these kind of grand gestures all the time to lure women. But no. He just seems so genuine. So thoughtful. The tabloids got him all wrong. I had him all wrong.*

"I guess I'll take one too," Anders mumbled.

"What'd you say, Anders?" John asked incredulously.

"I said, I guess I'll take a cat home too," he put his hands in his pocket and rolled his eyes in one coordinated maneuver. "Happy birthday to me, you know."

"Fuck yeah!" John said and slugged his friend lightly on the shoulder.

"Language, John! You're being disrespectful to Janice."

"Oh, fooey," Janice fanned the air. "I don't give a rat's ass."

Everyone laughed and Bo elbowed Winter, playfully. Her cheeks warmed.

Gilbert spoke loudly. "Okay, anyone who can adopt, please head over to the adoption office. We have a few staff staying on for the evening, but I think the rest of you can go."

The room soon filled with banter, moving chairs, and shuffling feet.

"Winter," Bo said. "Which kitten was your favorite? Black and white Edgar or white and black Elmira?" He smiled coyly, like he'd just realized how handsome he was.

"I love them both," Winter said.

"If you could only choose one and your landlord let you have a pet…hypothetically."

"Oh, then definitely Edgar. We already have this bond thing going on."

"Really? I'm jealous."

All she could think to do was to comb her hand through her hair and flip it.

He turned his chair to her and leaned forward, one elbow on his leg. "So Edgar's your favorite?"

She nodded.

"Well, he's yours," he said.

"What do you mean?"

"He can stay at my place forever but he's my gift to you. I'll be his friend and love him and stuff. But Elmira will be my girl. Edgar will be your boy."

Winter shook her head, smiling. "Wow."

"What?"

"You're really laying this charm thing on thick."

"Is it working?"

She smiled.

"Hey guys," Gilbert startled her. "You were both amazing. I have a feeling your handy computer posts were the reason we got the word out and got that huge donation."

Bo stood up and shook his hand firmly. "It was honestly a pleasure to help—this whole weekend was pretty damn enjoyable, to be honest."

"Yeah." Gilbert put his hands on his hips. "It's not too bad helping out animals, right?"

"And your passion is what helped push me. You're a good man, Gilbert. And your son, too. I'm glad I met you both."

"Thanks, Bo," John said from across the room.

He was slumped in his chair, exhausted, while Camilla and Anders talked about what sounded like a controversial moment in a recent soccer game.

"Yes, this was a really rewarding experience, Gilbert." Winter said. "Thank you for everything you do."

"Well, at the end of every month we have volunteer weekend. So, I hope I'll get to see y'all again. And I'm sure it won't be as demanding as this weekend."

"Count me in for next month," said Bo.

"I'd love to come back, too," said Winter.

"Okay, then, just call in to confirm or use that app thingy."

Gilbert gave Winter a hug and then squeezed Bo's shoulder before departing.

"You know," Bo said to Winter, "I had a very different idea of him when I first met him. I'm glad I gave him a chance... So, are you ready to adopt our children?" Bo asked, cupping his hands.

Winter laughed. "I'm ready to be a furball mother. I just gotta say bye to Camilla."

She could feel him watch her walk away...and she liked it.

Bo folded the paperwork and put it in his pocket. They carefully opened Suite 4 in the cat wing of the shelter building and closed the door behind them. Both kittens hid under the cement bed, armed with nothing but squeaky meows.

"Okay, I'll be in the office," Janice said through the glass. "Gilbert has an extra carrier for you, Bo, so I'll get that ready, as well as a few goodies for them."

"Okay, thank you, Janice," Bo replied.

"Wish us luck," Winter said.

"Oh, they'll love you." Janice slowly walked out the door and headed left before she realized she needed to go right.

Winter knelt down and made a clicking sound with her mouth. "It's okay, kitties. We're not going to bite," she said softly.

Bo knelt down as well. Janice said the kittens were about nine weeks old and had never lived anywhere but shelters, most of the time with their mom, until she died. The kittens had tiny little faces, big, round, greenish-gold eyes and long whiskers, and they looked up at these humans with a mix of shock and curiosity.

"It's okay," Winter said even softer than before. "Remember me, Edgar? I held you earlier."

Edgar tilted his head toward her but didn't budge from his spot.

"Hey, Elmira," Bo said quietly. "I'm the guy that was on the computer and my phone earlier. Remember me?"

Winter laughed and the kittens backed up.

Bo said to her, "I read that if you make eye contact with them and blink slowly or close your eyes for a second or two then open them, it signals to them that you're not a threat. It's almost like a hug. And if they do it back it means they trust you."

They tried this tactic on the kittens and after about a minute, the kittens slow-blinked back. Soon enough, the kittens got close enough for Bo and Winter to pick them up and pet them. The purring commenced and after a while they traded kittens, then traded them back again.

"They're sweethearts," Winter said, kissing Edgar's head.

"Yeah they are," Bo said, slow-blinking at her. "But they're not the only ones."

Winter'a stomach flitted. *He was good,* she thought.

By the time they walked out of the front doors, the sun was long gone, and the wind had picked up just enough to warrant coats to be buttoned up to the very top. Bo held the incessantly meowing kitten carrier and Winter held a bag of supplies—plastic toys, catnip, and new cat owner pamphlets.

"I'm over there." Bo pointed to a blue sports car parked on the street, directly under a streetlight, mere feet from the shelter lot.

"Damn, are you a street racer or something?"

"Not yet but I think I still have time," Bo said. "The Dodge Challenger Demon can go from zero to sixty in 2.3 seconds." When they stopped at the car, he looked at how unimpressed she was. He set the carrier on the trunk. "I don't know why I had the urge to tell you that."

"Trying to impress me?" Winter smiled.

"Maybe."

She walked around the car and looked at the custom skull decal rims, the hood vent, the body lines, the curves. "Well, you have good taste. It's definitely a nice car."

"I'm glad you think so," he said and opened the front door, "because this bad boy is going to take you out tonight."

"I thought plans changed since you just—you know—adopted."

"Well, I was thinking I'd show them their new home, then I'll probably have someone watch them tonight."

"Don't you need to stop at the store and get a litter box and pet food and stuff?"

"Oh, I had someone get that for me earlier and set it up in my place."

"Who is this 'someone' you keep referring to?"

Bo hesitated before answering. "The concierge or one of the apartment attendants."

Before Winter could say anything, Bo held up the meowing carrier so she could see inside. Elmira was pushing her head against the mesh, trying to get out, and her brother was scratching the back.

"Goodbye kittens." She waved. "It was nice meeting you."

Bo briefly put the carrier up to his ear and nodded his head. "Edgar and Elmira wanted me to tell you that this isn't goodbye. You'll be seeing them again very soon."

Winter raised her eyebrows. "Is that right?"

He set the carrier in the passenger seat and Winter handed the supply bag over. The moon was like a dimly lit bulb, with half of it tucked neatly into a blanket of cloud. Bo's eyes… they were like two gemstones that ignited when light hit them at just the right angle.

Bo took Winter's hand…and kissed it.

After a few moments he asked, "Can I walk you to your car?"

She bit her lip, hard, holding back the urges that were bubbling up inside her.

She pointed. "It's okay, I'm only a few cars up."

"So, is nine okay?" he asked.

She nodded.

"I'll pick you up." He leaned against the car. "Just text me your address."

"Oh, um…" She impulsively pulled her hand away and folded her arms. "You know what, I can just meet you wherever."

He squinted slightly, studying her. "No problem. I want you to feel comfortable." He squeezed his opposite shoulder and neck. "I was thinking we could grab dessert and a drink at the Multnomah Liquor Library. Unless you want to do something else."

"That members-only bar?" She perked up.

"Yeah, my great-great-grandfather founded it with his college buddies in, like the 1920s. So, I guess I can say I'm… grandfathered in as a member."

Winter's heart sped up thinking about all of the rumors she'd heard about that bar throughout the years. Back in high school, Wendy, the captain of her volleyball team, told her that only the Portland elite were admitted to the Multnomah Liquor Library, and they held secret meetings there. Cory, Winter's partner in Sophomore Physics 102, told her that illuminati rituals happened in a back room of the bar—that a certain liquor bottle on the shelf was actually a lever that opened a secret passage to a secret room. Even Winter's own mother told her weird things went on in "that expensive hole in the wall."

"I'd love to go there with you," Winter said quietly.

A fluttery feeling started in her chest…but the breeze blew it away, kept it from consuming her.

CHAPTER TWENTY

The moment he started the Challenger up and heard that roar, the kittens' meows morphed into howls.

"It's going to be okay," he said as gently as his low voice could muster.

They clearly didn't believe him, though. They tried clawing, biting, and scratching their way out, but luckily Gilbert let Bo borrow one of his personal, heavy duty, cat-proof carriers. Bo watched Winter get into her silver Camry as he turned the passenger seat warmer on its lowest setting. He enabled his phone on the car screen, turned the volume to medium-low, looked up soothing cat music on Youtube, and played the first video in a playlist titled *Calm Cat.* Winter drove away and Bo waited until she rounded the corner before he drove away too.

She said she trusts me but recoiled when I said I'd pick her up, he thought. She had a wall up and Bo felt like every other day she either took away or added a brick. *What happened to her?*

After Winter had abruptly ran out and left Bo to finish

cleaning the Home Suites alone on that first day of volunteering, he had spent hours online, looking for more background information about her. She didn't talk much about her parents or her childhood, other than random tidbits that could be tied to a style she was modeling or topic she was discussing. And the only thing that he could find about her dating life was in a recently posted video tagged with her name on Nanogram. It was a repost of a VHS filtered video Winter posted a couple years ago on StyleSlap. In the video, Gorgeous Winter wore a short black skirt and a long-sleeved white shirt that had the words *Directed by Stanley Kubrick* scribbled in black. She sat on a swinging porch chair, sidesaddle, with bare feet—other than the black polish painted on her toes.

The person filming was pushing the swing and Winter was giggling…yet something in her eyes looked scared…like she really wanted the person to stop. The post description read: *Winter Smith is a Slut. Just ask her ex*. When Bo clicked on the page username *Gomer_lyles13*, the banner displayed *This Account is Private*.

By the time Bo was on the freeway, the kittens' meows became more sporadic and the howling had subsided completely. He continued talking to them, telling them about his day or pointing out various Portland landmarks as they passed them.

"And there's the Hoyt Arboretum," he said. "Maybe we can go on a hike there sometime."

One of the kittens meowed, as if answering him, and it made Bo laugh.

Bo held the carrier and the supply bag and headed toward the resident parking garage elevator. The kittens were extremely vocal and trying to get out again.

"It's okay. We're almost home."

Though he pushed the top level button, the elevator made a stop on the first floor. The doors opened and Sarah, in full uniform, stood there in anticipation.

"I just got to work, but I heard you got kittens," she said, putting her hand between elevator doors to stop them from closing.

"Yeah." He held the carrier up proudly.

"Oh, my God," she squealed and got in the elevator with him.

The doors closed and the elevator jolted slightly as it ascended.

"Oh, fuck," she continued, "they are the cutest little things."

"They're too cute for their own good," Bo said. He pointed at each kitten. "That one's Edgar and that one's Elmira."

"Wow, those are some emo names."

Bo laughed. "I guess so."

"This is so not like you. I never took you as a taking-care-of-living-creatures kind of guy."

"Why do you say that?"

"Oh, I don't know. Cuz you're a bachelor with a massive bachelor pad." The doors opened. "You just always seemed so busy being Bo Blaine."

They started walking down the hallway toward Bo's apartment.

"So how've you been Sarah?" Bo asked.

The kittens' howling started up again and Sarah talked

louder. "I've been good. My friends and I are thinking about pitching in on this amazing property in Happy Valley."

They got to his door and Bo unlocked it.

"Get this," she continued excitedly. "120 acres of farmland with a barn, two grow houses, and a four-bedroom house."

"Holy shit."

"Yeah."

"You'll have, like, a weed commune."

"Slash paradise," she added, following Bo into his home. "So, I've assigned myself to help you with the kittens tonight. Jerry said he dropped off the stuff you requested and put it in one of your guest rooms."

"Sound good," he said. "But I'm thinking I should spend some one on one time with them for a bit. You know, just so they'll get used to me."

"Oh, okay." She sounded a little hurt. "I can come back."

"Sarah…" Bo set the carrier on the couch. Both kittens were trying to dig a hole beneath them. "Is there something off-putting or untrustworthy about me? Like, if you didn't know me, what impression would you get?"

"Wow, that's kind of a loaded question," Sarah said, leaning against the counter.

"I know, but I honestly want to know the truth."

Sarah thought for a second. "Well, if I didn't know you, I'd think you were a womanizer and a bad boy that gets in trouble every second and that doesn't know what he has and how lucky he has it and—"

"Okay, okay. I get it." Bo sat down.

"Hey, you asked!"

"Yeah… I did."

"But the thing is, since I *do* know you, I know that you're kind and thoughtful—I mean, what other rich guy gets Christmas presents for all of his apartment staff or gives them and their friends first dibs on job opportunities? And you're definitely not a womanizer. I mean, girls throw themselves at you and yeah, you've brought some women home, but you always seem to treat them with respect. I mean, the staff—myself included—expected to see girls leaving your place crying or calling the front desk screaming or something."

Bo stared at the floor, nodding.

"I think you're just misunderstood." She sits down next to him on the couch. "The things you've told me about Noah. Or some of the assholes you have to interact with on a daily basis." She shook her head. "Man, it would kill my buzz on a daily. You're a stronger man than me."

Bo chuckled. "You're way stronger. My dad is your boss. I don't know how you do it."

Sarah smiled. "A lot of ass kissing and a shot of whiskey. Usually gets me through any meeting or phone call with him."

"Maybe I should try that."

"All I know is, if I was your age—"

"Sarah, you're five years older than me."

"If I was your age," she repeated, then cleared her throat, "and I hadn't just gone through a horribly messy divorce, I'd consider dating you—you're *that* much of a catch."

"You're a catch too, Sarah. Your ex must be crazy to have let you go."

The kittens were not happy. They howled and scratched and bit the mesh front of the carrier. Bo slowly unzipped the opening and the kittens jumped out. Elmira hid under the couch. Edgar was braver, walking cautiously around the house, investigating through sniffing and pawing.

"Okay, I'm gonna go. But you better believe I'll be back." Sarah stood up.

"Yeah. I'm going on a date tonight so I'd love if you could watch them."

"A date, huh? Is it with the person you were thinking about last time?"

Bo shrugged, but he couldn't stop a smile from forming on his face.

"Good for you, Bo." She turned to leave, then asked, "Would I know her?"

Bo thought for a second, watching Elmira slowly crawl from under the couch to join her brother, who was fixated on a cluster of fake, felt cacti under a hallway side table.

"Her name's Winter. She's this fashion girl—"

"Wait? Winter Smith? You're dating Winter Smith?"

He nodded.

"I love her!" She pulled out her phone, showing him she followed Winter on StyleSlap.

"Whoa, that's cool."

"Oh, but…" Her face dropped.

"What?"

She sat back down next to him. "Supposedly, she's from a very weird relationship."

"What do you mean by 'weird'?"

"I shouldn't say anything else because I heard it from a friend of a friend who interned at a lawyer firm her and her boyfriend worked at. So, it could just be a rumor and I hate spreading gossip. Oh, fuck, I really shouldn't have said anything."

"No, I'm glad you did."

"Really?"

"Do you know who her ex-boyfriend is?"

"I wouldn't tell you even if I knew."

"But I'm sure you could find out."

"Yeah, and I would go to prison for aiding and abetting a murder. Because I know you'd murder him."

Bo nodded and stared into the middle distance. "Probably right."

"And Bo, you're like a brother to me, which is kinda gross because we've slept together. So, we're more like—long lost Alabama cousins."

Bo laughed and shook his head. "You're ridiculous."

Sarah got back up. "I'm just saying I don't want you to get in trouble. You're doing so good, other than that whole beating the shit out of Matt thing."

"If you do end up getting a weed commune, will you let me vacation there?" Bo got up.

"Of course." She winked. "So, I hope I didn't scare you too much about Winter. I just heard the guy was awful and it motivated her to quit and start her own online brand. She actually seems like an amazing girl."

"Thanks Sarah. I'm gonna go find the furry emo twins. I'll see you later."

"Okay."

Bo headed for the back hallway and when he looked back, Sarah was still standing there. And he could have sworn she whispered, "Just be careful, Bo."

CHAPTER TWENTY-ONE

Winter barely had any time to obsess over her date because she was still a style post short for the week and had intended on posting one Sunday evening. Of course, she thought she would have a lot more time. She hadn't scheduled a shelter fire into her usually impeccably-followed weekly planner, though she was more than happy to have been able to help. She couldn't remember the last time she felt so rewarded. The last time her heart felt so full. The last time she felt…valuable. And Bo asking her out. It almost felt like the ending of a long, tumultuous, fairy tale.

She ran into her room and rummaged through her closet, looking for something that could work with her setting idea: *Standing on the back porch...no, too cold...sitting on the couch...no, too lazy... Aha! Standing in the shower, under an umbrella.* Yeah, it was weird, but Winter had a hunch it would probably be one of her most talked about and reposted photos.

She decided on a simple, high-waist, pleated, above-the-knee skirt in burgundy, paired with a faded, black, Hank William's t-shirt, tucked in, and black thigh high socks and rain boots (though she knew she wasn't going to show the boots in the shot).

It took her twenty minutes to set up the shot, ten minutes to get dressed, ten minutes to put on her makeup, five minutes to put her hair up in a high ponytail after breaking two hair ties, and another fifteen to find her damn universe umbrella. She had never produced a photo so fast, and when she could finally sit down to see the result, she almost wanted to cry from happiness—it came out exactly how she envisioned it and she barely had to make any edits.

She posted to StyleSlap and Nanogram with the hashtags *StyleOnABudget* and *DontRainOnMe* and some of the other stock hashtags, like *Style*, *Mood*, *Fashion*...

She took another quick shower (without the umbrella) and as she was toweling off, she got a text from Mia: **My favorite photo of all time! I can't wait to see you boo bae!! I'll be back tomorrow.**

Winter wanted to tell her everything that happened over the weekend, but she decided against it, knowing there would be follow up questions and that she was running out of time—Bo was going to contact her any moment. Instead, **Winter texted back: Can't wait to see you too. We got a lot to talk about.** When Mia texted back, asking for more details, and then subsequently tried to call when she didn't get a reply after literally thirty seconds, **Winter typed back: Can't talk now.** ♥

It was about 9:30 p.m. when Winter realized Bo hadn't sent her the time he wanted to meet. Wrapped in a towel, she touched up her makeup and took her uncomfortably tight ponytail out. After applying some pomade, hairspray, and ironing a few unruly pieces, Winter's hair was down, shiny and slightly wavy—a beach-hair look. *Hopefully it doesn't rain,* Winter thought, *or I'll be on a bullet train to Frizzville.*

She looked down at her phone again, then after a few seconds of contemplation, checked her text, skimmed all of her social media inboxes, and even checked her email, hoping that Bo didn't lose her number. She smiled when she realized her shower photo was gaining traction. Her StyleSlap followers, in particular, were so sweet. One person wrote: ***So creative! Your feed makes me so happy!!*** And another person wrote: ***You look so fab! ffs now I have to get that outfit and that umbrella.*** And there were a lot of: ***I just can't,*** and ***I love you Winter!*** The high from her successful post quickly faded, however, when the digital clock struck 10:00 p.m.

A ball of anxiety formed in her stomach. *He was lying,* she thought. *He's not going to ever contact me again. He was just being nice.* She took deep breaths and changed into her date outfit—an outfit she and Mia put together a long time ago and what Mia referred to as "Sexy Casual," but Winter had never gotten the chance to wear out. It hung in her closet more as a symbol, to remind her that she was going to date again…when she was ready.

She put on the black, slim-fit, one piece pant suit that showed just a hint of cleavage. Put on her red suede ankle boots that matched her red lipstick. Then put on her red and black tweed topcoat. And looked in the mirror. And smiled.

As Winter contemplated adding red hoop earrings, her phone suddenly vibrated on the nightstand, making her heart skip a beat. For all her body knew, someone had just thrown a brick through the window. *Maybe that's Bo telling me he can't go out,* she thought. She hesitated for a few long seconds before she allowed her feet to move toward the phone. A text notification from an unknown number read: **Wow. Just, wow.**

It took Winter a few foggy moments to realize the number was Bo's. She sat down nervously on her bed and replied: **What happened?**

Bo: Excuse my language… Fucking amazing post, Winter! The colors, the composition, your straight-faced expression, just like those tintype photos. It's so damn good.

Winter closed her eyes and put the phone to her chest in relief. He wasn't mad at her. He didn't hate her. He wasn't saying she was a "slut," a "whore," or "desperate for validation"—he was complimenting her on her creativity.

Lyle would have been calling her by now to tell her to take the photo down. He'd probably be telling her the skirt was too short, or that he didn't want people thinking of his girl taking a shower, or any other crappy reason he gave to make her feel like something she created wasn't good enough or was sending the wrong message or—*Ahh!* If it were up to Lyle, Winter would be rotting as a receptionist for a law firm that specialized in screwing people over. She used to go home feeling worthless, wondering when her boyfriend would be coming home that night after going out "with friends." Wondering if he'd even make it home since he often drove drunk. Wondering if she'd do something to upset him. Wondering if he'd make her—Her heart started to vibrate, and Winter realized it was another text coming through.

Bo: I hope you're still down to go out. Wanna show you something at the bar

Winter: Hi Bo. Thank you so much for the nice things you said about the photo. What time should we meet?

Bo: Well, I'm ready now if you are

Winter: I'm ready 😊

Bo: Are you sure I can't pick you up?

Winter: I'm not that far really. I'd like to just meet you

Bo: K

Winter stared at that letter, in awe of the many possibilities of subtext it possessed. Annoyance, maybe? Indifference? Or could "K" mean "Hey! I don't understand your brain! Why are you so weird, Winter? Why?" The possibilities were endless.

Bo: I can't wait to see you again.

Winter bit her bottom lip. She almost replied, "Can't wait to see you too" or at least "u 2," but her fingers just wouldn't follow commands.

Winter: cool

She mimed banging the phone against her head. She couldn't write "u 2"—even though she really wanted to see him—but she was able to write "cool." *Cool!?* She waited for what felt like forever (about two minutes) and the next text from Bo said, **Just in case,** followed by the Multnomah Liquor Library address…and a Winking Face emoji.

Winter jumped up and twirled around. She put her wallet and lipstick and compact mirror and gum into a black clutch with red strap and took a final look at her reflection. She turned her bedroom light out, filled her water bottle up, and decided she'd leave the kitchen light on. Just as she was walking out the door she heard a fence gate shut hard but shrugged it off as merely her cottage neighbor Meryl, *taking out the trash or something*.

She drove down the main strip of Multnomah Village, and noticed every other tree twinkled with orange and white lights. Because it was so late, the bookstore, bakery, clothing, antiques, and home décor shops were already closed. The cozy taverns, restaurants, and cafes, however, were buzzing with life, and Winter rolled her window down a smidge to hear the conversations as she passed by. Her heart raced as she turned the corner and saw the library sign: A fifties, minimalist, silhouette of a shot glass and *Multnomah Liquor Library* written in retro cursive lettering, the same kind of font they used in the old Coca-Cola advertisements.

A valet person sat in a small booth on the other side of the parking entrance, and Winter almost pulled in before realizing she didn't really want anyone driving her car.

Luckily, the street was mostly empty, and she immediately found a spot. She turned her headlights off but had to keep the car running in order to keep the heater on. She watched as a few cars pulled up to the valet booth. The first car was some flashy-looking white sports car, and a man in a three-piece suit jumped out and threw the keys to the valet without even a greeting or eye contact. *Rude.* The next car was a black Escalade, and three people took their sweet time getting out, talking and laughing. The valet seemed to know them though, and they talked to him for a second before heading in.

"Well…they seem cool," Winter said out loud, as if trying to comfort herself.

She was twenty minutes early and wondered if Bo was already inside or if she should go in and wait for him or if she should call him or text him or— Just then, Bo's car slowly pulled into the parking entrance but didn't stop. The valet briefly leaned out of the booth, giving a familiar smile and wave, and Bo's car pulled into the lot and out of sight. Winter realized her heart was trying to leap out of her chest, just by knowing Bo was in that car. *Get yourself together, Winter,* she thought. *How are you going to get through this date if you—* Her purse vibrated and Winter pulled out her phone. The text read:

Bo: Let me know when you get here 🍸

Winter stared at the text but didn't reply. She was going to wait until the last moment to get out of her car, if she was even going to get out at all. She touched up her makeup and hair in the visor mirror and killed some time by looking at the newest comments on her latest post. *Pacific Northwest Herald* even reposted her on its Nanogram, with a link to a small article on the official website, stating that Winter was voted "Social Influencer of the Week." She was just about to email a thank you to the PNH editor, when she thought she saw Lyle's blue Mercedes-Benz speed by. She froze and didn't blink until it drove to the end of the street and turned sharply with what sounded like a skid. She fanned her misting eyes to keep her makeup from getting ruined, and knew she needed to act fast in order to stave off an impending panic attack.

First of all, she rationalized, there was no way it could have been Lyle because he didn't like Multnomah Village, once saying it was for "boring, hoity-toity people or well-off hippies."

And after they broke up, he moved over the bridge to Vancouver, and rented a house from his mother. Apparently, within a few months, he opened an extension to the Portland firm in Washington and rarely visited Oregon. One of the lawyers at the firm, Shelly, messaged Winter with the update.

She had also mentioned that at a recent office party, Lyle got drunk and said something horrible. Shelly asked Winter if that horrible something was true and if it was, she'd "call the cops on the bastard, immediately." Winter was moving on, she wanted nothing more to do with the guy, or the firm for that matter, so she made the decision to deny the horrible something.

Messaging back with something like: **"Oh, thanks Shelly but he lies a lot when he's drunk."** And she was technically telling the truth because Lyle lied a lot. Most of their relationship was a lie. The reasons she fell in love with him were based on lies. Heck, most of his life was a lie, including his career, in which he got paid to lie on behalf of other liars. Second of all, there were many other Mercedes-Benzes in the world and blue was probably one of the most common car colors and how would he even know where she was, anyways?

It was all so preposterous that Winter laughed, and realized it was a few minutes after she was supposed to meet Bo. She looked in the mirror with relief—her makeup was still intact and the red from her eyes had dissipated. She took a sip from her water bottle, took a long, deep breath, texted Bo…and opened the door.

As Winter approached the front door she looked through the windows to see a small, empty lounge with a right arm facing chaise couch, and a sleek, silver, square shade lamp. The three surrounding walls displayed a gray-toned nautical mural depicting a blue whale breeching next to a ship. She was just about to grab the silver octopus tentacle handle, when the door slowly opened for her. Inside, she wondered if she should sit down, but decided to stay standing. She looked all around for any semblance of another door handle, tentacle or not, but the walls in the lounge were doorless and completely smooth. After about a minute, one of the walls opened, revealing a wide corridor illuminated with blue light.

"Your reservation is ready," said a female voice that sounded like it was playing from an old timey radio. "Please enjoy your visit to the Multnomah Liquor Library."

Winter entered the corridor and heard the wall close back behind her. She slowly walked forward until she got to a door with no handle. She stood there for a while before the same female voice told her to "Please knock."

So she knocked.

"Who is it?" asked a familiar low voice.

"Oh, uh…Winter."

The corridor was quiet, and she could hear a mechanism revving up. Then the door creaked open, allowing old-timey bluegrass music and bar crosstalk to fill her ears.

Standing in front of her was a deity in a brown trench coat, black sweater, black twill chinos (rolled up just a tad), and cognac brown, chukka calf boots. Bo stood there, eyebrows high, shaking his head slowly.

"What is it?" Winter asked, self-consciously.

"Every time I see you," he said, "I just can't believe how stunning you are."

Her ears warmed. He held out his hand and she timidly took it.

"This place has an amazing entrance," she said.

"Nah. That's reserved for VIP only."

"Isn't this a VIP club?"

"Some are more VIP than others." He winked.

They walked, hand in hand, through another lounge that had two doors, but instead of a breeching whale on the mural, it was an octopus taking its turn harassing the ship in the middle of an ocean. The right door opened automatically, and they entered a large bar area with small clusters of people sitting throughout. Winter was suddenly overcome by the striking aesthetic: The room was dimly lit, save for the sections under industrial light chandeliers, or next to one of the three electrical fireplaces built into the dark walls; these sections consisted of buttoned, red velvet chesterfield sofas and fauteuils arranged around black coffee tables, or black velvet chairs set around circle dining tables; and the bar, fit with a line of black swivel chairs, was backed by light blue tiling and clear glass shelving that seemingly held every liquor bottle imaginable.

Winter watched as a bartender in a red vest moved a rolling library ladder to the left, climbed it, and carefully grabbed a bottle of Hennessy Black, before handing it to another bartender who opened it and started making drinks for two customers who seemed to be in a heated conversation.

"Wow," Winter said. "I can't believe I'm in here."

Bo smiled and guided Winter to the other side of the room. Every dining table and seat was full; a few people were eating desserts; a few others were in the midst of a full course meal, but most were drinking. Bo put his hand on the small of Winter's back and she shivered—not the scared kind, the happy kind—and they walked to the very back table, next to a fireplace. He pulled out a chair for her and she sat down.

"Can I take your coat?" he asked.

She handed it to him, and he hung it on a brass hook on the wall behind them. He hung his coat as well and rolled up his sleeves, showcasing his colorful tattoos… Or maybe he was just warm? He sat down and nodded to a red vest, who walked quickly over. The man was in his early forties, tall, and had a full head of gray George Clooney hair. He set menus down in the middle of the table.

"Good evening, Bo," the man said with a genuine smile, then looked at Winter. "And who is this enchantress?"

"Oh, Jeff, this is Winter," Bo said. "And Winter this is one of the managers and co-owners."

"Hello," she said.

"Winter is a fashion marvel, an amazing photographer, and probably the most creative person I've met so I really want to show her the Green Room later tonight. Were they able to fix that one thing that needed to be fixed recently?"

"Oh, yes, they did," Jeff said. "Well, she's in for a treat."

"Oh, good." Bo sat back, relieved.

"The Green Room? What is that?" Winter asked.

Jeff and Bo looked at each other.

"Well, it's something I came up with. Kind of an experiment and it's not open to the public yet but I'm hoping it will be soon."

"You designed a room here?" Winter asked.

"Bo helped a lot in the redesign of the MLL. I'm sorry to admit but it used to be boring and spiritless. Now, well..." Jeff looked around like he too was seeing it for the first time. "It's a marvel."

Bo shook his head. "Don't listen to him. Jeff helped out just as much as I did."

Jeff scoffed. "Preposterous. Bo's a visionary."

"Well, it sure seems like you're a great team," Winter interjected. "It's wonderful."

"You're wonderful," Bo said and took her hand.

She blushed and all she could think to say was, "Silly."

Jeff cupped his hands together. "Okay, it was nice meeting

you, Winter. Take as much time as you need with your order and I'll—"

"Oh, no, Jeff, I'll grab our order."

"No can do. You're going to experience full service tonight." He patted Bo on the back, then said to Winter, "It's hard to get this man to sit down."

Winter grinned. "Thank you, Jeff. It was so nice meeting you too."

Jeff headed for the bar.

"The menu's pretty extensive." Bo opened a menu.

"Whatever you recommend. It's your place after all."

"Well, I own a part but not a controlling part—you know what, I know a great dessert and drink pairing. Mind if I order it?"

"Please."

He jumped up and ran over to Jeff who was leaning up against the bar, conversing with another worker. Bo said something and Jeff chuckled as he went through the kitchen door. The other worker talked with Bo, glanced over at Winter, and smiled as they fist bumped. Winter looked around at the décor as Bo walked back to the table, so she wouldn't make him feel weird. He sat down.

"What did you order?" Winter asked.

"I ordered Salted Caramel Vanilla Crunch Cake with warm cider and whiskey for you, and chocolate molten cake with whiskey coffee for me."

"Ooh, I'm so dumb. I should have told you that chocolate is one of my favorite things in the world."

"I was hoping you'd say that. So…" He shrugged. "I guess we're gonna have to share."

She laughed. "I guess so."

Bo shifted then pulled his seat closer to the table. "I feel like you're too far away from me."

"We can move our seats closer to each other."

"Yeah, but then I won't be able to see your beautiful face."

He took her hand and kissed it. Winter's stomach was doing back flips and she didn't know how to respond to that.

"I'm sorry," Bo said. "I'm probably coming on a bit strong. I'm just…" He leaned back. "I'm just so happy to see you."

Winter ran her fingers through her hair and flipped it. "Not happier than I am," she said.

"Oh, this is a competition, huh?"

She nodded, smiling.

"Well, I think we're both the winners then." He winked at her.

"How are the kittens doing?" she asked. "Adjusting to your home okay?"

"Surprisingly well. It took a little while longer for Elmira. At first she hid anytime I took a step toward her, but by the time I left she was asleep in my lap."

"Oh, God, that's so cute. And Edgar was just cool out of the gate?"

"Yeah, he led the charge in the sniffing party—he investigated every crevice of that place. I think he's looking for you."

"Maybe he was making sure there weren't any predators."

"Making sure my dad wasn't there."

Winter bit her lip. "Can I ask you a personal question? And I completely understand if you don't want to answer."

"Why do I hate my dad?"

"Yeah."

He sat up and pulled his sleeves down. Then massaged the back of his neck.

"Please don't feel obligated to answer," she said.

"No, I want to." He stared at the table. "He's just… He's a bad person. A clinical narcissist." He looked up at her and Winter nodded understandably. "I've watched him abuse my mom since I can remember."

"I'm so sorry, Bo. Did you ever see him hit her?"

"No, it never got physical…as far as I know. It was mental abuse—he'd constantly tell her she was ugly or fat or worthless. He'd embarrass her in front of friends. Cheat on her and laugh about it. He'd control her every move, like she was some kind of slave."

Mental abuse? Winter bit her nails. "That's horrible," she finally said.

"Yeah."

"So is that why you got in fights with him? Your dad."

"Yeah, I don't know if it was because I was the youngest —my brother and sister were kind of wrapped up in their own stuff or didn't want to believe it even when I told them. But I was really the only one who stood up to him. And…and my dad didn't like that very much."

"That must have been so hard for you, Bo. And unfair—your own siblings didn't believe you?"

"Well, my brother is a lot older and moved out of the house when I was young, and my sister is a daddy's girl. When they did see something, they'd just rationalize it away." Bo slouched down. "It almost became—like a sick game. My dad liked me the least. I gave him the most shit. So he wanted everyone to think I was crazy or a bad seed or whatever."

Winter felt a burst of confidence shoot through her, culminating with her squeezing Bo's hand. He closed his eyes and squeezed back, like he was trying his hardest not to lose it right there.

"You do know you're not any of those things, right? Your mother is so lucky to have you in her life. And I can't believe that I just ate up that crap online despite what my gut was telling me. You're caring and you have a big heart, Bo. I know it."

He looked at her, his eyes slightly bloodshot. She would have held his hand all evening but just then a waitress brought a platter and greeted them. They let go of each other to make room for the desserts and drinks.

"Thank you, Hannah," he said.

"You're welcome, Bo. And as per your request..." Hannah pulled out a small gift box from her side pocket and handed it to him before almost skipping off.

Bo smiled and relief seemed to sweep over him. "I got this made for you. I'm so glad they got it here in time."

"Made for me?"

He handed her the box. Inside were two stuffed animals—so small they fit into the palm of her hand.

"It's Edgar and Elmira," he said. "Photorealistic."

Her mouth dropped as she studied the stuffed animals. "Oh, my wow. You got this made in the last few hours?"

"Mmm-hmm. So whenever you miss them—I mean, Edgar is technically yours after all— If you ever miss them you'll have them with you in spirit."

"I love this!" She jumped up and hugged him. "You're so thoughtful."

"Adopting those kittens mark a particularly special day for me."

"Really? Why?" she asked, still examining the kittens in her hand.

"Because you were there."

She bit her lip and looked at him, expecting to see a smile but his expression was serious.

"It was a special day for me too," she said.

The sweet aroma of caramel, apple cider, and chocolate filled the air... Or maybe she had just finally noticed it? Despite how intoxicating the smell of their desserts were, Winter craved something else...in the form of the misunderstood, tattoo covered, chiseled wonder sitting across from her.

Winter put the kittens back in the box, tucking it into her purse. Bo moved his chair closer to her and they shared both desserts and he put his hand on her lap and she rested her head on his shoulder and they talked about their childhoods and their mothers and their favorite music and the last movie they watched and their career goals and their thoughts on the upcoming elections and the funny things the kittens did and the most recent, crazy story in the news, and art...

And Winter felt comfortable and safe for the first time in years.

CHAPTER TWENTY-TWO

The bar slowly emptied, and Bo and Winter moved to a couch next to one of the fireplaces. The bartenders had supplied them with a steady stream of beverages, but Bo knew Jeff had instructed them to make sure they were watered down—some were even non-alcoholic—so Bo wouldn't get drunk. He tended to indulge in alcohol when he got nervous, like the night he had a big FFS meeting the next morning or the night his dad made an appointment to talk to him the next day. Let's just say, Jeff had to call a driver for Bo on many occasions.

Winter wasn't making him nervous. He'd never felt so connected to someone. So comfortable. But in the back of his mind, something or someone nagged at him. Warning him not to say or do something wrong. Telling him that he was a fuckup, a loser—that he'd never really amount to anything. Winter had a gentle demeanor. An innocence. A fragility that kind of frightened him. He wanted to protect her, yet he was convinced he was going to hurt her in some way.

Winter left to get a coffee and Bo stared at the fire. For a second he thought he saw a figure of a person standing in the yellow flames, flipping him off, but when he shook his head and blinked repeatedly, it disappeared. The dark, brooding, indie song *Depraved* by Mammals started playing through the speakers, and Bo rolled his eyes because it was a perfect soundtrack to what he was feeling…and what he was trying to deny.

Winter came back with a glass of water, and a smile on her face that touched her big, beautiful eyes.

"Hi," she said, sitting down.

Bo sat up straight and smiled back, his nerves relaxing just by seeing her face. "Well, hello."

"They said they don't have any more decaf coffee. But since they're almost closed, I don't want them to bother making anymore."

"There's a twenty-four-hour coffee shop around the corner. We can stop there when we leave."

"Ooh, I know that place. Sounds great…" She paused. "Shall we head there now?"

"Yeah, but I wanna show you the Green Room on the way out if that's cool?"

"It's definitely cool."

Bo stood up and stretched and helped Winter up. He wanted to put his arms around her but didn't know if it'd be appropriate. He put his hands in his pockets and looked at the ground and started walking away when he felt a light tug at the back of his shirt.

"Everything alright?" Winter asked.

He turned and nodded, probably unconvincingly. He took her coat off the hook and helped her put it on and then put his own coat on, and for some reason, could not look at her. *What the fuck is wrong with me?* he thought. *Your dream girl is standing next to you and you're...malfunctioning.*

"Shall I turn the Green Room breaker on?" Jeff asked, approaching them.

"Oh, yeah, we'll just be in there for a few minutes. Thanks."

"No problem," Jeff said. "And it was a pleasure meeting you, dear. You're welcome here anytime. With or without this guy."

Winter laughed.

"Hey, man," Bo said with a light chuckle.

Jeff backed up with his hands in the air, flashing a foolish shit-eating grin on his—*No... He's just being funny,* Bo assured himself. *Get a grip.*

"Ready?" Winter asked, but her words were soaked in defensive annoyance.

He finally looked down at her and she was watching as a small group of men said their goodbyes to Jeff before he disappeared into the back room...and she was biting her lip. The chandelier directly above illuminated her face and her eyes soaked up the light like a sparkler in a dark cave. *God, she's the sexiest woman I've ever seen,* he assessed.

He tried to take her hand, but she quickly tucked both hands in her coat pockets. Jeff came back out behind the bar and gave a thumbs-up.

"Which way?" Winter asked quietly.

Bo gestured toward a door in the corner and she hastily went through it.

"We'll probably go out the back door, Jeff," Bo said. "Thanks for everything."

Jeff waved and Bo felt guilt for thinking anything negative toward such a good man.

———

The Green Room had turned out exactly how Bo envisioned: A bar backed with emerald tiles; an electric fireplace built into the side of a tree that protruded from the wall and extended all the way to the ceiling, its leafed limbs and thick roots extending the whole of the room; an artificial forest floor, complete with soil, grass, leaves, twigs, and, bark; forest pathways leading to rectangular wooden tables surrounded by tree stump seats; moss walls; clusters of fireflies hanging from the ceiling by invisible strings; and hidden speakers playing forest sound ambience.

Winter's whole demeanor changed the second she walked into the room. Her eyes widened and she put her hand over her mouth, spinning around to see it all.

"Bo, this is unbelievable," she said. "You designed this?"

She walked over to the tree and ran her hands over the wood, following it halfway across the room. Bo took his phone out of his pocket and typed something into it before putting it back. The forest ambience quieted down, and a slow, acoustic song started playing. Winter turned around slowly.

"Did you put that music on?" she asked.

He smiled from the side of his mouth and nodded.

"Well…don't you think it's kind of…romantic?" she asked and crossed her arms.

"I can turn it off if it's making you uncomfortable."

"Isn't it making *you* uncomfortable? I mean, I can tell you want this night to end."

"That couldn't be further from the truth." He went over and sat down on the edge of a table closest to her. They didn't say anything for a few, long seconds before Bo added, "You just make me nervous."

"Wait…what?"

"Come here and I'll tell you."

She looked around as if she wanted someone to save her or talk her out of it or at least give an opinion, but he was the only other soul in the room. She looked down and moved a piece of bark around with her foot.

"You come here," she said, almost inaudibly.

"How about we meet in front of the fireplace?"

He got there first, and she sauntered her way over to him, again, avoiding eye contact. He slowly pried her arms uncrossed and lifted up her chin. The fire flickered in her eyes and they locked into each other. His spine tingled and he knew there was no turning back for either of them.

"You're so perfect. I'm scared I'm not good enough for you," Bo said.

"I'm not perfect."

He felt his brows knitting. "Perfect for me," he said and meant it.

She smiled shyly then after a few seconds lightly grabbed his sweater and pulled him closer.

"I want to show you something," he said.

He briefly pulled out his phone, typed something, and the fireplace dimmed to a low light. He then placed his hands on her waist, under her coat. And she put her hands on his arms, like she was holding on for a ride.

"Look up," he whispered.

They both looked up at a ceiling full of stars.

Winter gasped. "Wow," she said.

His eyes went back to her. "Wow," he said.

Her hands moved up and he pulled her against him, and she started breathing hard when he lightly kissed her neck. She ran her fingers through his hair, and he closed his eyes briefly before meeting her soft lips. The music swelled just as they kissed, her tongue periodically touching his. Teasing him. Bo didn't know kissing could feel like that. He knew Winter could feel his excitement because she pressed herself closer and he wrapped tighter around her…

And, Jesus…

He could barely fucking take it…

Bo and Winter walked hand in hand into the Halloween decorated coffee shop. The beams were covered in fake spider webs, multicolored ghost string lights were strung above the counter, and a few fake pumpkins with cartoon painted faces were placed around the shop.

Surprisingly, about a dozen customers filled the seats, despite it being so late. Boisterously, happy, drunken banter permeated the room, but was actually inviting when mixed with the calm coffee shop music. A blond man with a crewcut and corporate beard sat in the back corner with his feet on a table, wearing sunglasses and sipping from a mug. *Drunk people watching is definitely an entertaining pastime*, Bo thought, admiring the guy's Sunday night, devil-may-give-a-flying-fuck attitude.

Only three people were in line ahead of them: An older man who could barely keep balance as he stood at the register pondering over what he wanted and where on his person his money was; and an oblivious and talkative young couple—the guy, sporting a black faux hawk, and the girl with a platinum white mullet.

Bo brought Winter's hand to his lips and waited for her to look up before he kissed it. She blushed and looked away before flipping her hair. *Damn*, he thought, *she must know how cute she is when she does that.*

"So, do you want to drink it here or get it to go?" Bo asked.

Winter didn't say anything. The man at the register had apparently ordered, staggering to the closest seat. The couple started their order and Bo was about to ask Winter again if she wanted to drink her coffee there when he realized her hand was shaking.

"Are you cold?" he asked. "Here…wear my coat."

Bo started to take his coat off when Winter abruptly ran out the door…

He had a small audience consisting of a few customers that noticed his surprised expression before he ran out the door after her.

"Winter!" he yelled.

He caught up to her under an old fashioned streetlamp on the corner, and she looked frantically from side to side.

"I can't remember where I parked." Her voice was shaky, and tears ran down her face.

Bo tried to hide his worry behind the calmest demeanor he could summon. "What's wrong?"

She pointed toward the coffee shop and she was breathing in short bursts.

"Winter, breathe. You're going to hyperventilate. Take long, deep breaths."

She didn't listen and carbon dioxide loss made her more and more panicky and discombobulated.

Bo took her trembling hand and held it in his, palm side up. With his other hand he pressed a finger in the middle of her palm a couple times, as if he was pushing an invisible button. She looked at him, bewildered. He then moved his finger in small circles. Her eyes widened.

"What are you doing?" she asked frailly.

He repeated the movements—pressing and circling—and her breathing slowed.

"I'm calming you down," he said. "My mom used to do this for me when I had my…angry spells."

"It's not going to work. Nothing works." She wiped her wet face with the front of her coat sleeve.

"I think it already has." He smiled at her.

Her face was still red, but her expression relaxed with the realization.

"If you tell me what's going on, maybe I can help," he assured her.

"My…" She looked past Bo. "My ex."

"Your ex is in there?"

She nodded, then pulled her hand away and crossed her arms tightly. "I have to get out of here."

She waited for a red jeep to pass before crossing the street. He followed her.

"Maybe it wasn't him," he said.

"I thought I saw him drive by earlier and…and he was sitting in the back. I know it was him."

"Wait, the bearded guy with sunglasses?"

She nodded. His heart raced and his muscles tensed, and he contemplated running back into that coffee shop to beat the guy to a pulp.

"So he's stalking you," he stated.

She didn't deny it. At her car she fumbled in her purse for her keys, looking over her shoulder every now and then, paranoid.

"Winter," he said firmly, "Where are you going?"

"Home."

"If some weirdo is following you then I don't think you should go home. Especially alone."

"Oh, no," she said with fake nonchalance. "It was probably just a coincidence that he was there…and I overreacted because I'm exhausted. It's been a long day and —I didn't know he was in town and… I just didn't want to see him, that's all."

"Oh," Bo said sarcastically and threw up his hands. "That's all."

She looked down, her voice wavering again. "I…don't want to talk about it."

"Okay, okay, we don't have to talk about it," he said delicately. "So, do you have anywhere to go?"

She opened her car door. "Well, Mia's not back yet and my mom…" Her voice trailed off. "And it's too late to call Camilla…" She sighed and turned to look him in the eyes. "Bo, I had the most amazing night. I'll be fine."

"Stay over at my place."

"What?"

"Stay over at my place tonight and it will give you time to think about what you want to do about…him."

"Oh'm, I." Winter looked surprised. "I know this is the age of Tinder but—"

"No, it's not like that. I'd worry about you all night if I just let you go home with some asshole 'coincidentally' coming to town and showing up places you go. I have a few guest rooms." He cleared his throat. "And Edgar would love to see you."

"I don't know."

"If you want, I'll stay in one of the empty apartments or—hell, I could even stay at the bowling alley. But there's security at my place and at least I'll know you're safe."

She bit the inside of her mouth. "I don't have anything to wear."

"I'll take care of that."

She thought for a second, then hesitatingly replied, "Okay."

He put his hand on his heart with relief. "Oh, good."

She breathed in deeply through her nose, and exhaled… *Finally.* He tried to hide how elated he was that he didn't have to say goodbye to her yet. Didn't want to scare her away. And hopefully she'd tell him more about the guy in the sunglasses. They stood there, under a moonless, cloudy dark sky, in silence. Questions raced through his mind. *Why did she react like that? What did her ex do to her? And will I have the willpower to stop myself from killing him if I hear something I don't want to hear?*

"Thank you," Winter said and flashed a small smile for the first time in a while.

Butterflies convulsed inside him. Arms still crossed, she rested her head on his chest. Her warmth made him realize how cold it was outside, and he embraced her.

"Your heart's beating fast," she said.

He chuckled, a little embarrassed that his secret was discovered. "I'll drive your car, okay? You should rest."

"What about your car?"

He could feel her breath on his neck. His skin prickled. "I'll leave it in the lot and get it tomorrow."

"Bo," she said quietly.

"Yes." He matched her tone, and watched a yellow Lexus Sedan pass by, followed by a blue Mercedes-Benz with tinted windows.

"I trust you," she said and looked up at him, "Please stay there with me."

CHAPTER TWENTY-THREE

Winter was exhausted. It had been one of the longest days of her life—the shelter fire, getting her post done, going on a date, seeing Lyle. Aided by the relaxing classical music on the radio, she unsuccessfully fought falling asleep, opening her eyes once to see nothing but dark and winding, forest-lined pavement and once more to see a mostly empty, dark highway.

"We're here, sleepyhead," Bo said.

Winter woke up with a start and her eyes took a while to adjust and realize they were pulling onto the driveway of a building so massive, she could barely see the top. Bo stopped the car in front of the underground parking gate and fidgeted with his cell phone until the gate opened. The first level parking lot was full except for the back corner. A gray Tesla sat next to the wall and Bo parked behind it.

"Is that yours?" Winter asked, stretching.

"Mmmhmm. But technically it's a company car so I don't drive it much. My Challenger—I paid for that with my own money."

She nodded understandingly.

"Come on," he said with side smile. "It's been an *eventful* day, to say the least."

He jumped out of the car and ran over to her side, opening her door and helping her out.

"Thank you," she said.

His hands were so warm in the cold garage and she couldn't help but imagine them all over her body. The back of her neck tingled, and her stomach tightened. She wasn't scared to stay the night; she was scared she was going to freak out again—about whatever—and he'd want nothing to do with her. And what the heck was Lyle doing in the city anyway? Was he really following her? Was it just a coincidence? Maybe he was visiting someone? But the way he just sat there, alone, leaning back, staring—well, she only guessed he was staring, since she couldn't technically see his eyes behind those dark sunglasses. And the fact he was wearing sunglasses at night…and indoors… What a weirdo indeed. But then again, maybe he didn't even see her. Or maybe she should call the cops or— *Oh, my gosh*, she thought, *what if I hallucinated the whole thing?*

"You sure you don't want me to go somewhere else for the night?" Bo asked.

She shook her head and he put his key in a box next to the elevator. After a few seconds the elevator doors opened, and he gestured for her to go in with a playful nod. She leaned against the handrail and wanted to fix her hair in the mirror opposite her but resisted. He pushed the *up* arrow and the doors closed and Winter noticed there were no numbered buttons, just icons indicating up, down, open, close and emergency. *Was this his personal elevator?* she thought. He leaned next to her as they ascended, and she thought he was going to kiss her, but he didn't.

"Look at how beautiful you are." He pointed at the reflection.

She looked away, embarrassed. The elevator doors opened, and he held her hand all the way down a quiet hall decorated with random landscape photographs and mirrors framed with golden floral designs. He stopped at an unmarked door, held two fingers in front of a digital panel on the wall, and the door opened.

"I wonder if the kittens are asleep," Winter said.

"I hope we'll be able to find them before you go to sleep."

Winter was overwhelmed by the cozy yet sleek apartment. Besides the massive kitchen, and the living room that was about the size of her whole bungalow, all of the earthy toned furniture and décor tied together beautifully. Bo hung their coats on a wall coat rack and went into the kitchen. Winter scanned all of the framed prints and posters, noticing the Oregon or nautical themes, and got a closer look at the *Wanderer above the Sea of Fog* print displayed above the breakfast nook.

"Caspar David Friedrich is another one of my favorite artists," she said.

"Really?" He took a teapot out of the cupboard and set it on the stove. "Mine, too."

"When a scene is shrouded in mist," she said in a bad German accent, "it seems greater, nobler, and heightens the viewers' imaginative powers, increasing expectation—like a veiled girl."

Bo smiled and raised one eyebrow. "Did he say that?"

"Oh, sorry," she said back in her normal voice, "Yeah, I took Art Appreciation in sixth grade and I chose Casper to be my second semester essay subject. I just— I always imagined that's what he sounded like."

"You remember that from middle school?" He shook his head.

She crossed over to a small side table and picked up a replica of the *Fight Club* soap, examining the details. Then she picked up a coaster depicting a minimalist rendition of the stairs and blue sky backdrop in *The Truman Show* movie. *Dang, he has such good taste in movies and art,* Winter thought. She wondered if she should tell him but decided that he probably already knew.

"Winter, can you do something for me?" Bo asked.

He had the teapot warming up on the stove, took two light-green mugs out of the cupboard, and placed two stringed tea bags inside them.

"Of course." Winter walked over to him and waited for instructions.

"I'm making us some nighttime tea since we weren't able to get anything at the coffee shop."

"That sounds nice. What do you need?"

He moved a strand of hair from her face. "I need a favor."

"Shoot."

"Actually, it's two favors."

"Yes?" she said with slight wariness.

"And feel free to decline either favor, it won't hurt my feelings."

"What is it?" she laughed.

He pat the counter, and it took her a few seconds to realize he wanted her to sit on top of it. She jumped up, beyond curious at what he was up to. The warm kitchen light highlighted the sharp angles of his face and presented her with a whole new perspective. His green eyes looked at her with a mixture of intensity and tenderness, and she contemplated any girl in the world that could resist them.

"Okay." He scratched his head. "I'd love it if you could help me find my kittens and, I don't know, another kiss, I guess."

She smiled. "Yes to both… I guess."

She opened her legs so he could stand between them, then she inched closer to him and he cradled a side of her face with his hand. The second their lips met electricity moved around her chest and settled in her upper abdomen. He kissed her softer, gentler than before and she knew why. *He found out I'm fragile*, she thought, and a sadness gnawed at her. *He thinks I'm...unstable.* She stiffened from the stinging realization.

"What's wrong?" he asked.

She placed one hand on his chest and moved even closer to him.

"Nothing," she said convincingly, and initiated the next kiss, letting herself melt into his soft lips.

His hands moved around her waist and hers moved gently around his neck. When she came up for air, he started kissing her jawline, then back to her lips, and he moved his hands to her legs…until he suddenly pulled away.

"We should stop," he said, breathing heavily.

She shook her head and tried to pull him closer. He didn't budge so she wrapped her legs around him. He closed his eyes and took a sharp breath before opening them again.

"You don't understand how much I want you," he said. "But I don't want to take advantage."

"What do you mean?" she asked, unwrapping her legs. "You're not taking advantage."

"You've been through a lot today and—I mean—you saw

your ex, and I couldn't live with myself if I swooped in and tried something when you—when you've been through a lot."

"Okay," Winter said, trying to hide the hurt in her voice.

Lyle caused enough destruction and somehow he was still controlling her; he was a puppeteer and she was a puppet that desperately wished it could find sharp enough scissors to cut those last few strings.

The teapot faintly whistled, and Bo turned the burner off and filled the cups before squeezing drops of honey and a splash of coconut milk into each. Chamomile perfumed the air, giving Winter a soothing, peaceful hug.

"Even your tea-making is artistic," she said.

He laughed and shook his head. "This is the way my grandma made me tea when I couldn't sleep."

Winter took a sip and her eyes widened. "Oh, my, whoa, it's so nice."

He kissed her forehead and she flashed him an exaggerated wry look.

"Hey," she said. "No funny business, remember?"

He chuckled. "Yep, you're right."

Before Winter could even get to her third sip, a door creaked open from inside the apartment.

"Well hello, handsome! You're back so late," a random voice said.

Seconds later, a pretty, petite, ombré-haired woman wearing black slacks, a buttoned-down work-like top and an oversized green cardigan, shuffled in. She was maybe in her early thirties and could barely open her eyes despite grinning from ear to ear.

Bo almost dropped his tea. His expression went from surprise to mortification to fake acceptance.

"Sarah, this is Winter. Winter…" Bo cleared his throat. "This is Sarah."

"Winter? Oh, my God, how exciting!" Sarah squawked, running over to the other side of the counter and holding her hand out. "I'm a big fan!"

"Oh." Winter put down her tea and shook Sarah's hand. "It's nice meeting you, as well. Um…how do you two know each other?"

"She's the concierge manager here." Bo's words were cheerful but dipped in irritation.

"Oh, come on, Bo. I'm more than that," Sarah said.

A wave of anger seemed to pass over Bo, but he quickly masked it with a forced side smile.

"We're good friends," Sarah said. "We go *way* back."

"Well," Bo clapped his hands. "Didn't think you'd still be here but I think we're going to sleep soon so…"

"Sure, Bo, I was just watching the kittens, you know. Like you asked." She laughed and Winter noticed her eyes were bloodshot and some of her words slurred into the next. "Unfortunately, I ate a little too much of this pot brownie, and to counteract it I took a shot or two of your whiskey. Hope you don't mind. But it's cool, I slept it off."

"Where are the kittens?" Winter asked.

"Don't worry, they're safe. They were sleeping with me."

"Oh, they're in a guest room?" Winter asked apprehensively.

"No, in the master suite. Best room in the place."

Winter looked at Bo, hoping for some kind of explanation or at least opposition to the fact that the concierge manager was sleeping in his bed. Instead, he pursed his lips and his eyebrows furrowed so hard they almost joined.

"Well, I'll be leaving now," Sarah said, and smiled in an

unsettling kind of way—like she had just gotten away with something.

Bo's angry expression remained as he opened the door. He had started to move his tongue around in his mouth, pushing it against the inside of his cheeks.

"I can tell we'll be good friends," Sarah said and winked at Winter. "I'll see you around."

Winter couldn't get herself to say anything.

On Sarah's way out the door she said in a quiet, whiny tone to Bo, "I'm sorry. I had no idea you were bringing her back home."

"Bye," Bo said curtly.

He slammed the door behind her and when his eyes finally met Winter's again, his expression morphed from anger to worry.

"Winter, I'm so sorry for that."

He walked over to her, but she backed away, standing in the living room at a safe distance, cradling herself.

"I had no idea she'd still be here," he continued, stepping a few feet closer. "And she's not usually like that. I don't know what's gotten into her."

"Sounds like your whiskey got into her...and something else," she murmured.

He shook his head. "Tomorrow I'll talk to her and let her know how unprofessional that was."

Winter realized her face was all screwed up, and she forced herself to relax. *There has to be an explanation*, she thought. *It's all a big misunderstanding. Maybe Sarah has a crush on him or something. You have to change, Winter. You have to trust. You have to stop running away from people.*

Bo had calmed himself and carefully picked up both

teacups. "Will you please drink some relaxing tea, and we'll go visit the kittens?"

Winter swallowed. After a few seconds of contemplation she said quietly, "Yes."

He handed her the tea, and they went into his bedroom. Both kittens were curled up on Bo's bed, the pillows were on the floor and the blankets were hanging halfway off. Winter drank a few sips, set her tea on the nightstand, then sat down and lightly pet Edgar, then Elmira. Edgar curled tighter at Winter's touch and Elmira put a paw over her eyes.

"They're so adorable," she said quietly.

"Should we get them up?"

"Oh, I'd feel so bad doing that."

"Yeah, you're right. Probably wouldn't be too happy with us if we messed up their sleeping schedule."

She nodded and smiled. He sat down next to her and put his hand on hers. They sat for a while together, watching the kittens sleeping, before Winter couldn't hold it any longer.

"Why was she sleeping in your bed?" she asked.

He took a deep breath through his nose. "I had no idea she'd do that. I definitely didn't give her permission."

Winter nodded slowly, her eyes wandering to the floor. He nudged her playfully.

"She's a stoner," he said. "Sometimes she doesn't even know what planet she's on."

"Okay, cool. So you're not sleeping with your concierge manager?"

She asked this plainly without much thought behind it, expecting an obvious and immediate "no" from him. He put his tea down and tried to say something, but no words came out and Winter started feeling nauseous. She stood up and the kittens opened their eyes briefly, Elmira stretching, before going back to sleep.

"Wait...you're sleeping with her?"

He stood up. "Not anymore. I don't want to lie to you."

He tried to grab her hands, but she wouldn't have it.

"I think I need to go," she said.

"Winter, she means nothing to me."

"Oh, that's supposed to make me feel better? It's just really weird to have someone you're...*effing*...just chilling at your home, sleeping in your bed, while you're taking me out, convincing me you like me. It's so—it's so gross."

She hurried out of the room and he followed her. As she put on her coat, he stood in front of the front door.

"Please don't leave," he said. "I heard some things about your previous relationship, and I don't want you to be—"

"Heard what, exactly?" Her eyes started to well up and her weakness made her angry.

"I don't have specifics. But I heard it was weird. I was hoping you'd fill me in on what that meant."

"Why would I? I'm just another notch on your belt. You want me to tell you so you and your buddies can make fun of me?"

"Winter, I've wanted you for—" He sighed. "I slept with her because I was lonely. Because I couldn't have you."

"Oh, please."

She reached around him to grab the doorknob. He reluctantly moved out of the way and she walked fast down the hallway, with him following close behind.

"Winter," he pleaded. "It's so late. Please just stay here tonight. You can lock the guest room if you don't trust me. But I promise I'm not a bad guy. I don't know what I have to do to prove that to you."

She turned to him, tears rolling down her cheeks. "Why do you have to be like him? Why? I thought you were different. I really did."

It looked like the wind had been knocked out of him. He approached her slowly and she could see his eyes were reddening.

"Like who?" he asked delicately.

"Like *him*! Like Lyle!"

"Your ex?"

She closed her eyes, and a tear dropped onto her hand.

"How am I like him?" he asked.

She opened her eyes and he gently wiped her cheek with his thumb.

"You," she sniffled. "You'd sleep with other women and get a sick pleasure of dangling it in my face."

He shook his head, bringing his eyebrows together.

"And I know what would happen next," she continued. "You'd forbid me from going out and you'd accuse me of—" She spoke fast, and her words jumbled, almost collapsing on each other. "And you'd come home, and you'd think it was funny to—to scare me or—or to hurt me and—"

Somehow, Bo was already holding her. She was trembling and sobbing, burying her face in his soft sweater.

"And you'd—you would—force me to do things," she whispered.

His voice cracked. "I'd never do any of that to you."

And he just repeated those words over and over.

And before she knew it, she was drifting off to sleep in his guest bedroom. With Bo lying next to her. And the kittens curled up and sleeping between them.

CHAPTER TWENTY-FOUR

Bo woke up first. He quietly stopped in his master bedroom restroom to brush his teeth and swish his mouth with mouthwash and try to tame his bedhead hair.

The kittens were already awake, using the living room as an obstacle course that involved chasing each other, taking turns using the cat scratcher set up in the hallway, and playing soccer with fish shaped cat toys stuffed with cat nip.

Bo selected the latest episode of *The Joe Rogan Experience* podcast on his phone and put it on speaker as he made eggs, hash browns, toast, and sliced fruit.

Curious, the kittens checked on what Bo was doing, repeatedly, and he had to shoo them away more than once when they jumped on the counter and got a little too close to the food. By the time Bo set the breakfast nook table with drinks and the plates, Winter had gotten up.

"Smells amazing," she said, rubbing her eyes.

He paused the podcast and almost forgot how to breathe: She was a vision to behold in his black sweater, leaning against the hallway entrance, with her long, toned legs, beautiful, painted-pink toes, one bared shoulder, and messy ponytail. *She knows exactly what she's doing*, he thought. In the back guestroom closet, Bo kept packs and packs of undergarments, t-shirts, and socks, as well as grooming toiletries for any guest that needed it. Though Winter happily opened a new pack of undergarments and a toothbrush/toothpaste package, she insisted on wearing Bo's sweater because she needed something "warm." He happily gave it to her, and she put it on over her outfit. Then, like a magic trick, her outfit and panties dropped to the floor. He had to get up and take a lap around his apartment after seeing that. He was only a man after all.

"Were you listening to JRE?" she asked.

"Wh-yeah? You listen?"

She nodded. "I've heard a lot of 'em. You're listening to the last one with Joey Diaz, right? I love when he's a guest."

"Yeah. His stories are so funny."

"One of the best storytellers out there." She laughed as the kittens ran around her. "Do you have any episodes you'd recommend?"

"Definitely Elon Musk," he answered.

"Oh, my, that episode was marvelous. Some of the things he said though—it's kind of terrifying. Just knowing where A.I. is headed. And how he answered Joe's questions…he was so ominous."

"Yeah. I think the future of technology is terrifying but also really fucking exciting."

She smiled. "I agree."

He watched her in awe as she walked over to the couch and picked up a feathered wand cat toy. She knelt down in the middle of the living room and waved the wand. Elmira immediately started chasing it. Edgar hid behind the ottoman, wiggled his butt, and then pounced, missing the feather by a few seconds before jumping into the air and clasping it between his paws.

"Damn, Edgar!" Winter laughed. "Did you see that?"

"I sure did. Guess we know which one will be an athlete when they grow up."

Elmira had already lost interest and was clawing up a small throw pillow, thumping it with her hind feet. Winter played with Edgar a little while longer before he got distracted by the curtains automatically opening by the magic of the remote in Bo's hand. Edgar jumped on the right side, just as it stopped. Elmira sniffed the left curtain first, but quickly made her way over to the right—to which her brother almost landed on her head.

"Still think you can handle two kittens?" Winter asked and walked over to Bo.

"Well, I have you to help me, right?" He winked at her.

She bit her lip and seemed to think about something, crossing her arms.

"Oh, shit," he said. "You must be cold."

He grabbed the gray knit throw blanket from the couch, unfolded it, and wrapped it around her. She stood there, looking away, as he rubbed her shoulders slowly to help her warm up. She uncrossed her arms and bit her fingernails. After a few long seconds, she finally looked up at him, stood on her tippy toes and kissed his cheek.

"Thank you," she said.

"You're welcome."

Then she turned to the table. "You cooked all this?"

"Mmmhmm. I want you to have a good morning."

"Well…I already am."

He gestured to the plate in front of the corner bench, and

she sat down. He sat in a chair across from her. They ate and Winter gushed over the taste of her breakfast, and Bo regaled her with a very interesting story (not really) about how one of his teachers at boarding school insisted on teaching him to cook because he didn't even know how to make toast back then. She laughed so hard she choked on her orange juice.

When they were done, Winter jumped up and insisted on washing their dishes, even though they were going into the dishwasher.

"Oh, I gotta feed them," Bo said.

"Can I help?"

"Sure, can you refill their water?"

Bo put two elevated pet bowl sets on the counter. Winter filled one side of each with water, and Bo put half of the can in each of the other. The kittens, smelling their breakfast, were at their feet meowing. The meows stopped the moment the bowl sets hit the floor, however.

"Join me on the couch?" Bo asked Winter as he washed his hands.

She sat close to him, wrapped tightly in the blanket, except for her exposed legs outstretched on the ottoman. He wanted so bad to put his hand on her knee…run it up her thigh… have it disappear under the blanket and–*Keep it together, Bo*, he told himself.

"You need to call the cops and tell them everything you told me," he said matter-of-factly. "You can use my lawyers and they're gonna need you to gather any proof—like photos, witnesses, even the people you just told secondhand—"

She stiffened and put her legs down. "I don't think I can. I never really told anyone. At least, not the extent of it." Her voice trailed off.

"Why?"

"Because," she said, shamefully.

He sat forward, resting his elbows on his knees. The kittens were still eating, and both tails looked like little black and white question marks from his view.

He looked back at her. "You know you didn't deserve any of that..."

She nodded.

"No, really," he continued. "I feel like you don't know how smart and sweet and confident you are."

She rolled her eyes. "I'm not confident."

"Are you kidding me? You put your creativity out there in the world. Do you know how long it took me to even let people see some of my stuff? I mean, *Blaine's Lanes*, for one thing, was like something I've been wanting to do for years."

She nodded slowly. Bo stared into space, thinking about everything.

"That piece of shit," he finally said, his knee bouncing uncontrollably. "He wanted you to believe you were worthless. But that couldn't be further from the truth."

She sucked on her bottom lip and her eyes started to mist.

"Will you at least get a restraining order on the guy?" Bo continued. "He's stalking you. I'm your witness."

"Yeah, but how can I prove he's stalking me? He was at a coffee shop and I don't even know if he saw me."

Bo shook his head. "Okay then, I need you to give me his address."

"Are you serious? To do what?"

"I'll figure that out when I get there."

She shook her head. "And risk you going to jail or something worse? No way."

He started popping his knuckles and sat back to attempt to

relax. Winter leaned against him and he put his arm around her.

"It's okay, Bo."

"Yeah?"

"Yeah."

She nuzzled in the crook of his neck and a calmness washed over him.

"I have a meeting in an hour for the Lanes' Halloween party. I really have to be there so—please promise me you'll stay here until I get back and we can figure out what to do. I don't want you being alone, especially at your house."

She put her hand on his and his muscles slackened. Then she lightly kissed his neck and he almost melted into the cushions.

"Just..." He closed his eyes. "Just please...stay here, okay? I'll be back in a few hours. There's cameras here and security."

"And the concierge manager?" She lifted her head up and smiled.

He made sure not to smile back though he really wanted to. "I'm just saying, you'll be safe here."

She nodded. "The kittens will keep me company."

"Okay, good."

He slowly pulled his arm back from around her to reach the remote, and pushed a button, summoning the ceiling projector.

"Fancy," Winter said.

"So, you can watch Netflix, use any of the other apps, go on the internet, whatever, using this remote. And if you need a laptop, it's in my office. Oh, and the wifi info is written on a piece of paper in one of the kitchen drawers."

"You really know how to host somebody."

"Oh, and if you wanna take a shower, make sure to use the one in my bedroom. It's a lot bigger than the others. If you need anything just call the concier—the front desk."

"A few hours?"

"I promise. It'll only be a few hours. I have a meeting and then I have to show Jeremiah his work room."

"Wait…*Mia's* Jeremiah?"

"Yeah. I didn't tell you? He's working for me full time now."

"That's wonderful, Bo," she beamed. "I love that kid."

"He's an alright dude. And damn talented."

"He's so good. Can't even put into words how much he's helped me and Mia with our posts and with building our brands."

"Well, I'm really happy to be working with him." He stood up, admired her for a few moments, and then said, "I'm gonna take a shower. I'd ask you to join me but then I'd never leave."

She put her legs back up on the ottoman and he had to turn away quickly before he saw too much. *This girl*, he thought.

After his shower, the kittens were curled up again like the yin-yang symbol on the cushion next to Winter, who was watching *Ex Machina* with a blanket over her legs…*thank you, lord.*

"Damn, talk about a terrifying glimpse into the future of A.I.," he said, looking at the screen.

Winter was seemingly startled out of a trance and paused the movie. She sprung up, wrapping the blanket around her waist. *Oh, thank you*, he thought. Elmira opened her eyes for a second to see what the fuss was about, then closed them.

"Have fun at work," Winter said, in good spirits.

"I can't wait to see you again."

He caressed her cheek. They kissed, softly, closed mouth. Bo knew if her tongue felt his, he wouldn't be strong enough to leave. And kissing her then…it was different—tender and earnest, but also…*absolute*—as if a difficult math equation had just been deciphered between them. And a strange sense of relief settled inside him that he'd never felt in his whole life.

CHAPTER TWENTY-FIVE

Winter sat down in a daze.

"Wow." She mouthed the words but didn't make a sound.

The feeling was so foreign to her. She'd heard about it, read about it, but it never really clicked inside her until that very moment. Like many times before, she was dizzy, but for once it felt...good. She was floating, vibrating. She felt both a lightness and heaviness in her chest. And the taste of him lingered on her lips. She remembered his genuine smile as he left out the front door, and it brought on that magical, tingly chill that she'd only previously gotten when she heard really good music or watched a compelling part of a movie or TV show. She once read that those special tingles occur when one's brain is flushed with dopamine for whatever reason, but she couldn't help but think it was caused by something deeper. Something not so scientific. Something spiritual. She grabbed a throw pillow to bury her face in. She felt like a hormonal schoolgirl whose crush just asked her to prom. *Where did he come from?* she screamed inwardly to whomever would listen.

Her movements inadvertently woke up the kittens, causing Elmira to lethargically walk to the very end of the sofa and sit against the armrest. Edgar, however, sniffed the throw blanket before climbing onto the warm lap underneath it. Winter pet the kitten and scratched his chin and he thanked her with a loud purr and three, short, squeak-meows before turning himself into a mini loaf and closing his eyes. With a slow reach and maneuver as to not disturb the ball of fluff, she got the remote in her hand and started the film up again.

Possibly due to the fact that Winter had seen *Ex Machina* at least three times, her mind wandered. After wandering far enough, she came to a wonderful and satisfying conclusion: Bo was absolutely, unequivocally, *nothing* like Lyle. Had her ex-boyfriend ever comforted her when she cried? Had he ever asked if she was okay? Understood what she was saying even when her words didn't come out right? Did he ever look at her with any semblance of compassion? Sleep in the same bed with her without expecting something in return? *Nope. Nope. No. Nah. And heck no.*

Her phone vibrated on the end table and when she picked it up her heart sank: The battery flashed red and a prompt told her she was an idiot for not bringing a charger in her purse. It didn't actually say that, but it definitely implied it. The prompt closed, revealing Mia's fluttering glider butterfly gif. Winter quickly—yet gently—moved Edgar to the sofa, then answered the video call.

Mia appeared on the screen, her red hair French braided into two pigtails. Her makeup was more toned-down than usual, except for the crimson lipstick.

"Well, hello!" Winter said.

"Biiiitch! I missed you."

"How was the trip?"

Winter remembered the battery level and began looking around the apartment for a rogue Apple charger.

"Oh, my gahhh!" Mia said excitedly. "It was so fun but also a nightmare because I accidentally lost the car keys right before the shoot and Jeremiah blamed me."

"Wait, but you just said you lost the keys."

"Really, Winter? You're taking his side?"

Winter laughed. She spotted a charger in the master bedroom and sat down. *"Just a sec, Mia."*

Winter plugged the phone in and sat down on Bo's bed, putting two pillows against the headboard to prop her up.

"Wait what?" Mia squinted. "Where are you?"

Winter took a deep breath. "I don't know if I want to tell you."

"Are you at a guy's house?"

"Maybe." Winter squeezed her eyes closed.

"Oh, my God! Who is it? Do I know him?"

Winter opened her eyes and smiled slightly. "I…stayed the night at…Bo's."

She pulled the phone away expecting a loud shriek or even a cackle, but Mia didn't reply. She just sat there on the phone screen, blank-faced and unblinking.

"Mia?" Winter continued. "Did you hear me? I stayed at Bo's. There was no hanky-panky but we did make out and talk and stuff."

After a few more seconds, Mia fanned her face as if she were about to cry. "I just…can't believe it. I can't believe my plan worked."

"Yeah. Well—"

Mia's voice wavered. "I knew there was a glow about you

—in your face and in your voice and—oh, my God. You deserve to be happy. And your whole aura changes around him. In a positive way…"

Winter said softly, "Thank you, Mi."

"So, I'm assuming the animal shelter gig went well?"

"Oh, yeah. It was amazing. I met this girl Camilla there, she's a singer and she's really cool. I think you'll love her."

"Shit, yeah. Hey, invite her to Bo's Halloween party."

"You're going to that?"

"Well, duh. Jeremiah's working for him now and I'm going to take advantage of any and every perk he gets. And you're going too."

"Okay, I'll go."

"I can't freakin' believe my plan worked. Sorry not sorry about that by the way.

"I forgive you…" Winter readjusted a pillow. "Oh, I have so much to tell you. The Lake Oswego Rescue burned down and—"

"I heard about that on the news. It was so sad."

"I know, but we worked all day to help and we were able to get so many of the animals homes."

"Oh, I'm so glad. Jeremiah is lucky I wasn't there. I would have probably adopted half the place myself."

"And Bo and I got paired together in the beginning, to wash the cages. And that's how we kind of got to know each other."

"Winter, sorry in advance, but I'm about to be extremely pushy and annoying."

"Oh…um, go ahead."

"So, I can tell you're giving me the condensed version. I want you to tell me every detail—down to every word you exchanged and the cologne he was wearing. So, how about you tell it all to me at once, when we shoot the video?"

"What video?"

"What do you mean?" Mia put the phone an inch from her face. "We have the Gym Cloak stuff to shoot today, remember?"

"Oh, sh—" Winter put down the phone for a second.

"What the hell?" Mia's voice was muffled by the bed.

Winter slowly brought the phone back up. "I completely forgot."

"Damn, I knew I should have reminded you…" Mia put her phone on something as a makeshift tripod so she could use her hands to pluck her eyebrows using a compact mirror. "Well, you still have time," she added.

"I don't have the outfit with me."

"Then stop at your house on the way."

"I promised Bo I'd stay here."

Mia stopped plucking. "Huh?"

"I'll explain later."

"Okay then, get your toned behind to the gym, pronto. I'll be there in about twenty minutes, but I'll wait for you…" She smiled. "Maybe."

Winter thought about it. "Okay, I'm sure he'll understand," she finally said.

"Huh?" Mia said again.

"Nothing. I'll see you soon. Bye."

As Winter was hanging up, she heard Mia say, "Care Bear Stare to you, my friend."

Winter sprawled herself out on Bo's bed and could faintly smell the mouthwatering citrus, vanilla, and amber scented product he used in his hair. Then she realized Sarah, *the concierge manager*, had taken a nap in or on the blanket and it gave her a spurt of energy to gather her stuff and go.

She got dressed in last night's outfit, made the guest room bed, found her keys on the kitchen counter, grabbed a can of nitrogen infused coffee from the fridge, remembered to say goodbye to the kittens—consisting only of her petting them (*Gee, cats sleep a lot,* she realized)—turned the lights down, and lost momentum when she remembered she was going to have to do her makeup when she got home.

Before she shut the door and rendered herself officially locked out, she tried calling Bo, but it went straight to voicemail. On her fourth and final try, she left a short voicemail telling him how much fun she had with him and how she forgot about this workout clothing advertisement thing she had to do with Mia and how she would be fine since she'd be hanging with a friend all day and how the kittens were cute and still sleeping…

…and how she hoped she'd be seeing him again really, really soon.

CHAPTER TWENTY-SIX

Bo readjusted his scarf as he leaned on the railing. He didn't usually take public transportation, but he knew the *B. Lane* parking lot was going to be a nightmare; the rental companies, all the staff, and the caterers were all scheduled to be there in the early afternoon. Bo hadn't ridden the aerial tram since the city voted to build a second one, in order to minimize the increasing tourist traffic cluttering up the OHSU and VA line intended for local workers, students, and patients. Though Bo's family had helped fund the second aerial tram, and despite Bo building his business around it, he preferred to drive or be driven up the hill just in case he needed a quick exit. For what? He didn't know. Maybe he had a sixth sense that Mt. Hood would erupt while he was at work and he'd be able to drive faster than the lava? That beautiful, menacing mountain was only around 100 miles from Portland, after all.

There were a few touristy gawkers standing next to him, pointing at "cool" looking houses. A man with his whole family—who looked like he could headline the Dad Jokes

World Tour—gave Bo a courtesy smile, and for some reason that compelled Bo to smile back and look out the window as to not ruin the family's fun. His mind wouldn't let his eyes focus on the scenery below, however. All he could see were vibrant hues of greens, grays, yellows, oranges, reds, and browns, all running together like rain on a chalk drawing. *There has to be a catch,* he thought. *Winter's just too interesting, too gorgeous, too talented, too...too. There has to be a catch.*

"Hey, man," said a voice from across the tram. "It's me, Tate."

Bo turned around to see the cabin operator—a massive unit of muscle that stood about 6'4", with long black hair tied back, and arms full of tribal tattoos.

"Oh, shit. Hey, man! It's so weird to see you out of—"

Bo stopped himself when he realized Mr. Dad Jokes had pointed at something out the window and made some inaudible dad joke to his family. The guy's wife playfully hit him in the arm and his two kids chorused a groan.

"Out of jail?" Tate said, loudly, then laughed. "I never thought I'd get out of there either."

Bo and Tate bro-hugged it out.

"What are you doing back in Portland?" asked Bo. "I thought you said you were moving back to the reservation in Washington."

"You know what? I finally realized I had to change things. I stayed here and went to this rehab and lived in this house, man, and they got me a job."

"That's amazing news. I was kinda worried when you stopped emailing me."

"Oh, yeah, fuck man. They wanted me to stop talking to

anyone connected to that old life, but man. You were the purest man I knew. Real talk."

"Well, pure isn't how I'd describe myself."

"I just mean you're a good man. Didn't have a bad bone in your body. Just some anger but only for shit that made sense, you know? Like your douche of a dad. For a while, I wanted to get out just to beat his ass."

Bo couldn't help but laugh. "You never told me that."

Tate walked back to his post and Bo followed.

"It's all good now," said Tate. "I'm a changed man."

A woman in the corner looked up from her book and Tate smiled and tilted an invisible hat to her. She looked away.

"Well, I'm proud of you," said Bo. "That dragon is hard to kick."

"Tell me about it. They got me on this Buprenorphine stuff and it took me forever just to wean off that. But I did it, man."

Bo gave him a congratulatory fist bump, and seconds later, Tate had to man his station. Buttons were pushed, a lever was pulled, and the tram jerked to a stop. The doors opened and the commuters started exiting. Bo noticed there was a long line of people on the other side waiting to get on.

"Thank you for driving the sky bus for us," said a little girl holding the hand of her mother as they passed Tate.

"Well…" Tate cleared his throat. "You're very welcome." He bowed his head then looked at Bo once everyone had stepped off the tram. "See, *that's* why I do this shit."

"Hey, man, stop at *Blane's Lanes* down the street anytime —maybe during one of your breaks? I'm pretty sure I sent my phone to your email. You know what, just in case I'll send it again. Call or email me anytime… I owe you so much."

Tate shook his head.

"Yes, I do," insisted Bo. "You taught me a lot of shit about the world, man. Like, street smart shit."

"Man, whatever." Tate smiled.

He pushed a button and the other door opened. A fresh batch of commuters walked on and Bo hurried out the exit before getting swallowed up.

"Good to see you, man!" shouted Tate. "I'll contact your pure ass!"

A cluster of old ladies with giant purses gave Bo a dirty look—as if he were the one who said it!—just as both sides of the aerial tram closed. He chuckled and felt one drop of rain hit his nose. Above him, a fluffy gray cloud crept toward the sun. He put on his hoodie and trekked toward work.

Just as he thought, *Lanes* was in a chaotic disarray. He greeted the rental company workers while they unloaded stage pieces, he answered questions from both front of house security guards, and helped staff pull in boxes of Halloween decorations before the boxes succumbed to the usual Oregon weather. Bo couldn't take it anymore; he had to call Winter. He finally found a second to duck into his office, shutting the door and blinds behind him. He sat down and put his feet up on the desk, savoring the minuscule amount of minutes he would probably have alone, and took out his phone.

"What the—?" he mumbled, realizing Winter had tried to call him four times. *Four times!*

His pulse quickened and he jumped up, pacing back and forth as he listened to her message. *Why the fuck did I leave her at home? Why didn't I just have her come with me to work?* He tried calling her over and over, but it repeatedly went to voicemail. He was so mad at himself he didn't know what to say, so he just kept hanging up.

A knock on the door distracted him from his self-scolding, and Jeremiah slowly opened the door.

"Well, well, well," said Jeremiah. "What's up, boss?"

"Oh, you don't need to call me that," Bo said, too worried to even fake a smile.

"Okay then, how about I call you Bo for short?" Jeremiah laughed, but stopped when he realized it wasn't reciprocated. "Everything cool?"

Despite the room being *cold as shit*, a band of sweat formed on Bo's forehead.

"Yeah, man." Bo sat on the edge of his desk. "I think I need to go."

"Oh, sh—something happen? Can I help?"

Bo thought for a second. "Actually, yeah. I can't get a hold of Winter. Could you call Mia and—"

"Oh, yeah, dude! Mia just told me Winter slept over at your place. Good for you man. Good for you."

"Damn, word gets around fast doesn't it?"

Jeremiah shrugged and pulled out his phone. "Girls, man. You know, they can sometimes be a gossiping succubus."

"Um…"

Jeremiah put it on video mode and Mia answered on the first ring.

"What?" she whined.

"Hey, babe, have you seen Winter yet? Bo wants to talk to her."

"No, but she's on her way. Is everything okay? I thought they were still in the smitten faze?"

"Oh, yeah. I think so," Jeremiah replied.

"Hey, Mia," said Bo. "I'm a little worried about her so can you please have her call me?"

"Yeah, we're about to shoot our workout videos. No thanks to Jeremiah, but I guess he has better places to be."

"Yeah, like my new job," Jeremiah said incredulously.

"So, what's going on, Bo?" Mia asked.

Bo stared into space.

"Bo? Jeremiah, is he still there?" she continued. "I don't see him in frame."

"Yeah, he's still here," Jeremiah answered.

Bo got in frame. "We saw her ex last night and I just—I don't think she should be alone."

"You saw Lyle? Where?"

"Multnomah Village."

"What the hell? Man, that guy's such an ass. A freakin' succubus in the flesh, or would he be an incubus?"

Jeremiah's eyes widened and he mouthed the word "freaky" to Bo, who nodded in agreement. Yet, Bo didn't know if Jeremiah was reacting to his girlfriend's word choice or the fact that Lyle was in town.

"I think he's dangerous," Bo said. "I just don't want her alone—"

"But Bo, she's a grown woman who can definitely fend for herself. I mean, she left him, didn't she?"

He sighed. "Yeah."

"I really don't think there's anything to worry about. He didn't take their breakup very well, but it was mostly just, you know, him firing her and then making some vulgar comments on her posts and stuff. But that's about the extent of it. For the most part, he's been kind of laying low, keeping his distance."

"Until last night," Bo said. "But I guess there's a chance it could have been a coincidence."

"Um, yes. I'm *sure* it was just a coincidence," Mia said firmly, and her conviction made Bo feel better.

Bo crossed his arms and looked over at Jeremiah, who gave a half-hearted, tightlipped smile of support.

There was a short hard knock on the door and a split second later it swung open. One of the bar managers ran in, frantic. "Bo, the walk-in fridge isn't working. Just went kaput."

"Is Lori here yet?" Bo asked.

"No, she's here tomorrow. I'm the only manager on today for load-in but there's no way we'll be able to fit everything in the back fridge."

Bo stood up. "Okay, if there's any perishable food that we can't fit in there, please have the staff fill buckets with ice and —and put the food in there until I can get someone out to work on the walk-in and—"

"Want me to help?" Jeremiah asked.

"That'd be great," Bo answered. "Then we can go over some stuff to post—"

"Oh, I already posted videos and flyers and in thirty minutes…" Jeremiah looked at his watch. "…the newsletter's gonna be sent out."

"You're fucking awesome," Bo said.

"Okay, then!" shouted Mia through the phone. "I'll have Winter call you. And I'll see you at the Halloween party."

"If we have one," said Bo.

"Very funny," she replied. "I already picked out my Halloween costume. So you're having a party, one way or another."

"Succubus." Jeremiah coughed.

"Incubus," Mia retorted.

Jeremiah hung up the phone before she could say anything else.

"Are you and Mia doing okay?" Bo asked as they all walked out the door.

"Oh, yeah," said Jeremiah, genuinely confused. "Why do you ask?"

CHAPTER TWENTY-SEVEN

Winter waded through her closet, searching for a blue and pink and white speckled, mid-rise workout pant, and a white mesh, long sleeved workout top with a heart shaped cutout on the back. *I really need to get more organized*, she decided. This happened whenever she had a sponsored post to shoot months after she received the product. She'd stow it somewhere for safe keeping, then forget where that safe place was.

Mia called her two times in ten minutes to tell her to "hurry it up, girl," but Winter didn't let it stress her out. She was still high off of her magical night with Bo. She saw his face, could hear his encouraging words, remembered what he felt like, smelled like… Oh, and the warmth she felt in his arms. The safeness she felt. It was like he was in every crevice of her. Every molecule. He just moved in. Pitched a storm proof tent. Claimed land. And she welcomed it. Yes, she knew thinking about him so much was hindering her searching skills, was slowing her down like trying to run through molasses. But she couldn't stop. She was addicted to her new heart inhabitant. She felt…happy…and… alive...knowing that he wanted to see her again.

"Yes!"

Winter spotted her workout clothes, perfectly folded under her bed. At the same time, she noticed Mia was calling…again. She denied the call, texted Mia that she had just found her outfit and would be out the door in two minutes —adding three heart emojis as an apology—then silenced her phone and threw it in a small gym bag, along with a charger, an unopened water bottle, a protein bar, and a small baggy full of almonds. She quickly put on the outfit. Even quicker, she put her hair in a high ponytail. And as fast as humanly possible, she touched up her makeup. She heard a car door slam shut and wondered why her neighbors were home during their work hours.

She peeked out the window and the world looked like it had been filtered with the gray hued, low brightness, high contrast filter theme pack she used for some of her more moody posts. And of course, it was raining. Not hard, but enough where she would need both a hood and a beanie to combat her hair's affinity for frizz.

She zipped up her black-lined, transparent, button-up raincoat, grabbed a pink beanie from her dresser drawer, turned around and a man stood in the doorway. He wore a green, Oregon Ducks Nike baseball hat pulled low and a black scarf wrapped around the lower half of his face.

She screamed and backed up until she couldn't back up anymore. The man took a few steps closer and unraveled his disguise—it took a few long seconds for her eyes to relay to her brain that it was Lyle. He still had a crew cut but it looked like he had tried to shave his beard in a hurry, leaving random patches. She tried to control her trembling by clasping her hands together.

"What are you doing here, Lyle?" she asked flatly.

"I wanted to talk to you," he said gently.

She moved down the wall, but for every step she took away, he stepped closer, holding up his hands as if to show he wasn't holding a weapon.

"How'd you get in here?" she asked, without accusation in her tone.

"Oh, that's not important. You wouldn't talk to me and this was my last resort." He exaggeratingly shook his head. "Oh, God, you look so good."

"I think you should leave, Lyle." Her voice started shaking and she fought back tears.

"Winter, I'm not going to hurt you. I stopped drinking and I've had time to think about things—like how I took you for granted. I was such an idiot. Your mom helped me work out what went wrong—"

"You've been talking to my mother? Since when?"

"Just the last couple months. I think. I don't know, Winter. But I want to—Winter—" He laughed. "Can we please sit down and talk? I'll leave right after…from your life…forever if you want."

She shook her head.

"Come on," he insisted. "Let's talk for a few minutes. Then I'll leave, I promise." He looked at her with puppy dog eyes and put out his lip like a child. "Come on, Winnie. My therapist really encourages me to make amends with people."

"You're seeing a therapist?"

He smiled slightly. "Yeah. Who would have thunk it, right?"

They stood in her messy room surrounded by thick, fuzzy

silence. She was suddenly so cold, and the sensation of goose bumps formed on her arms, though when she pulled her sleeves back a little to investigate, her skin was unblemished.

"Winter? Hello?"

"Okay," she finally said so quietly, as if she didn't even want herself to hear it.

She followed his lead, which brought them to the living room sofa. He sat at one end and she at the other, and he angled himself toward her, but she refused to do the same, tucking her hands underneath her legs.

He swallowed and seemed to consider his words before he said them, something he rarely did when they were a couple.

"You're so special, Winter. I took advantage of you. I didn't treat you with the respect you deserved. I'm truly sorry. I was so lost when you left me. And I had no right to take away your job *just* because I was hurt. We both knew how to push one another's buttons and I took it too far sometimes." He held out his hand for a few seconds then put it down when he realized she wasn't going to take it. "Do you believe that I'm truly sorry?"

"I don't know."

"Okay, I understand."

Her eyes filled with water and she turned her head so he wouldn't see. "You should leave."

His knee started to bounce. "Winter, I—"

"No!" She wiped away tears and sat up straight. "You know how many times I've heard you say 'sorry' and other crap like that? I'm not falling for it again. I hope you really did get a therapist and stopped drinking because you used to be a very, very bad person, and leaving you was the best thing I did for my life."

He put his cap back on and after a while, stood up. "I'm

sorry you feel that way." He turned to leave then turned back around. "If you want your job again, just let me know. The team misses you. I'm working in Washington now so you wouldn't even see me that often."

"Thanks, but I have a job."

"What kind of job?"

"Social media."

He laughed. "Come on, Winter. That's not a job."

"Actually, it is," she snapped.

"Winnie. Winnie. You don't have to prove to anyone that you're pretty. It's something that brings you attention, I understand that. But it's not a career."

Winter's brows furrowed and he almost seemed amused by her expression.

"Winnie, you have changed. It's a little scary."

"What?"

"It's just—look at you, you look like a little bull ready to charge." He smirked. "You never used to be preoccupied by this vapid, shallow, soul-sucking, social media stuff."

"I used to have my cell phone taken away from me every other second by some…insecure asshat." She fumed.

He stumbled back, feigning shock. "It's like I'm not even talking to the same person anymore."

"Maybe I finally developed a backbone."

She heard him stifle a chuckle. "It's cute… But the job offer still stands. The firm would love you back. And hopefully one day you can find it in your heart to forgive me."

He took something out of his pocket—a key. He held it up briefly before hanging it up on the wall key rack. "Your mom let me borrow hers a while ago."

Fuming.

"But I don't think it is right for me to have it anymore," he continued. "I'm so sorry. Just…please consider letting me take you out sometime. I'll prove to you—"

"Nope. Not gonna happen."

He looked at her silently for a couple seconds, then left, carefully making sure not to slam the door.

Winter let out a long sigh and forced herself to get up and secure the locks. She discreetly looked out the window, and watched his car leave and disappear around the corner. She fixed her makeup again, then grabbed her gym bag. On her way out, she looked at the key he left and didn't recognize it —it was newer and a shade lighter than the copy she gave her mother.

She wanted to run to her mother's, but she knew Mia would never forgive her—even more than the sponsor money, she didn't want to leave her friend in the lurch. She couldn't believe she stood up to him. Since they had broken up, she felt a forbidding shadow following her, like she was waiting for something horrible to happen… He seemed different too. He wasn't drunk. He spoke to her with, well, with a lot more respect. And she was able to break away from his manipulative tactics. A weight had been lifted from her shoulders and she wished Bo could have been there to witness her newfound courage.

The rain fell harder, and she ran to her car, barely seeing a soaking wet note taped to the driver side window. Sitting in her car, it took her a while to decipher the words.

Paraphrased, it read:

Save me a dance at Blaine's Lanes' Halloween bash. We belong together. By the way, you and Bo Blaine had a lot of fun saving those poor animals, right? Believe me, he is not who he says he is. When it comes to bad, bad people, I'll show you that he's way worse than I ever was. I have proof, Winter. Just don't tell him because he is dangerous. I still love you, Winnie. Please believe me. Remember the good times we had. And I promise I'll make up for everything else.

CHAPTER TWENTY-EIGHT

"Man, you sure you want to get that much touched up? It's gonna hurt like a bitch, especially this one…"

Craig pointed to a large tattoo mimicking Vincent Van Gogh's *A Starry Night* on Bo's lower abdomen.

"I don't mind," Bo answered. "I'll pay you extra."

"Oh, no that's cool, man…" Craig adjusted his black and red flannelled Irish cap with the back of his arm. "Fuck, you know what, actually, yeah, that'd be awesome. Just think of it as socialism...share the wealth, and shit."

A familiar classical piece started playing through the speakers, except it was remixed to an electronic dance beat.

Bo chuckled. "Mozart must be rolling on MDMA and moshing in his grave right now."

"Huh?" Craig looked confused before it sunk in. "Oh, yeah. I have that on my iPod, you know, ironically, and shit."

"I get it, man."

Craig turned on the tattoo gun and that familiar buzz comforted Bo. He closed his eyes, smelling the aroma of stale air, Green Soap, and disinfectant.

After a few minutes he heard the doorbell chime, and a burst of cold air slapped his chest. His whole stomach area was numb, and it almost made him angry that it wasn't hurting more. His trips to the tattoo parlor were cathartic for him. A place he could meditate. A place he could punish himself for whatever it was he had fucked up. What was unusual about that particular visit to the parlor was that Bo had absolutely no idea *how* he fucked up.

He had called Winter when he got off work Monday, and she didn't answer. When he got home, called and texted her, she didn't answer or reply. He realized Winter and Mia were shooting their videos, so he sat in a chair, outside on his master bedroom balcony, and waited. The kittens sat on the other side of the sliding glass window, and they all stared at the mini waterfall pouring off of the awning.

He thought of Winter's beautiful smile. He thought of holding Winter again. Making love to her. *Damn that escalated quickly*, he thought, and went inside to cool off, despite it being about forty-two degrees outside.

He watched a few episodes of *The Office* until he heard a light knock on the door.

"It's Sarah."

"I don't think you should come in," Bo said.

"I just want to tell you something. I don't have to come in."

Bo opened the door just enough to see a sliver of her face. She sighed.

"Bo, I'm so sorry. I guess…" She looked away for a second. "I guess I didn't realize I kind of…like you."

He opened the door a little wider. "What?"

"I got jealous and I wasn't lying when I said I was high and a little buzzed."

"I understand, Sarah. I'll talk to you later."

He tried shutting the door, but she put her foot in to stop it.

"Bo…I have to tell you something."

He begrudgingly waved for her to come in and closed the door. She nervously sat down at a chair and he stood, arms crossed.

"Okay, what is it?" he asked.

She took a moment, then looked up at him, shamefaced. "I did some research to try and find her ex. You know, I was just curious… And I found him and messaged him. Asking about Winter and stuff…"

"Well, that's weird, but go on."

"So we've been talking a little and it just came out that that, well—I told him you and Winter were dating."

Bo clasped his hands behind his neck. "Wh—why? Why did you feel the need to tell him that?"

"Like I said, it just came out. He seemed like an okay guy once I got talking to him. He insisted every rumor was false and—"

"That's bullshit. He's scum."

"But how do you know?"

"Because Winter told me."

"Yeah, but what if she was lying?"

He shook his head. "Nope. Winter told me and I trust her."

She threw up her hands. "Okay."

"Thanks for telling me, Sarah, but I hope from now on you'll stay out of my business."

"But he was going to find out you two were dating eventually," she said. "I just, jumped the gun."

"Oh, then, I guess I should be thanking you," he said

sarcastically.

She stood up. "You look very handsome today."

"Sarah, I'm sorry if I led you on but," he shook his head, "I—"

"I get it," she went to the door and didn't look back. "Goodbye, Bo."

Bo had waited until nightfall, getting some work done in his office, ordering special cat treats and cat toys online, eating dinner, when Winter finally called back. She said the shoot with Mia went well and she was excited about the Halloween party, but something sounded…off. Like she wanted to tell him something, each word loaded with uncertainty.

"Can I see you?" Bo asked.

"Um, I'm a little busy…with some stuff."

"Are you home alone? Because—"

"Actually, I'm staying at Camilla's house. So I'll be fine. I'll think about what to do about Lyle."

"Oh…okay. Say hi to Cam for me. Hey, you can invite her to the party too."

"Thanks." She laughed softly. "I already did."

He laughed then they both went silent. It felt like he just rode a fun water slide that ended off a cliff.

"Winter…" he finally said. "I miss you already."

She responded an excruciating five seconds later. "I'll see you soon, Bo."

She said those last words so cordially, it might as well had been a razor sharp spiked handshake. Then she hung up and he just sat there. *Dumbfounded.*

"What the fuck?"

That night, he suffered through one of the worst invasive-thoughts episodes. He contemplated calling Sarah. Contemplated calling another girl in his phone. But knew he'd never go through with it. Winter was doing it again. Pushing him away. Convincing herself that he was the enemy. Why couldn't she accept that he wanted to keep her safe? What was she thinking now? Will he see her again? Could she be lying about Lyle? *Of course not! I can't believe I would even entertain the idea!*

What if Lyle got to her again? What if she's not really over at Camilla's, but actually at that sack of— What if they're having sex? What if he's hurting her? He got as far as putting his coat on before he realized he didn't know Camilla's address. He looked on every social media platform, but she didn't have her last name listed. He was about to message her to ask what her address was but thought better of it. *Winter has every right to stay anywhere she wants without some random person showing up and trying to tell her what to do. Shiiiiiit!*

When he woke up the next day to no messages from Winter, he logged onto *Nanogram* while he ate breakfast, and the first post was Winter and Mia working out. In each post, the girls looked like they were having fun, but again, something in Winter was off-kilter. He knew he didn't know Winter for that long, but they had shared intense, intimate moments with each other. He knew when that spark in her eyes dimmed. Wanting to distract himself from his own thoughts, after breakfast he went straight to the tattoo parlor. After all, the party was the next day and Bo was due for some relaxation...and soul soothing pain.

CHAPTER TWENTY-NINE

"Okay, I'm almost done," Winter said.

Camilla shifted around in her seat. "Ah, I can't take it anymore. Just let me have one more bite."

Winter smiled. "But you just had one."

"Don't judge me!" Camilla said as she reached for a donut.

Winter pulled her eyeliner pencil out of the way and Camilla took a giant bite. She offered Winter a bite, who ate it without hesitation. Then she got right back to drawing black whiskers on Camilla.

"So, you gonna tell me what's going on?" asked Camilla.

"Please don't move, or I'll have to start over. And, um… I don't know—"

"You know what? If you don't tell me, I aint gonna go with you to the party."

Winter rolled her eyes. "Mmmhmm."

"I won't."

"You'd do that to me?"

"Uh-huh."

"Nuh-uh."

Camilla cleared her throat. "Uuuuhhh-huhhhhhh," she sang with her usual beautiful tone.

Winter stopped what she was doing. "Oh, my God, Cam, you know I can't resist that voice."

"Just tell me…." Camilla blinked her eyes rapidly. "Purrrty please."

"Did I tell you I can't wait to meet your son?"

"I get him next week. And I'm sure he'll love you. And yada yada yada, you've said that a million times. Stop changing the subject, buenona."

Winter finished the last whisker, then put a yellow tabby cat ears on Camilla. "Okay, we're done. You look adorable."

Winter tightened the tie on her plush white robe and sat back in the vanity chair.

Camilla turned around and looked in the mirror to analyze the cat inspired makeup. "I look aight…so if anyone asks, I'm some famous movie cat, right? What's my name again?"

"Cat."

"I know, but what's my name. If anyone asks, y'know?"

"That's the cat's name. Cat, from *Breakfast at Tiffany's*."

"You gonna get ready?" Camilla grabbed another donut and went over to her closet.

"Uh, in a sec. Thanks for doing this. I was gonna hold a stuffed animal cat but you're much better."

"Yup." Camilla's mouth was full. "Okay, I think I have a yellow sweater here somewhere…and is it cool if I wear blue jeans?"

"Yeah, that's fine. Hashtag catcasual."

"Oh God."

"I apologize for that."

"Hell, yeah. Gotcha!"

Camilla pulled a sweatshirt from under a pile of clothes and shook the wrinkles out. She put the sweater over the white t-shirt she was already wearing and changed into jeans. Then she plopped down on her bed, exhausted. "Spill it, girl. I can tell something's wrong and maybe I can help."

"Oh, it's just—guy problems."

"Try me."

Winter sighed. "To summarize…my ex showed up and warned me about Bo."

"About Bo? The softie?"

"I know. I shouldn't be even listening to Lyle—that asshole."

"Damn, didn't know you had such a filthy mouth." Camilla laughed. "So what did he say?"

"He said he'd show me some kind of proof tonight."

Camilla perked up. "Wait? So this party's not gonna be boring after all?"

Winter rolled her eyes. "I hope it is…I don't know, maybe I shouldn't even go."

"Oh, we're going."

Winter pulled her chair closer to the mirror. She brushed her hair briefly, before styling her hair in a low, half ponytail. "Thanks for letting me stay here for a few days."

"Anytime. You ready to tell me what *else* is going on?"

"Um…I'll…"

"It's okay. When you're ready."

"Thank you," Winter said softly.

Camilla reclined against a giant body pillow and the headboard and immersed herself in her phone.

Winter put on a lacy bra and panty set, rummaged through her suitcase, and pulled out an oversized, white, Tuxedo-style, buttoned up, night shirt. She slipped it on and just like Holly

Golightly in the *Breakfast At Tiffany's* sleep scene, it fell almost to her knees. Underneath, she wore teal high waisted booty shorts, just in case she had a Marilyn-standing-over-the-subway-vent moment. And since it would be cold outside, she wore Tiffany blue, knee-high socks and black loafers. She then positioned up on her forehead, a gold lined, Tiffany blue sleep mask with the closed eyes and eyelashes design. To top off the look, she put on blue and golden tassel earrings, to resemble Holly's earplugs. By the time Winter was done with her makeup, the sun had gone down, and Camilla was asleep again.

Winter tiptoed out to the living room and turned on her phone. She closed her eyes for a few moments before taking a look. She had received five calls and two messages from Mia asking her where she was and why she's not getting ready for the party with her; one call and one text from Jeremiah, asking her to call Mia; and one lone text from Bo that said he couldn't wait to see her again and that he thinks she'll like his costume. Her heart skipped a beat as she read his text, imagining his voice whispering the words in her ear instead. *Lyle's lying*, she thought. *Bo has a kind heart. There's not a bad bone in his body.*

She wanted to talk it all out with someone, anyone, but she didn't even know where to start. Mia knew that Winter and Lyle had a volatile relationship—heck, Mia hated him from the second she met him—but she didn't know the extent of it. Winter was always too scared to tell her. Too ashamed. She had thought, for so long, that if she were to say it out loud, then it would make it real. She never wanted it to be real.

Her new friend Camilla definitely didn't deserve to have Winter unload such heavy crap on top of her. And though she had only skimmed the surface, she was already regretting telling Bo, someone she had just started dating.

Then there was her mother, who Winter *did* confide in when Lyle had pushed her into a file cabinet in the back office, just for giving him the wrong file during a meeting. Winter asked her mother what she should do, and her dear mother said those comforting words, "Maybe you shouldn't have given him the wrong file, honey. You probably embarrassed him." After that, whenever Winter even hinted to her mother that Lyle had done something, her mother would rationalize it, sometimes even laughing it off. And he always knew how to talk to Cassandra—how to manipulate the situation to make her think that Winter was hard to deal with. She always took his side. Always.

Winter's cheeks burned with anger when she thought of her mom handing Lyle a key to her home, her mom thinking she knew what was best for her daughter, her mom thinking that Lyle was the only person capable of taming her stubborn offspring. Winter thought about it and vowed right then and there that she needed to cut Cassandra Smith out of her life. Her mom was comfortable being miserable and misery was contagious. Since there were no such vaccines, Winter would just have to stay away from the infected.

"Damn, what are you thinking about?" said a groggy Camilla. "You look so…intense."

"Oh, um. I'm just thinking about how much I hate my mom."

"Pfft," Camilla shuffled into the living room. "Welcome to the club. I can't even talk to my mom anymore. I'll say something and she'll railroad over me and just talk and talk. It's exhausting."

"Dang. Well, my mom's just a cold bitch."

"What has gotten into you, Winter?" Camilla looked shocked. She sat down next to Winter and held her hand. "I like this side of you, though. You're feisty and don't take no shit from anyone. You need to keep that attitude."

Winter smiled. "I think I will."

"So, you look amazing. You gonna change out of your nightgown?"

"No, this is Holly—"

"I'm just kidding. I looked up Holly Golightly."

"Yeah, I kind of had to adapt the costume to Oregon weather, but hey, I tried."

"Bo's gonna be drooling over you…but that's as per usual."

Bo's smile and green eyes flashed in Winter's mind and her heart warmed.

CHAPTER THIRTY

Bass vibrated Bo's soul as he studied his reflection in the mirror. His hair was styled into a tousled, just got out of coma look; he wore a buttoned up white shirt, tucked into black pants, and a long, black coat that looked like it was actually made in the 1800s. *Not bad*, he thought, as he pressed on Edgar Allen Poe's signature mustache above his upper lip. Even from his back office, he could smell the Mexican appetizers: most notably, the nachos, chicken fajitas, and spicy black bean enchiladas, which were specifically chosen to be paired with the event's Tequila and Margarita mix sponsors.

"Hey, man, mind if I go grab a plate before it gets crazy out there?" Jeremiah asked.

In the lounge area corner of the office, Jeremiah sat in a gray armchair with his legs crossed on a checkered gray and black ottoman. He wore blue jeans, Chuck Taylor shoes, and Johnny Lawrence's red Cobra Kai jacket with matching black Cobra Kai headband from 1984's *The Karate Kid* film. Mia lay on the couch next to him, typing into her phone. She wore a blonde, shoulder-length wig, curled and pinned up on one side, and black spandex pants. Bo noticed that she also wore one of those black crop tops with a Bardot Sweetheart neckline, a variant of the classic crop top shirt styles that his mother had used in her fashion line.

"Yeah. For sure," Bo replied, spiritlessly.

Jeremiah practically jumped up. "Dude, don't take this the wrong way, but you look fucking tight."

"Jer,' oh my God," said Mia. She put down her phone for a second and raised her eyebrows. "Damn, Bo. You do look tight."

"Hey, girl," Jeremiah said. "We're sharing a bro moment here."

Mia rolled her eyes and Bo took one last look at himself. "Guess I kind of do," Bo replied.

"Yeah." Mia sat up. "You look just like a hipster Charlie Chaplin."

Bo and Jeremiah looked at each other.

"Babe, he's Edgar Allen Poe. You know, *The Raven*, 'Nevermore' guy?" Jeremiah said as he walked over to the mirror behind Bo to readjust his wig.

"Same diff," she replied as she typed into her phone again. "Damnit, Winter just won't call me. The only thing I got to know she's alive was a SpongeBob gif that said, 'See you soon.' Wow, she's such a brat."

"Hey, that's more than I got. She just sent me a smiley face emoji," Bo said.

He walked over to his desk and sat down, swiveling the chair back and forth as he checked his phone.

"I'm gonna grab you something, Bo," Jeremiah said. "I haven't seen you eat all day."

"Thanks, man."

"What about me?" Mia whined.

Jeremiah turned around, confused. "I thought you said if you ate anything else your lard would rip the seams of your Sandy costume?"

"Babe, I was literally kidding. You were supposed to tell me that I don't have an ounce of lard on my whole body. It's a freaking test and you failed."

Jeremiah shook his head and went out the door. Moments later, he stuck his head back in to say, "You're beautiful baby and you don't have an ounce of lard on your body. Facts."

Bo couldn't help but smile and was thankful for the distraction. Mia played something on her phone and laughed.

"I should be mad, but she is just so damn cute," Mia said.

"Who?"

Mia grabbed her purse from under the table and pulled out a makeup bag.

"Look at your soulmate's latest post," she said before reapplying lipstick using a compact mirror.

Bo navigated to Winter's StyleSlap page on his phone and turned the volume up.

A bored looking Camilla, wearing cat ears and cat makeup, sat in a chair in front of a mirror. Winter walked into frame, wearing Holly Golightly's nightgown outfit from *Breakfast at Tiffany's*. She did her best impression of Holly as portrayed by Audrey Hepburn. She squinted, walked like she just got woken up from sleep, and held a cocktail glass in her hand. She twirled around so the camera could see her outfit… *Fuck, she's so gorgeous*, Bo thought. Over the short video, a sound snippet of the movie played, the one where Holly explains that she goes to Tiffany's when she gets a case of the "mean reds."

Bo watched it three times before setting his phone down.

"You really like her, huh?" Mia asked, staring at him.

He ran his hand through his hair and leaned back. "You could say that."

"Well, I'm not sure if you know this but she sometimes gets—how do I put this? Overwhelmed by certain things, like she'll freak herself out."

"Yeah. I've witnessed it."

"You have?"

"When we saw her ex at the coffee shop."

"I'm sure that's why she's been acting weird…or weirder." Mia shakes her head. "I didn't want to freak her out even more, but it *is* kind of odd that he was just in town, hanging out in Multnomah village of all places. What the frick was he doing there? God, he's such a prick."

"Yeah, he is. I'd love to get my hands on him."

Mia lit up. "Oh, yeah, what would you do?"

"I'd…I'd rip him a new one."

"And then what?"

"And I'd—I don't know," he said. "I'm not good at this."

Mia laughed and typed something fast into her phone.

Bo sighed. "He deserves to rot in prison. The way he treated her."

"That'd be awesome." Mia looked up from her phone. "Those mind games. And it didn't help that he's a lawyer. They're master manipulators. Some use it for good, some are douches like Lyle."

"Do you know if she ever documented any of the physical stuff?"

Mia tossed her phone down beside her. "What physical stuff?"

Bo opened his mouth to talk but stopped himself.

"Bo?" she added.

Jeremiah walked in holding two plates stacked to the brim. "It's starting to fill up out there so I put a velvet rope around the last alley for us."

"Thanks, man," Bo replied as Jeremiah set the plate in front of him.

"So, we're gonna share this one," Jeremiah told Mia, sitting the plate down on the coffee table in front of her. "You know, to curb the lard."

Mia ignored her boyfriend and looked at Bo piercingly. "Bo… Did that asshole physically abuse my other half?"

Bo started picking at his food. "Mia, I don't know if I was supposed to say anything."

"Bo!" Mia demanded.

"Okay, okay, yes. She said he hurt her all the time and—"

"Oh, my God," Mia said, over and over again. Her eyes filled with tears and she sprung up and ran to grab a tissue from a table across the room.

"Who hurt Winter?" Jeremiah asked with a mouth full of food.

"*Lyle*." Mia's nose already sounded stuffed up. "Why didn't she ever tell me?"

"Oh, shit," said Jeremiah.

"Great…" Mia patted each tear that escaped down her cheek. "Now I'm gonna have to put on my makeup all over again…I mean…why didn't she tell me? Her own flesh and blood?"

"You two are related?" Bo asked.

Jeremiah shook his head. Mia sat back down and typed again into her phone.

"Baby, she was probably just scared or embarrassed," Jeremiah said, his hand on her leg. "You know she loves you."

"And don't worry," Bo said, pointing his fork at the sky. "Lyle's gonna pay for what he did."

Mia sprung up again and walked over to Bo, holding out her pinky finger. "Promise?"

Bo took a second to realize what she wanted. He wrapped his pinky around hers and they shook on it.

CHAPTER THIRTY-ONE

Winter and Camilla walked arm in arm, following the music from the tram to the entrance of *Blaine's Lanes*. The place was packed, and Winter felt on edge knowing that Lyle could already be there.

They politely pushed their way through the crowd to the closest bar they could get to, and Camilla's drink-ordering voice somehow cut right through the heavy banter and deep bass coming from a new song by *The Weekend.*

Winter's much needed scan of the room was cut short by a young couple who told her they loved the Holly Golightly post, and wondered if they "could please get a selfie." She happily obliged and hoped her smile hid that spark of anxiety that was creeping up her spine since she walked through the door. *Why did I come here?* she thought. *I'm so freakin' stupid. Stupid. Stupid.*

"Vegan White Russian with Coconut milk!" Camilla shouted, holding up the glasses in the air so no one would knock into them. "And yes, I am describing my mom."

"Whoa, that sounds great," said Winter.

When they emerged from the bar crowd, Camilla handed Winter her glass, then noticed the line formed near the farthest bar. "Come on," she said. "They got food."

"Okay, but first I'll see if my friends are here," said Winter. "I want you to meet them."

"Already met Bo."

"I mean my friends Mia and Jeremiah."

"Well, maybe they're in the food line?"

Winter thought for a second. Shrugged. And Camilla yanked her so hard toward the mouthwatering fragrance of Mexican cuisine that both their glasses spilled a little.

They got to the back of the line and sipped their drinks, admiring and commenting on the décor. The waterfall had slowed to a small stream, pooling into a cloud of fog. Translucent ghosts floated in and out of the rocks, which Camilla and Winter deduced must be from some kind of hidden hologram machine.

The ceiling was covered in cobwebs, and a giant animatronic spider sat in a ceiling corner, watching the party with its eight eyes that moved back and forth, along with its eight twitchy legs. Orange lights twinkled throughout the room, framing the bars, wrapping around columns, and lining the bowling lanes. Carved pumpkins—big and small—were placed on almost every tabletop surface, a giant, color changing bone face hung behind the DJ, and cauldrons full of candy sat next to each entrance and exit door.

After taking in the spectacular surroundings, Camilla and Winter turned their fascination to the costume dedication of some of the guests: A zombie nun holding her own head like a football; Samus Aran in full exoskeleton from the *Metroid* games; a *very* voluptuous Jessica Rabbit; *Game of Thrones'* Daenerys Targaryen wearing a dragon backpack; Inspector Gadget with motorized helicopter hat; the twins from *The Shining*; a gaggle of ghosts; a blood soaked killer clown; a sexified version of Sandy from Spongebob Squarepants; and a giant loofah coupled with a giant bar of soap.

"Cinderella?" asked Camilla to a costumed woman that stepped in line behind them.

The woman turned around to reveal a tablet built into the back of her frilly, blue dress, displaying the login screen for the Tinder app.

"Tinderella?!" exclaimed Winter.

"You got it," said the woman.

In less than a minute, Tinderella and Camilla were talking about the most annoying dating app dates they experienced.

Winter stood on her tippy toes and looked around, spotting who she thought was Mia, but was just some girl in an Ariel costume from *The Little Mermaid.* She knew Mia, who was never late for anything, had to be there. She knew Bo was there—it was his party, after all. She knew that she was hiding. She could text them. She could have Cat and Tinderella hold her spot while she walked around, but something was holding her back. *Shit was about to hit the fan, is why,* she told herself. *I'm not in that much of a hurry to find out what Lyle's gonna present to me. What if he does show me proof that Bo is not who he seems? Would it matter? Would my feelings change?* Winter bit her lip, wondering what to do, what to say, what to think, what to feel, what to-

"Hey, Winter," Camilla said.

"Oh. Hey…you…" Winter replied, noticing they were already halfway to the buffet.

"I was saying you look great," said Tinderella. "*Breakfast at Tiffany's*, right?"

Winter nodded. "Thank you. Yeah, it's one of my favorite movies."

Just then, a familiar looking Cobra Kai walked out of a door marked *Private*, with his arm around a forlorn looking Sandy from *Grease*.

Winter watched as her friends walked through the crowd, to a stanchioned off lane at the opposite end of the building. Thirty seconds later, Edgar Allen Poe—that is, if the author lived in modern day Portland and had the facial structure of a model—walked out of the same door. He had a realistic looking raven perched on his shoulder and a small mustache that kept slipping off and Winter forgot how to breathe as she watched him greet people and eventually join Mia and Jeremiah.

"It looks like Bo reserved the lane at the end," Winter said.

"Hell yeah," said Camilla.

Winter stayed quiet, staring at the ground, until they were almost to the buffet.

"I don't care," she muttered.

"What was that?" asked Camilla.

"I don't care what Lyle has to say…I want to be with Bo," Winter said matter-of-factly.

"No matter what Lyle has to say?" Camilla turned to Tinderella. "Her ex is trying to cockblock."

Tinderella raised her eyebrows and nodded slowly, understanding completely.

"Yeah, I'm not under Lyle's spell anymore. I just know Bo and I are meant to be together." Winter shook her head and spoke as if realizing each concept as she said it. "I know it sounds like a fairytale, Tinderella, but you out of everyone should understand."

"Well, go get him," demanded the app princess. "Pretend he has your glass slipper or something."

Camilla nodded. "Yeah, what she said."

Winter tilted her head up and did her best Holly Golightly impression: "No matter where you run, you just end up running into yourself."

She took a pretend sip from her empty drink and bid her line mates both "adieu" before departing to that place that calmed her down, that made her feel beautiful, that encouraged her—that kept her safe—Bo's arms.

Though there was a mob of people between them, Winter could see a direct path. She had decided that she would tell Bo and her friends everything. She would stop feeling ashamed. Stop letting people like Lyle and her own mom walk all over her. She'd do what felt right to her. She'd be proud of her art and not let any damn person weaken her spirit. An electronic beat matched her heartbeat as she approached her happiness… The DJ booth was to her right and a man with a baseball cap and a hand adorned with golden rings, bobbed his head as he typed into his computer and turned various nobs on a rig in front of him. The music vibrated through her as she got closer to the DJ monitors, and just as she passed the crowded main bar again, a hand clasped her so hard she yelped from the pain. No one seemed to notice as the hand, connected to a person in a black, hooded cape, yanked her into the crowd and practically dragged her out the front door.

"Let me go!" Winter screamed, trying to wriggle free, but the more she pulled the more it hurt.

"She's drunk," said the cloaked man as they passed a security guard.

And it took a few seconds for it to sink in that the man's voice belonged to Lyle.

"No, I'm not!" she screamed even louder.

It looked like the security guard nodded to Lyle, before exchanging glances with two people that were smoking in the front. Before she could figure out what they were saying or doing next, Lyle had dragged her to an empty alleyway on the other side of what looked like an office building next to *Blaine's Lanes*. The sun was almost down, and she could only see a hint of wavy glimmer peaking between the buildings below.

"Just let me go and I'll walk with you, Lyle," she pleaded.

He looked back at her and decided she was telling the truth. When he let go, another shot of pain circled her arm and she rubbed it. *Don't cry*, she thought. *Do not let him make you cry ever again.*

She looked around for somewhere to hide, contemplating if she could run away fast enough. When they got halfway down the alley, the wind picked up, blowing Winter's nightgown up. She quickly pushed it down and held it there with both hands.

Lyle stopped abruptly, swaying a little. "I can't believe you wore that out."

Winter recognized that red, glazed over look in his eyes, and knew he was drunk. She made an effort not to show her horror because that always made it worse.

"Happy Halloween," she said as sweetly as she could without throwing up. "Are you here to show me something?"

"Slut," he snarled.

"I—I'm Holly Golightly from *Breakfast at Tiff*—"

"I'm Holly Go-blah-blah from Blah Blah Blah," he said in a mocking tone. "I know who you are—you said it in your stupid post… It's slutty."

"Thank you for sharing."

He looked at the ground for some time, seething, when finally he put his arm up as if to hit her but quickly put it back down.

"I'm sorry, Winter," he said, remorsefully. "I just want the best for you and—"

"Thank you, Lyle. But we're not together anymore."

He leaned on the wall next to her and she stepped away. The bass in the distance now thumped once for every four of her heart beats. Winter crossed her arms, and he took off his cape and tried wrapping it around her, but she stepped out of reach, shaking her head.

"So, it's true," he said, throwing his cape on the ground. "You're fucking that piece of shit from that piece of shit family."

"What do you mean?" she asked quietly.

"Do you want to know?" He raised one eyebrow. "D'ya really wanna know?"

She didn't answer.

Lyle pulled his wallet out of his back pocket. "You know, you act like you're such an angel." He laughed. "Your mommy told me you volunteered at a doggy shelter. Anything for your image, right?"

"I never told her I volunteered."

"Okay, well… Some teenager tagged you and Bo getting all chummy together. He took it down after an hour. But it's okay 'cuz I saved it to my phone." He laughed again. "Proof you're a slut."

"I don't have to take this anymore."

Winter only took a step or two before Lyle flew in front of her, blocking her way. He wavered a little but regained his balance fast enough to block Winter when she tried to go around him.

"Why are you doing this, Lyle?" Winter's voice cracked.

"Just—I'm sorry. I love you, Winter." He had actual freakin' tears in his eyes. "You're the best thing to ever happen to me and you know I'm fucked up, okay? You know what I went through growing up. I promise I'll get therapy. Since you left I've had time to think about it, okay? I get it. You don't have to prove anything anymore. I need help. I'll get help…for you."

Winter focused on taking deep breaths.

"Here, here…um, this is what I wanted to show you." Lyle opened his wallet and pulled out a folded piece of paper.

"Winter!" she thought she heard a voice scream in the distance.

Lyle unfolded the paper. "He's a bad, man, sweetie. The whole Blaine family…they're shady as shit."

"Winter!" the voice was closer.

"What do you mean?"

"My colleague has represented FFS Industries for years but recently Noah Blaine asked him if he knew how to hide funds overseas, without co-owners or stockholders knowing. My colleague has reason to believe…"

"Winter!" The voice was louder now. And it sounded familiar. It sounded like…*Bo's* voice.

Lyle didn't seem to hear the voice, but he grew more and more agitated that he didn't have her undivided attention. "Winter! Damnit. He has reason to believe Noah's embezzling money."

Winter shook her head.

"And he—" Lyle handed the paper to her. "This is a copy of one of the accounts. He wanted the secret account set up under Bo Blaine's name… The family is so idiotic they left a paper trail."

Winter looked at the paper. "If this is true, why wouldn't your colleague go straight to the police?"

"Because he… I don't know. I think he has stock himself and doesn't want the company to go under and I don't know…I think …he thinks maybe he's complicit in some other— And Winter, that family is so shady that he's terrified of what they'll do to him. I'm telling you, they're bad news."

Winter looked up and saw Bo standing at the end of the alleyway, watching them. The fake mustache was gone, and the raven fastened to his shoulder had slumped backwards. He slowly walked forward and every ounce of worry in her body disappeared. She quickly folded the paper and put in in her purse.

"Wait—don't you care?" Lyle asked. "Your new boy toy is a fucking criminal! Embezzlement. Money hidden overseas. What the fuck?"

Winter shook her head. "I trust him."

"You've got to be kidding me. You're even dumber than they are."

"Lyle, maybe you really should try therapy because you obviously have some demons to work out."

Lyle looked at her sideways. "What has gotten into you?"

Winter thought for a second, then shrugged. "Self-respect?"

Livid, Lyle lunged forward and grabbed her purse. "Give me back that paper you fucking whore."

When Winter wouldn't let go, he pushed her against the wall.

"Hey! Get your hands off of her!" Bo shouted.

And in the split second Lyle turned his head and realized they weren't alone, Winter kicked him in the balls...hard. He let go of the purse and doubled over in pain.

Bo and Winter jogged away hands interlocked.

The sun had gone down, and they followed the path lamplight back to the bowling alley. Before they went in, Bo thanked the security guard for telling him he saw "that Winter Smith girl" being dragged away by some drunk, then he instructed the guard and everyone standing in the front not to let Lyle inside the building.

"Will do, boss," said the security guard. "And Winter, a shoutout on your Nanogram wouldn't hurt."

Winter smiled. "Of course."

"Tight. I'll DM you tonight to remind you."

Bo and Winter entered the premises, but Bo stopped near the door, in the same spot they had that special moment the first night they met. The crowd seemed even denser, and clusters had formed around each lane: some people were bowling, some people were cheering the bowlers on. Others danced to a popular rap song that the DJ was playing for them.

Winter looked up at Bo.

"You saved me back there," she said.

"No. I think you saved yourself." He smiled warmly and pet her hair.

"You're one of the most handsome Edgar Allen Poe's ever."

He laughed. "Yeah, I can't really compete with the O.G."

"He's okay. But I'm thinking about Edgar the kitten. He's just a tiny bit cuter, I'm sorry."

He put his arm around her and pulled her in. "Do you understand how happy I am to see you?"

"How happy?"

He caressed her cheek and just stared at her. "Gorgeous Winter."

Winter put her hands under his 1800s jacket and clasped her hands around his waist. They kissed and she caught her breath by resting her head on his chest.

"Did he hurt you?" he asked.

"No, I'm fine."

Bo cleared his throat. "I heard what he said, Winter, and I promise I had no idea my dad did that."

Winter looked up at him. "I trust you."

He kissed her forehead then held her head with his hands. "Come on, let's go party."

Mia squealed when she saw Winter approaching and met her halfway to give a big hug.

"You're here!" Mia screamed.

"Mia!" Winter screamed.

Bo backed up. "Um, guys, I'll be right back."

"Where are you going?" Winter asked, still in her friend's embrace.

"Just gotta run to the aerial tram really fast. Tell the worker something."

And he was swallowed up by a new group of party guests walking in.

"You gotta let me go," Winter laughed. "It's my turn to bowl."

She was sitting on Mia's lap and the cloud had bumped

into the side of her leg, reminding her to grab her pink bowling ball that sat precariously on top of it.

"No!" Mia shouted. "Not until you tell me I'm an amazing friend and that when you and Bo get married, you'll put me in your vows because I made it all happen."

"Married? We just started dating, Mia."

"I don't care. Promise me."

Winter rolled her eyes and put one hand behind her back. "Okay, I promise."

"You're crossing your fingers."

"No, I'm not."

"Yes, you are!"

Mia tried to look, and Winter twisted and turned to hide her crossed fingers.

"Come on, guys," Jeremiah said, slumped in his chair, exhausted.

"Zip it, Karate Kid!" shouted Mia.

"I'm Johnny Lawrence, dude," Jeremiah replied, annoyed. "Maybe you should actually watch the movie sometime, it's a masterpiece."

One of Winter's favorite James Blake songs came on and it gave Winter a jolt of adrenaline. She slipped out of Mia's grip and took her turn. The ball released from her fingers awkwardly and rolled slowly down the middle of the lane.

"Oh, what's it gonna do? What's it gonna do?" Camilla screamed.

They all watched in anticipation as the ball hit the middle pin down, followed by most of the other pins. Only two remained. Winter put her head down in shame.

"Yes! That's your best one yet," Camilla said, patting Winter on the back.

"Yeah," Winter laughed. "Cuz I haven't knocked down a

single pin until now." She rolled again and the ball went straight to the gutter.

"That's the spirit!" Camilla said, dancing as she rolled her turn, knocking down every pin as usual.

"Dang, you're good," Mia said to Camilla.

"Oh, why thank you!" Winter usurped the compliment and winked at Mia. "No, seriously. I have a feeling Camilla's amazing at anything. You should hear her sing."

"Oh, she had me sing her a whole Banks song before you got over here," said Camilla.

Mia nodded excitedly. "I heard her humming and damn—I mean, honestly, I would have turned around for her in a heartbeat if I was a judge on The Voice."

Bo and Kevin walked up.

"Holy shit!" exclaimed Jeremiah. He jumped out of his chair, shook Kevin's hand excitedly, and then turned to his girlfriend. "Mia! This! Now, *this* is a Karate Kid!"

Kevin wore a crisp, white karate uniform with the bonsai tree and sun logo on the back, a black belt, and a Miyagi Dojo headband, an exact replica of Daniel LaRusso's outfit from the original 1984 *Karate Kid.* He promptly did a 360 degree show-off of his costume, complete with karate stances.

"It's fucking incredible," Jeremiah said in gleeful giddiness.

"Oh, my God, I've literally never seen Jeremiah this happy," said Mia.

"Your costume is the shit too, man," said Kevin. "A perfect Johnny Lawrence! Down to the Chuck Taylors and everything."

Jeremiah and Kevin bro-hugged and Mia almost hurt herself performing the most impressive eye roll of her life.

"Jeremiah, this is Kevin," said Bo. "He's the one I told you about."

"Oh, no shit?" Jeremiah smiled from ear to ear.

"Told about what?" inquired Mia.

"Kev's a tech genius. We're thinking about making an app together."

"I'm down," said Kevin. "Just say when."

"Hey, I work for a video game company." Camilla threw back a shot of something and winced before continuing. "Maybe I can hook you guys up with designers or something."

"No shit?" Bo said.

And they asked Camilla questions about her job and seemed really excited by the new business connection they just made.

Mia finally took her turn to bowl and she did some Sandy dance moves as she walked up to the cloud holding her bowling ball. Bo put his arms around Winter's waist, holding her from behind.

"You're one sexy Sandy," Winter told Mia.

"Are you making fun of me, Riz?" asked Mia, doing her best Sandy impression.

Winter answered her in her best Rizzo. "Some people are so touchy."

As Winter watched Mia take her turn, Bo put his lips on the side of her neck. She closed her eyes and put her hands on his hands. She heard pins being knocked down and her eyes flew open to the sound of Camilla cheering and Kevin whistling.

"Damn, girl, you were holding out!" said Camilla, giving Mia a high-five.

"Whatever," mumbled Jeremiah, sitting down in a chair—his *Karate Kid* high had obviously run its course.

Soon enough, Mia and Jeremiah got into an entertaining argument over the true meaning of sportsmanship, with Camilla and Kevin acting as referees.

"Lyle's not gonna bother you anytime soon," Bo whispered in Winter's ear.

She turned around. "What do you mean?"

He smiled slightly.

"What happened?" she asked.

"My old friend, Tate, is a tram operator, and he—" Bo seemed to think about how to put it. "He was able to convince Lyle, in a manually stalled aerial cabin 500 feet up in the air, mind you, to stay away from Winter Smith."

Winter was stunned. "Do you know what he actually said to him?"

Bo seemed to think about answering her but they both became distracted by their friends, who were back to eating at their seats while Kevin stood over them, passionately presenting a case that Grandpa Joe from *Charlie and the Chocolate Factory* was one of the scariest villains in cinema.

"Well…" Bo finally answered her. "I wasn't there, but Tate said he gave him advice on how to treat others and the consequences that could arise when people treat others wrong."

Winter nodded reflectively.

"And…" Bo continued.

"And?"

"And he may have mentioned to Lyle that he has friends on the outside *and* the inside, and that they were watching… or something of that nature."

"Are you talking about prison?"

"Yeah."

"Well, how do we know if Lyle's going to listen?"

Bo put his hands on her shoulders. "Winter. I promise. He listened."

Winter opened her mouth, then closed it.

"I'm sorry, I had to think fast before Lyle got away," Bo continued. "And, I mean, I'd much rather you call the police on him—"

"No, I just want all this behind me…" she insisted.

"Well, will you at least consider meeting with a therapist about all of this? I'll pay for it."

"What are you whispering about over there!" shouted Mia. "Camilla wants to know."

"*Mia* wants to know," said Camilla.

"Well, we *all* want to know if Camilla can sing here sometime." Mia stood up and got a bowling ball from a cloud and put it gently on Jeremiah's lap...to his annoyance.

"That would be amazing!" Winter said.

"Oh, yeah, no pressure man." Camilla readjusted her cat ears. "But you know, I have a band and stuff. No big deal."

"Oh, um. Yeah. Of course."

"You know what, before you decide…" Camilla took out her phone, her thumb moving like lightning. "I just sent you a link to my Youtube page. So let me know whenever you get around to checking it out. If we suck, no feelings hurt."

"Suck? Yeah right," said Mia.

"I'll check out your page, but honestly, based on what I've already heard, we can set up any night you want to perform."

"Her band's ridiculously good," said Winter. "It's kinda annoying how good they are."

"Oh stop!" Camilla said.

"Jeremiah," said Mia, "can you please get your turn out of the way so we can start shooting our bowling photos."

"Yeah, we should start posting," Winter agreed. "It's getting late."

Jeremiah begrudgingly got up and bowled his turn. When he got a strike, his mood perked back up and he did an endzone dance.

"Good job, baby," Mia ran up to him and kissed him. "You'll definitely be rewarded tonight for that."

Bo realized he had to go make rounds and thank people for coming. He left, conveniently, just as the mini photo session began. They bowled, danced, posed, did impressions… Within fifteen minutes, one of the videos they posted, featuring Mia, Winter, Camilla, and a few people in the lane right next to them dancing to a Diplo song, was trending on three different social media platforms under the hashtags *Halloween* and *HalloweenPortland.* Within twenty minutes, a photo of Mia and Winter standing next to each other, posing like Sandy and Holly Golightly, had garnered over 100,000 likes on Winter's StyleSlap page. Tinderella, whose real name was Betty, and who had evidently been stood up by her date, also joined in on the posting fun. She said that she "got like 1,000" new followers just because Mia and Winter tagged her in a few live videos.

They all took a breather. Mia drank champagne, sitting on Jeremiah's lap; Winter sipped water, teetering on the arm of Camilla's chair, who was texting someone; Kevin and Betty had fallen deep into conversation—discussing weird folklore regarding Disney theme parks. Winter, again, took in the intricate decorations and admired Bo's creativity. She felt like she was in some magical, immersive, Halloween land. The music slowly started to fade down, and Bo got up on the DJ platform. He said something and the DJ took a huge chug of water as he nodded. Then Bo grabbed a mic from underneath the rig.

"Hello, ladies and gentleman!" Bo said into the mic. He waited for the banter to quiet before he continued. "I just want to thank all of you for spending your Halloween here at *Blaine's Lanes*. This place is a passion project for me, and I can't even begin to explain how happy I am to see people enjoying themselves, and, man…" He shook his head. "I just, thank you for supporting this local business. Y'all are welcome here anytime. And I have a lot more ideas for this place. Now have a fucking great Halloween and don't forget to hashtag *BlainesLanes*. We'll feature some of the photos and videos on our social media pages and on our website." He put his arms up and together as if praising the audience.

The bowling alley erupted in cheers and applause and the music increased back up to full volume. Bo handed the DJ the mic and whispered in his ear. The music seamlessly transitioned to *Hearing Damage* by Thom Yorke and Bo jumped off the platform, making a beeline for Winter. She got up to meet him and they embraced.

"Can I tell you something?" Bo asked her.

She nodded, eagerly.

"This is one of the best nights of my life."

"Really?"

"Because you're here with me."

The room felt like it melted away, leaving Winter and Bo alone, but their kiss was cut short by a flash going off. Mia was standing in front of them, moving around to find another good angle.

"Oh, my God, you're stopping the magic," Jeremiah said, trying to pull his girlfriend away.

"I don't think that's possible," Bo said, without taking his eyes off Winter.

And in a small crowd next to the bar, Winter noticed two people holding up their cell phones, recording them. When she examined some of the people near the entrance, she saw a guy taking a photo of them. When he realized he wasn't being as discreet as he thought, he quickly turned around.

"Looks like we're gonna have to get used to this," Bo said, the moving spotlights created a dancing flame in his green eyes.

When his lips met hers again, Winter knew her life was about to change. And what surprised her the most was she wasn't even remotely scared about it.

They were all having "the best Halloween ever," as Mia put it, until Matt Graham and two drunk friends came stumbling from the food section. They were wearing droog costumes from Kubrick's *A Clockwork Orange*, and Matt was obviously trying his best to portray Alex from the film. He wore a black bowler hat and long eyelashes on one eye, but his eyeliner dripped like hot candle wax down his sweaty face.

"Aaaay! My man!" Matt shouted.

Bo sighed and peeled himself away from Winter as he approached.

"Thought you said there'd be food here." Matt jumped on top of an empty seat, landing in front of Bo. His fellow droogs followed suit.

"Oh, yeah, man," Bo said. "But you're kind of late, you know."

"Hey, can I have that?" slurred the shorter droog, pointing at an uneaten fajita on Jeremiah's plate.

"Sure. Yeah," Jeremiah said.

Jeremiah handed the plate over and the guy scarfed it down.

"You're hanging out with Winter Smith?" Matt said. "Dude. My sis is gonna be jello."

Bo didn't answer.

"Dude, these girls are hot," said the taller droog. His hair was disheveled, and he stumbled into the closest chair.

"You guys can bowl next if you want," said Camilla with a nervous laugh.

"Fuck no. We're party-hopping tonight and just stopping by." Matt slapped his hands on Bo's shoulders and squeezed. "I think the women here are a little stuck up, if you know what I mean."

"No, I don't, actually," said Bo with a straight face.

"God, you're no fun sometimes. I heard how you used to party, man. Probably broke the record for the most blow done in a single night in the Pacific Northwest."

"What?" Bo was pissed.

Kevin stood up. "Nah, man. Bo was never into that stuff. I've known him for almost fifteen years. I think I'd know."

"People have secrets, bro. And it's cool." Matt leaned against the wooden table monitor. "Don't have to fight your man's battles, though. Not that this is a battle or anything." He laughed.

"You know, it's been a long night." Bo started buttoning his coat. "You can believe whatever you want to believe. Have fun and—"

"Wait, you guys are leaving?" Matt asked.

Bo turned to Winter. "You maybe want to go? My place?"

"Ohhh! My Man's 'bout to get it in!" Matt high-fived Short Droog.

"You know what—" Bo said.

Winter braced for what was about to happen, but Bo remained calm.

"I'm sure catering have some leftovers," Bo continued, smiling. "I'll send you a few plates over."

"No shit? That'd be fucking legit. I guess we are kickin' back here, boys!" Matt said.

The original group vacated their seats to give it over to the droogs and said their goodbyes to each other. Before they parted, Mia gave Winter a hug and made her promise they'd hang out in the next few days.

"I have so much to tell you, Mia," Winter said.

"I know you do," said Mia, but refused to elaborate.

CHAPTER THIRTY-TWO

Bo turned the lights up and the kittens greeted them at the door, meowing, head butting, and rubbing up against their legs.

"Oh, I've missed you!" Winter exclaimed. She sat on her knees in the middle of the living room, taking turns petting Edgar and Elmira. "You both look a tiny bit bigger than I saw you last. Is that even possible?"

Bo watched her. She was a knockout and he almost couldn't believe she was in his home again.

"Anything's possible," he said.

"You know, Bo. Whenever we're with each other—" Winter looked up. "—I feel this strange feeling like we just spent a lifetime together. It's like we've spent all these lifetimes together already." She laughed at herself and shook her head. "Gosh, that's weird."

"No, I know what you mean." Bo was holding her backpack and purse and put it on the couch. "Every day with you is an adventure."

He bent down beside her and pet the kittens. His presence

seemed to give Edgar a shot of adrenaline, and he ran around the room a couple times before wrestling the edge of the curtain. Elmira got another pet session in before chasing her brother.

"It's so cute. They love it here," Winter said, amused by the whole scene.

"I love them here."

In the warm light, her eyes were deep brown but glinted with flecks of umber and honey. She ran her fingers through her hair, her face flushed with the knowledge that someone was admiring her. *Who the hell was this girl? She just came out of nowhere.* And she had some kind of…power over him. A good kind of power. Like a blanket of stillness right after a windstorm. An inspiring kind of power that made him want to strive to be powerful too. *Any other time*, he thought, *any other time, I would have handled that situation with Matt differently. Way differently.* But just knowing she was beside him, calmed him, cleared his thoughts. Up until that fateful moment he saw the firefly light up from across the bowling alley, he had looked at everyone with a predisposed cynicism. A suspicion. Something had changed in him. The rain picked up suddenly, pounding against the window, followed by a boom that made Winter jump and hold her chest. They both laughed and he helped her up.

"You're probably exhausted," he said.

"No… What about you?"

She stepped closer to him and took one of his hands. He knew if he looked down, her eyes would tell him all he needed to know. Suggesting something he'd been wanting since they met. It was fucking terrifying.

"Um…make yourself at home." He slowly pulled his hand away, went over to the window, and pulled back the curtain. "Stormy weather. Never change, Oregon." A hidden kitten swiped at his pants, a claw temporarily getting caught on the fabric. "Hey, you," he said.

Edgar emerged and ran around the corner, into the hallway. Elmira was already tired, and Bo watched as she jumped onto the couch and made herself into a loaf. Without looking back at Winter, Bo removed his coat, looked out the window again, then walked across the room, over to the kitchen to get a cup out of the cupboard.

Winter just stood there silently.

"Oh, um," he said, filling his cup with water from the fridge filter, "you can watch a movie, play a video game, take a bath, eat, drink, go to sleep. It's—"

"Did I do or say something wrong?" she asked.

He hesitated, then finally looked at her. "Of course not. Why would you think that?"

She sat down on the couch next to Elmira. "No reason," she finally said.

He downed his whole glass of water in one go. "Want anything to drink?"

"I'm good, thank you."

"The remote's in a caddy on the side of the couch."

"Thanks," she said curtly. At least, she seemed to try to be curt, but it just came off as adorable. She stared into space for a while. "It just kind of feels like you're avoiding me or, I don't know, maybe I'm tripping."

He sighed, then scratched the back of his neck. "If we start kissing and touching and stuff. It's gonna be hard to stop."

She looked at him. "Why would we have to stop?"

He felt his heart pause then start back up seconds later and his stomach ached from the butterfly shrapnel. She must have seen his expression because she sprung up and floated—like an angel would—over to him. She put her arms around his waist, and he smelled a hint of floral perfume on her—lilies and rose and...*raspberry*? And he closed his eyes. *Be strong*, he thought. *Be fucking strong*. He impulsively kissed her forehead. *Damn it, Bo!*

"Winter…you've been through a lot today and I just…"

"I'm fine, Bo."

"You might think you are." He set his cup on the counter, "But you're vulnerable."

She shook her head vigorously. "No. Not anymore. I made a decision to stand up for myself and not be taken advantage of. I mean, I didn't even have any—have that much anxiety today. And you helped me with that, Bo. I promise you did. I'm stronger now."

He examined the way she over-pronounced her words, her impassioned cadence, as if she was arguing her side of a debate in a speech competition. Before he knew it, he was gently running his fingers through her hair.

Bo pulled his shirt off over his head and threw it on the chair. Winter leaned against the dresser, mouth agape. The curtains lit up with light, followed by a thunder strike that shook the ground underneath them, yet Winter was completely oblivious to it.

"It must have taken forever to do all of these," Winter said, running her hand over the strip of paisley patterns, planets, and galaxy tattoos on his chest. "Did it hurt?"

"It wasn't that bad," he shrugged.

"Well, it's beautiful."

"You're fucking beautiful."

They kissed and it started off gentle at first, but slowly worked their way up to earnest, hurried, like they would devour each other if they kept the progression going.

"Just a second," he said, breathing heavily.

He pushed a button on a diamond shaped lamp sitting on the dresser, and it turned on, spinning slowly, projecting blues, greens, reds, and purples, that blended and moved with each other, creating a vivid aurora borealis effect on the ceiling and walls. Winter looked at the light in awe, then looked back at him, smiling.

"Is that okay?" he asked.

She nodded.

He had imagined seeing her under that lamp so many times, but nothing prepared him for the masterpiece before him. The changing colors illuminated her skin, her eyes, her hair, and every angle of her feminine features. She was a star in the galaxy.

He walked back up to her and put his hands under her nightshirt. She slowly pulled it up and off and threw it on top of his shirt. Then she slowly stripped off her shorts, letting them fall to the ground around her feet. He froze for a moment, taking in her beautiful figure. Voluptuous, toned, yet, a softness. *How am I going to last*? he thought, almost in a panic. Before she could take off her lingerie, he kissed her shoulder blades, her neck, and she stiffened for a second, then relaxed.

"Are you sure?" he asked.

"Yes," she whispered.

She put her arms behind her back and almost instantly her bra fell to the floor. They kissed all the way to the bed, and Winter lay on her back. He pulled off her knee-high socks, realizing that even her feet were perfect. He ran his hands on her smooth legs, kissed them, and worked his way up to her stomach. She was breathing fast but seemed to hold her breath as he moved up to her breasts. Her nipples rose in his mouth.

She propped herself up on her elbow and kissed his lips, slipping her tongue in before taking it away again. That took him a second to recover from. Then he kissed her chest and neck and up to her ears, and she unbuttoned and unzipped his pants before moving her warm hands inside them. Touching him. She lay back down and smiled when he drew in a sharp breath from her clasp.

He pulled his pants and boxers off clumsily and threw them across the room. The rain calmed to a steady patter against the window, and it relaxed his nerves. They caressed each other, her skin feeling like porcelain under his fingers. Then he gently pulled her panties down, and she lifted her knees to get them around her feet. She kept her legs together until he was done putting on the condom… Then she slowly opened them. A time-lapsed rose in bloom. The blood pumped through him and he thought, *What did I do to deserve her?*

CHAPTER THIRTY-THREE

He looked at her with eyebrows knitted, his lips slightly apart. She bit her lip, almost breaking the skin. No one had ever looked at her like that. Even before she opened herself to him, his eyes took her in with…she wasn't quite sure, but something like…grateful wonderment. The lights moved counterclockwise around the room, painting temporary strokes of colors across his tattooed skin, the outline of his muscles, his chiseled features…and his tattooless soldier that stood at *full* attention for her. She wanted him inside her but played as cool and composed as her body would allow.

He inched towards her, kissing her stomach again, but more tenderly. Then caressed her legs. Finally, he gently entered her. She moaned immediately. He moved slow and rhythmic, every now and then changing up the tempo. He moaned, then he went faster, and she lightly grabbed a tuft of his hair, as if holding on to a rein. He lifted himself up to see what the key looked like entering and reentering the mechanism, then he kissed her feverishly before mounting her again. And she wrapped her legs around him.

She moaned. And he moaned.

And he called out her name.

And they kissed again.

And she ran both hands through his hair. And arched her back.

And he groaned, slowing his rhythm. But going deeper somehow. And though she wanted him to stay inside her, *live* inside her, she felt herself release. Buckle. She embraced him tightly as he slowed down to a stop. And he stayed inside her for a while, catching his breath. Then kissing her. Soft. Really soft.

Then he slowly pulled out and moved off the bed and stared at her for a while, then excused himself.

And when he walked across the room to the bathroom, and the colors of the lamp hit his face, she could have sworn…

His eyes were watering.

CHAPTER THIRTY-FOUR

He drove over the Marquam Bridge, heading home after a fucking long, shit, ass day of work. The temperature outside was a whopping thirty-nine degrees, yet even with the heat off in the car, he was sweating. He loosened his tie and when that didn't help, he tore off his blazer jacket, losing control of the car for only a second.

"Oh, shut the fuck up! You think you own the road?" he screamed, pressing down on the horn.

The tiny man in the Kia Sorento flipped him off before admitting defeat and pulling back. He tried to commit the floppy-haired hippie's face to memory, just in case the guy ever walked into FFS and begged for a job like the pathetic man he was. The vision made him chuckle, and his mood lifted by at least two notches.

A Michael Finnissy composition that he couldn't remember the name of started playing on NPR, so he turned it up to an almost deafening level. It was a thing he did whenever he was in his car alone—or, of course, if he was being driven around. Only a certain volume level or higher gave him that weird sensation behind his neck, as well as a giant shot of dopamine. Looking in his rearview mirror, the waterfront buildings reflected the water and reminded him of — He did a quick U-turn off the bridge, almost hitting some slow round woman holding groceries while crossing the street. *Who the fuck walks in the evening? Doesn't she have a car?*

Getting closer to the building he visited the least, for obvious reasons, that familiar gnawing started in the middle of his chest. His prior physician insisted the sensation was caused by indigestion. "Too much spicy foods and fats," the idiot with a stethoscope had said. It wasn't that simple. Yes, maybe that's how it started—akin to a lit match. *But someone,* he reasoned with himself, *has to hold that match to the fuse that then lights an explosive device.* And there was one particular person that knew how to do that. That could write a book on bomb explosions…metaphorically speaking. *The kid's definitely not smart enough to write a book on anything*, he thought, and chuckled again.

"Sarah, please come into my office."

Sarah, whose annoying brown hair faded into blonde like she was homeless or in rehab–or perhaps, a halfway house for societal rejects—timidly walked in and shut the door way too slowly.

"Yes, Mr. Blaine?" she squeaked in that up-speak kind of speech pattern that always sounded like a question even when it wasn't. Of course, this time, it just happened to be one.

"Sarah, sweetheart. You're one of my best workers. I just want to tell you how much I appreciate you."

"Oh, thank you." She didn't know what to do with her hands so she put them behind her, like a child being lectured to by a teacher. It was a little enduring, but mostly gross. She was a grown woman, after all. "But, Mr. Blaine, I actually was going to talk to you. Um—"

"Call me Noah," he said, and swiveled his chair back toward his laptop.

"Um, Mr.— Um, Noah, sir, I actually was going to give you my two-week notice. I'm—"

"Absolutely not. Did I mention how valuable you are to me here?"

"Oh, yeah. I just, my friends and I just bought—"

"How much do you need to stay?" he asked, typing fast.

"Oh… I don't think—"

"You know what. I think you deserve a promotion and health benefits. What do you think?"

The dull, thirsty flower brightened at his proposal. "What kind of promotion?"

He swiveled back to her. "Double what you make now. If you perform well, it could possibly even go up upon evaluation."

She smiled and relaxed her arms beside her. And from the change in proximity of her bosom to the ground, the rigidity flowed out of the rest of her body too. *Hmmm. She actually wasn't that bad looking of a girl. A little weathered under the eyes. Some skin damage. Idiotic hair. But really not bad at all.*

"Okay, that's settled," he said. "Now, sit down and give me the rundown."

She sat down and her smile faded slightly. Noah toggled through camera footage, until he got to a camera on Bo's floor. He fast-forwarded until he saw Bo and Winter, holding hands, walking down the corridor.

"Well, she's been coming over almost every night—no, I think it was actually every night and—" Her voice trailed off. "They seem really happy."

Noah rolled his eyes and sat back. "Every night?"

"Yeah."

"And he hasn't brought anyone else here?"

"No, I don't think so."

"Are you sure, because I'm really not in the mood to go through all this footage right now."

"No Mr. Blaine—I mean, Noah—it's just been her."

He realized there was an imperfection in the bottom left corner of his half-framed wooden glasses and took them off to buffer them with a cloth from his breast pocket.

"So, do you think he's taking this girl seriously?" he asked. "She's—what did you say? *A social media harlot*?"

"I don't remember saying that."

"Oh, yes, you said it last week. I remember it clearly because I haven't heard anyone under the age of seventy say the word *harlot*."

She smiled. "Okay, maybe I said it."

Noah fast-forwarded the footage and watched Bo and Winter emerge from Bo's place. They walked down the corridor and the footage switched to the elevator, where Bo held Winter's face with both hands and kissed her passionately. He shut the laptop hard.

"You and I both know that they are not going to work out. But I need it to happen sooner than later."

She hesitated, then said, "Why is that?"

"He has obligations…to business and to people…and everything else equals wasting time plus money."

She looked confused, though, she usually looked like that.

Noah was beginning to think she got high on the job. *Fucking hippies. All over this damn city.*

"Come on," he said, standing up. "I'll explain more at dinner."

She blushed. "Dinner?"

"Oh, come on. It's not like that…" He put the laptop in the desk drawer. "It will be our first business meeting to go over your promotion… A christening, if you will."

Flustered, Sarah stood up fast and the chair flew back hard against his library cabinet. He sighed, taking off his glasses to examine the wooden surface with his nearsighted eyes.

He couldn't find a nick, even when he ran his finger on the surface to see if he could feel any invisible blemishes.

Lucky for her.

And just like he thought, she followed him out the door like a sad little puppy dog.

THANK YOU FOR READING

Did you enjoy this book?

We invite you to leave a review at your favorite book site, such as Goodreads, Amazon, Barnes & Noble, etc.

DID YOU KNOW THAT LEAVING A REVIEW…

- Helps other readers find books they may enjoy.
- Gives you a chance to let your voice be heard.
- Gives authors recognition for their hard work.
- Doesn't have to be long. A sentence or two about why you liked the book will do.

ABOUT THE AUTHOR

Savannah Thomas was born and raised in Podunk*, Oregon. She escaped her self-diagnosed Prison of Shyness Disorder by self-medicating with daily doses of Head in the Clouds antibiotics. Her severe daydreaming turned into poetry and story writing and at the age of 15 she was published in Anthology of Poetry for Young Americans. Years later she sold a story about her mother's mental illness to the now defunct *Elle Girl* (the younger sibling to *Elle* magazine), and earned a Bachelor's degree in Creative Writing from Southern New Hampshire University. Savannah has an affinity for creating tantalizing worlds with relatable characters, particularly in the romance and fantasy genres. Besides her passion for writing, Savannah loves making music, acting (check out her imdb page!), listening to podcasts, playing video games, and snuggling with her cat Jessie.

*Not actual name of town

Savmthomas@gmail.com
SavannahThomasAuthor.com

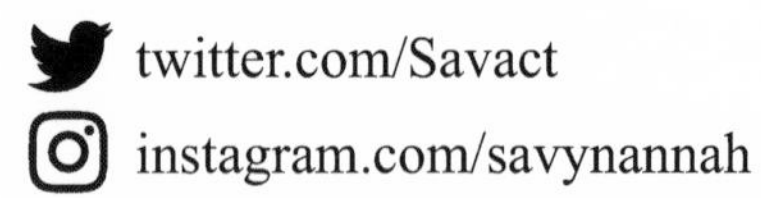

Made in United States
Orlando, FL
09 January 2022